"I cannot remain here!"

Elaine experienced a resurgence of distress.

"You have no choice, I fancy," Charles replied. "Besides, as you once said, sooner or later someone will come for you. What will I tell this—" the word seemed to choke out of him "—*husband* of yours, if you are gone?"

Elaine flinched. "You need not speak as if you do not believe in his existence."

"I don't want to believe in it!" Charles retorted.

She looked at him with pain. "But you must, Charles."

"I will not permit you to leave my house. Whatever the truth, I will see you safe. We will wait until the Runners have unearthed a clue. Unless I am given reason to believe otherwise, you will remain in my charge." He arched an eyebrow in the old, cynical fashion.

"Meanwhile, rest assured that my emotions will not tempt me to violate the sanctity of your refuge!"

* * *

A Trace of Memory
Harlequin® Historical #220—September 2007

ELIZABETH BAILEY

grew up in Malawi, then worked as an actress in British theater. Her interest in writing grew, at length overtaking acting. Instead, she taught drama, developing a third career as a playwright and director. She finds this a fulfilling combination; for each activity fuels the others, firing an incurably romantic imagination. Elizabeth lives in Sussex, England.

ELIZABETH BAILEY

A Trace of Memory

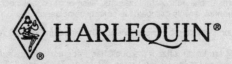

HARLEQUIN®

TORONTO • NEW YORK • LONDON
AMSTERDAM • PARIS • SYDNEY • HAMBURG
STOCKHOLM • ATHENS • TOKYO • MILAN • MADRID
PRAGUE • WARSAW • BUDAPEST • AUCKLAND

ISBN-13: 978-0-373-30529-2
ISBN-10:   0-373-30529-X

A TRACE OF MEMORY

Copyright © 2001 by Elizabeth Bailey

First North American Publication 2007

Printed in U.S.A.

DON'T MISS THESE OTHER
NOVELS AVAILABLE NOW:

#863 KLONDIKE WEDDING—KATE BRIDGES
When Dr. Luke Hunter stands in as the groom in a proxy wedding,
he doesn't expect to be *really* married to the bride! Luke's not a
settling-down kind of man, but beautiful Genevieve may be the
woman to change his mind.

#864 A COMPROMISED LADY—ELIZABETH ROLLS
Thea Winslow's scandalous past has forbidden her a future. So why
does her wayward heart refuse to understand that she cannot have
any more to do with handsome Richard Blakehurst?

#865 A PRACTICAL MISTRESS—MARY BRENDAN
She was nearly penniless, and becoming a mistress was the only
practical solution. The decision had *nothing* to do with the look
in Sir Jason's eyes that promised such heady delights....

#866 THE WARRIOR'S TOUCH—
MICHELLE WILLINGHAM
Pragmatic, plain Aileen never forgot the handsome man
who became her first lover on the eve of Bealtaine, the man
who gave her a child without ever seeing her face.
Now that he has returned, how can she keep her secret?
The MacEgan Brothers

#219 HER GENTLEMAN PROTECTOR—MEG ALEXANDER
Miss Emma Lynton was stranded in France, in the middle of a
revolution, totally alone! Handsome aristocrat Simon Avedon
came to her rescue and vowed to escort her home.

Chapter One

The girl lay alone in an alien place. The overhang of trees was utterly unfamiliar. Great swathing branches reached out from a clump of massy giants, to form a well of shadow above her. Where was she? She struggled up, looking about.

Light dappled through the leaves, casting pools of brown upon the petticoats of her white muslin gown. The girl shivered, and rubbed her arms, discovering an unwelcome feel of dampness to the black velvet spencer she wore over her gown. Her feet were chill, her ankle boots of soft blue kid affording scant protection against the dewy morn.

How in the world had she come to be lying there, beneath the bushes? She dragged herself to rise upon unsteady legs, standing to gaze in growing bewilderment as she took in the wooded surroundings in which she found herself. Was she mad, to have ventured thus lightly clad into a terrain studded with shrubs and undergrowth?

She put a wavering hand to a dull ache manifesting at the side of her head. Taking in vaguely that she wore no bonnet, she became aware of a sticky feel, and hissed in a breath at the abrupt stab of discomfort. Her fingers came away bloodied. The girl stared at them, blank with astonishment.

What had happened to her? A gust of panic shook her, and she whimpered, looking quickly away from the horrid sight. Hazy sunlight splintered in her vision, and she was obliged to bite down on a rise of sobs in her throat. She stumbled forward, swishing through the tangled brush that caught at her ankles as if it would stay her escape.

As she came clear of the trees, the sun's warmth hit her. The girl checked, casting a wild glance about her and catching her breath. Ahead the ground sloped upward in a sweep of open grassland dotted with low-lying scrub, and then rose further to another belt of trees. At either side, the woodlands stretched away.

Her heart spattered into pulsing frenzy. What place was this? What was she doing here?

But questions only strengthened the ache that emanated from her injured head, shifting pain into her brow. She must not think! Rather must she act—find help. But where, in this wilderness? In which direction should she go? In this inexplicable predicament, it mattered little.

Looking down as she picked up her skirts, she froze. The splodges she had taken for shadow revealed themselves in the brighter light to be stains of brown or green. The hem of her gown was dirtied, the boots below it clogged with mud, and there were rips in the muslin folds that hung unkempt below the spencer. That, too, had a tear across the bosom, and the gown was also damp. Small wonder she felt chilled. How long had she lain there?

A cold wind of alarm spread through her, and a quivering started up, spreading through her whole frame. No explanation for her sorry state presented itself to her questing mind, and she was only half aware of moving as she began slowly to make her way towards the open ground.

That she could be in such a place, quite alone, seemed more the stuff of nightmare than reality. The more so, because the only reward of desperate thought was a mindless blank that nagged the growing headache into tearing pain, forcing her to check in the middle of the open space, pressing both hands to her forehead, her eyes tightly shut.

For a moment or two she was convinced she must swoon. But the dizzying flare of agony receded, and presently she became aware that it had become overlaid with sound outside her immediate consciousness. A murmuring penetrated her mind, and its cause became suddenly clear. Voices!

Her eyes flew open, and she glanced up ahead to find that figures were emerging from the trees at the hilltop. An instinct of caution sent her flying back the way she had come, all thought of her discomforts swallowed up in fright. Before she knew what had happened, she was leaning into the hollows on the far side of a tree, panting and shaken.

It was several moments before she could hear anything above the sound of her own laboured breathing. But presently, as the panic began to subside, she was able to make out the growing rumble of speech, accompanied by the swish and tread of several feet thrusting through the underbrush. It was with an easing at her heart that she recognised the lighter tones of female voices alongside that of a man.

The girl peered stealthily around the edge of the tree that formed a present haven. Three people were descending the rise ahead: two women straggling slightly behind a tall man, who strode with a purposeful air. Even at this distance an impression of gentility pervaded the group. It was in the timbre of their voices as well as the form of their garments. These people came of no common country folk.

A breath caught in the girl's throat, the sensations in her breast compound both of relief and a little alarm. The instinct of her class gave her surety of imminent rescue. But at the same time, she felt acutely the lack of answers to the natural courtesy of enquiry.

The voices were growing distinct, one from another, faintly echoing as words began to batter at her uncomprehending ears. Words raised in argument, that kept her pinned in her hollow, seeking courage to accost these wayfarers.

'You do not fool me, Meg,' came drily from the male. 'I know just what brings you and Harriet here.'

'What do you expect, Charles?' This in a tartly critical tone from one of the females, who was seen to be fastidiously holding up her skirts of muslin, pulling them away from stray protrusions of gorse. 'Every year, we wait to hear at the end of the season that you are betrothed.'

'And every year we are disappointed.' This was the other female, who was sensibly clad in a habit of green cloth, and who stepped out vigorously in stout leather shoes. Her voice had something more of warmth, and the girl felt a faint relaxation of her tension. 'You must admit, Charles, that your recalcitrance is disgraceful.'

The gentleman kicked at an inoffensive root that happened to stand in his way. 'I admit nothing of the kind. I deserve, on the contrary, congratulation for evading the traps that are set for me year on year.'

'If you would only engage yourself to marry Belinda, there would be an end to that nonsense.'

The gentleman halted abruptly, and the women did likewise. 'Where had you this notion of my marrying Belinda? Have I ever shown the slightest disposition to be *épris* in that direction?'

'No, you have not. Charles has had five years in which to drop the handkerchief for her, Harriet, and since he has not done so—'

'More's the pity!'

'It is scarce likely that he will do so now.'

'I should not mind if he had shown the slightest disposition to marry someone else.'

'Find me a woman who does not bore me into a stupor with effusive charm, and I shall marry her with alacrity.'

Then the gentleman turned, resuming a rapid progress towards the tree where the girl stood peeking. She darted back out of sight. She could still hear the women's voices raised in argument. She must reveal herself now, or the opportunity would be lost. She willed herself to step out, but the sound of the gentleman's approach, his booted legs swishing through the undergrowth, kept her rooted to the spot.

She had taken in little of his looks, beyond the fact of his height and the ensemble to be expected of a gentleman taking a country walk. Breeches and a frock-coat of some dark colour, hair concealed by a broad-brimmed beaver. But his voice was easy and cultured. Even in his evident irritation with the women who accompanied him, there had been no violence in it. The recognition gave her courage.

She drew a long breath, pulled away from the tree, and thrust herself out of hiding, directly in the gentleman's path.

He stopped abruptly, and stepped quickly back with an expression of shock upon his countenance, uttering a startled exclamation.

Unaware that, a little way behind him, his sisters were staring with equal astonishment, Charles Clevedon, Earl of Wytham, gazed blankly at the willowy apparition that had manifested in front of him.

She was young and fair and, from the cut of her clothing, unquestionably genteel. But her gown was torn and dirty, her white features streaked with stains, and she was shaking pitiably. In the instant of taking in her unhappy state, it struck Charles that no amount of dishevelment could disguise the extreme loveliness of her face.

'Pray help me,' she uttered faintly. 'I do not know where I am.'

For a moment longer, Charles stood silent, his gaze riveted upon the appeal directed at him from a pair of clouded blue eyes. He was conscious for a brief instant of a sensation as of melting in his chest. And then it was overtaken by the instincts of a gentleman.

'Of course we will help you, ma'am,' he said, moving forward. 'What in the world is amiss?'

'Good heavens!' came from Harriet behind him.

'Are you hurt?' asked Meg, passing him as she ran quickly to the girl's side.

'My head.' The girl put her fingers to one side of the short fair locks that fluffed about her face, and winced. 'It is bleeding, and it hurts dreadfully.'

'What happened to you?'

The strained features turned in Meg's direction, and a muscle rippled in the wan cheek. 'I—do not know.'

'You don't know? But—'

'I cannot remember.' The willowy form swayed a little.

'Lean on me,' Charles said quickly, going to her side and putting an arm about her.

'*Merci.*' She sank into his support so that he was obliged to hold her up. The French word registered at the back of his mind, but he was too occupied to heed it. Her clothing was moist and cold to the touch, throwing a startled question into his brain. In a moment or two, the girl grew stronger, drawing a steadying breath and pulling herself upright.

'What do you mean, you cannot remember?' demanded Harriet, and a note of suspicion made Charles look quickly towards his sister. What did she mean by it?

'How did you come here?' asked Meg.

Charles felt the girl tremble within the circle of his arm. Looking down, he saw her eyelashes flutter.

'I do not remember that either.'

'But are you alone?' Harriet's tone was rife with disapproval.

'It seems so.'

'It *seems* so? Good heavens!'

'Harriet, be quiet!' snapped Meg. 'Can't you see that the poor girl is unequal to answering questions? Charles, can we not find somewhere for her to sit down?'

Glancing about, Charles noted a fallen stump some yards back towards the way they had come. Without a word of warning, he picked the girl up and began to carry her towards it.

The world swam, and the girl closed her eyes, clutching at his shoulders. A resurgence of distress had attacked her at the sudden flurry of questions. At some dim corner of her mind, she had expected them, and the knowledge that she had no answers was a thorn that pricked below the surface relief of rescue. Her headache nagged.

She was placed gently down upon the upturned hulk of a dead tree. Feeling the firm hands upon her shoulders, she found that the gentleman was bending over her, looking down into her face.

She took in hazel eyes in a strong countenance, sculpted in firm lines, with a good nose and a jaw that would brook no defiance. Under the beaver, his chestnut hair looked to have been not altogether tamed by the fashionable crop. A troubled frown that played between solid brows accentuated one arch. The voice was pleasant, but dry.

'Are you able to sit alone?'

'Yes, I thank you.' Nevertheless, she took a firm grip of the edge of the tree stump as he removed his hands. She was glad to find herself reasonably steady, and sighed in relief.

'Now, then,' came from one of the women.

The gentleman waved her away. 'Don't badger the girl, Meg.'

'I only want to find out what has happened.'

'If she cannot remember, there is no point in asking.'

'She must have hit her head badly,' said the female.

The girl found herself the recipient of frowning concern in a matronly face. It was plump, and its rounder features bore a resemblance to the man. They were softer, however, framed by richer curls worn pinned back below a fetching hat with a clutch of waving plumes that matched the colour of her riding habit. She wore a smile that radiated warmth.

'I dare say you feel quite dazed, poor thing. I expect it will all come back to you very shortly.'

The girl was indeed too hazy in the head to respond to this, unable to think beyond the immediate present and the comfort of no longer being alone. She was content for now to leave her future in the competent hands of her rescuers.

The Earl stood frowning down at her, wondering what thoughts might be passing in her mind. He did not think he had ever seen anyone look so white and frightened.

Harriet broke the silence. 'What is your name?'

Charles saw a faint line of concentration appear between brows so fair and delicate that the blue of her misted eyes appeared stronger by contrast.

'My name—'

'Yes, your name,' repeated Harriet impatiently.

'Harriet!'

'If this does not strike you as peculiar, Meg, then I can only say that I think poorly of your understanding.'

'I do not know what you are talking about.'

'Do be silent, both of you!' begged Charles, alert to the painful concentration in the girl's features. 'You are distressing her.'

Even as he spoke, the girl winced. Her fingers crept to her forehead and her eyes became dark and luminous. Words, despairing in their intensity, burst from her.

'I do not know my name.'

Charles' gaze remained riveted upon her face, caught by the haunting look that accompanied the words. A strangled sob escaped her. Ah, here came the tears. But, no. She swallowed them down, curling her slim fingers as she fought for control. A valiant effort, in the circumstances.

Glancing at his sisters, Charles saw that even Harriet had been struck by the girl's anguish. Meg was predictably moved. The girl spoke, drawing his attention. Her voice was a trifle husky, but controlled.

'Forgive me…I can remember nothing at all. I awoke just now, lying under some bushes. I have no notion how I came there, nor how long it had been. I could not think for the pain in my head, and I knew that I was lost. But it was only when you asked me, that it came to me…I do not even know who I am!'

She ended on a rise of panic, a wild look in the eyes that travelled across the Earl's face and those of his sisters. Charles was seized with the oddest desire—to catch her up into a close and comforting embrace. An absurd thought! He dismissed it, as the inevitable question loomed. What in the world were they to do with the girl?

'Well, you had better come home with us,' Meg said decidedly, as though she had heard his question.

The girl looked relieved, Charles thought, and her protest must be a mere formality, uttered for the sake of politeness.

'I do not wish to impose.'

'You can't very well stay here,' objected Harriet, with obvious reluctance.

'I should think not,' said Meg. 'What she needs is the services of a physician. Charles, stop staring at the poor girl in that hopeless fashion, and do something!'

Charles started, and nodded. He had indeed been distracted. A thought, stunningly novel, had occurred to him. Of course they had to take her home with them. To his home. Was it possible that this had been her object?

'Do you remember nothing at all?' he asked abruptly.

The girl looked vague, and shook her head. 'Nothing.'

'Perhaps something will come back to you once you have rested.'

Her lip quivered. 'I hope so indeed.'

Charles became businesslike. 'Then let us get you home. Can you walk, do you think? It is about a half mile to my carriage.'

The girl nodded, and, ignoring Meg's unnecessary directions, Charles helped her to her feet. She leaned heavily upon his supporting arm, but she was able to walk. He was tempted to pick her up and carry her, for they made but slow progress. Only the idea that was burgeoning in his head, if it had any substance, was so extremely irritating that he was damned if he was going to put himself out.

Every step but increased the girl's confusion of mind. She had been at first glad to leave matters to others, but the consciousness of her position very soon swept in on her again. It was difficult enough to walk, for her legs felt like jelly, and the ache at her head made her vision blur a trifle. But worse was the condition of her unforgiving memory. The explanation of her plight defeated her, but one troubled question lingered. Was this situation of her own contriving, or had she been left here by some ill-disposed person? The latter thought so wrought upon her senses that she lost her footing, and stumbled.

'Steady!'

Almost she had forgotten the owner of the supporting arm that upheld her. Through the numbing dispersal of her thoughts, she realised that she had not even thought to ask his name. She was tall, but he topped her by half a head. She turned to look at his profile.

'May I know whom I have to thank?'

She thought a shade of some odd emotion flickered across his features as he looked round, but she could put no name to it. He answered amiably enough.

'I am Wytham.'

'Charles Clevedon, the Earl of Wytham,' interposed the voice of the other female whom she had not taken in. Its acerbic quality drew instant, and unwelcome, attention.

'We are his sisters. No doubt you will tell us that the name means nothing to you.'

'Harriet, what are you at?' demanded the kindlier woman.

'Something that should be discussed at a more convenient time, I fancy,' said the Earl.

The girl saw him cast odd glances at the women. He must have felt her eyes, for his own turned back to her and he smiled. She became aware of his proximity, feeling it to be suddenly oppressive.

'Do not concern yourself, ma'am. I would not have you bend your mind to these matters until your hurts have been attended to.'

'Very sensible,' agreed the matronly female, coming in closer. 'How are you faring, my dear? Is the walk too much for you?'

There had been meaning in the snatch of conversation, in those strange looks, but it eluded the girl. Yet an instinct of alienation swept through her. She thrust away from the man upon whose aid she had been depending.

'I can manage, I thank you,' she said hurriedly.

'Take care!'

Too late she took in that her action had been precipitate. The woodlands around her spun. She threw her hands to her head, and was engulfed by blackness.

Charles caught her as she collapsed. 'Confound it! I think she has fainted.'

'How convenient!'

'Harriet, how can you? Charles, pick her up, for the Lord's sake!'

But her brother had no need of this injunction. He was already swinging the girl up into his arms. She weighed surprisingly little for so tall a female. Her head had fallen to one side, and he could see the red that stained her hair.

'One thing is certain,' he said aloud, as he began to move again, with swifter steps, 'she has definitely sustained some sort of injury.'

'Did you doubt it?' asked Meg, hurrying after him.

'I imagine there is every reason for doubt,' snapped Harriet, breathlessly keeping up. 'A more impudent ploy I have yet to see!'

'Ploy?'

'Whom has she to thank, forsooth! As if she was not well aware of his identity.'

'Harriet, have you taken leave of your senses? Charles, surely you cannot be party to this nonsense?'

But Charles was not of a mind to thrash out the subject at the moment. 'Whatever I may think, I repeat, this is not the time to be discussing it. Let us get her home first. Nothing is to be achieved by arguing the matter in the middle of the woods.'

With which, he hastened his pace, ignoring the protests of his sisters, who were soon lagging behind, leaving him thankfully to his own reflections.

It struck him that chance might not have favoured the female he carried in his arms. For he had come here today merely upon a whim.

He was not, the Earl flattered himself, a man easily ruffled, but it had been beyond what anyone might endure to have both his sisters descend upon him at once—and with but one mind! His decision to embark upon an inspection of the northern wood of one of the outlying sectors of his Teddington estate had been prompted by a desire to shake them off. To his chagrin, both had opted to accompany him, declaring that they had nothing better to do on a Sunday.

Preoccupied, therefore, and impelled to stride a degree more swiftly than the ladies might find comfortable, he had cast only cursory glances about him. Enough to see that his forest keepers were holding the wildness in check, for the thickly wooded area through which they had passed before discovering the lady in distress had been relatively clear of undergrowth. The gorseland had needed attention, and several of the massy trees could have done with pruning.

Had his attention not been taken up by the irritating insistence of his sisters on harping on the age-old matter of his continuing bachelorhood, he might have examined the state of the bark, and been quiet enough to catch glimpses of the wildlife his keepers were supposed to be encouraging.

A thought caused him to glance down at the female in his arms. Ironic, that enforced discussion, if it turned out that this was indeed another matrimonial ploy! If so, it was at least novel. He had been hunted by every means at the disposal of females possessed of even a modicum of ingenuity. But not one of them had thought of accosting him in his own woodlands claiming loss of memory!

It occurred to him forcibly that such a scheme—if it was one—must have demanded no small degree of forethought, not to mention acting skill. Improbable? Yes, but not beyond the bounds of possibility. They would discover soon enough whether the injury at least was genuine.

If so, it must partially allay his doubts. She might have abused her attire to create the necessary impression, but it would take an excessively determined female to inflict a wound upon her own head! And her clothes were damp, which argued a lengthy time in the forest. All night, perhaps? Confound it, she must be genuine!

The landaulet came into sight, and not before time. She was a lightweight, but he had carried her some distance, and the effort was taking its toll. Within moments, his groom was hailing him, plainly astonished to see him thus encumbered.

'Open the door, Parr,' he ordered tersely.

The groom made haste to obey, and Charles deposited his burden—a trifle ungently and with a good deal of relief—upon the cushioned seat of the open carriage.

'Who's this, me lord?' demanded Parr, and the coachman squinted over his shoulder from his perch in front.

'I have not the faintest notion,' replied Charles. 'We came upon her in the woods.'

She slipped down the seat, and Charles cursed. Jumping nimbly up beside her, he attempted to settle her more comfortably. The girl stirred, murmuring incoherently.

'Don't be afraid,' he said soothingly. 'You are quite safe.'

Her eyelids fluttered open, and the blue orbs stared up at him in an incomprehension that was singularly convincing. Charles straight away forgot his earlier suspicions.

'You are safe,' he repeated gently.

'Elaine,' she murmured.

'I beg your pardon?'

She blinked confusedly. 'You are…not Elaine.'

'I am Wytham. Do you not remember? I found you in the woods a short time since. My name is Charles.'

There came again that frown of concentration between her pale brows. 'Then who is Elaine?'

Charles eyed her consideringly. Was this some memory dredged up from her unwilling store? Or was it a carefully rehearsed piece of theatre? She pronounced the name with a French inflexion on the 'E', as *élaine*.

'Perhaps you are Elaine,' he suggested at a venture.

The cloudy eyes continued to regard him, a painful furrow between. 'If I am, I do not know it.'

She pulled herself up, unable to refrain from groaning at the protest in her head.

'Are you in pain still?'

'My head.' Her fingers rose waveringly to her brow, and thence to the place from where a concentration of discomfort emanated. They touched a point of tenderness, and she gave an involuntary cry. 'What have I done to my head?'

A warm hand closed about her fingers, bringing them down. 'It is better if you do not touch it. You have a wound there.'

She looked to the hand that held hers, and her gaze wandered up to its owner's face. A sliver of recognition penetrated the dull throb in her skull.

'I know you.' Her gaze travelled slowly beyond him, and she became aware of the confines of the carriage. Something leapt in her mind, and her eyes came back to him. 'You are taking me home. The women, where are they?'

'Good, you remember,' said her companion. 'My sisters will be here presently. I see them approaching, I fancy. You swooned, and I outstripped them as I carried you.'

The girl cast her eyes in the direction he indicated, and spotted the two females hurrying towards them, and a hazy recollection of an earlier meeting came back to her. In seconds, the whole sorry situation flooded in, and she made a moan of despair.

'I woke in the woods, did I not? My gown—my head—nothing made any sense.'

Her eyes went to her gown, and she fingered the soiled muslin, a resurgence in her mind of that bewilderment that had beset her—before she had discovered herself to these people. She was distracted by the arrival of the two women.

'So you have woken?' came breathlessly from one.

'Not only that,' said her rescuer, 'but she has discovered a name. She does not know whether it is her own, but for want of any other, why should we not use it? Elaine, these are my sisters. This is Lady Margaret Huntly.'

Elaine allowed her hand to be taken by the one she remembered now as being the friendlier of the two.

'Call me Meg. Everyone does.'

Smiling, the matron hoisted herself into the carriage and took a seat opposite. The second woman butted in.

'Give me your hand, Meg.'

'Lady Harriet Penderyn,' announced the Earl, as Meg helped her sister to climb into the carriage and step across to take the seat opposite her brother. She did not resemble him, Elaine thought, for though she was slim in the face, her nose was longer and her mouth pinched. She had cold, disapproving eyes, and her hair, under a bonnet as frivolous as the gown she wore—augmented only by a light pelisse, along with unsuitable kid sandals—was so streaked with grey that its original hue was indeterminate.

'That is a very pretty name, Elaine,' said Meg, settling herself more comfortably. 'We should certainly call you by it, even if perhaps it may prove incorrect.'

Elaine looked at her, and then shifted to the face of her sister. A sense of unreality began to pervade her, as she glanced thence to the gentleman—the Earl, was it not? All three eyed her back in varying degrees of interest. For a moment she felt as though she stood outside herself, an observer rather than a participant in the little drama. She did not belong inside it, for those involved were unknown to her, including that person inhabiting her own frail body. Her thoughts found tongue, though she hardly realised that she spoke, a low murmuring that drew even stronger interest.

'I feel as if I were drugged…so that nothing makes sense. They stare at me—and I at them. They had as well be ghosts for all they mean to me. The stuff of dreams, perhaps? *Alors, je ne sais pas qui je suis*…nor who they are. *C'est un mystère.* Is it possible that I will wake—and know?'

The hideous uncertainty of this thought set up a trembling within her. She had no notion that tears gathered at her eyes and trickled down her cheeks, nor that her fingers and her lips echoed the tremors inside. Only vaguely did she hear the hushed commentary about her, and the words made no sense.

'Did you hear that? She spoke in French.'

'Is she hallucinating?'

'I fancy she is only in shock.'

'She is not the only one!'

'Do be quiet, Harriet! How can you be so unkind?'

'Elaine? Elaine!'

Recognising that it was herself who was meant, Elaine turned her eyes towards the sound of the name, and blinked upon the strong features of her rescuer. A firm hand closed about her own, and a voice of authority broke through the distressing clouds about her mind.

'Listen to me, Elaine. It is a useless exercise to trouble yourself with these thoughts. Whatever it is that has happened, I will allow nothing further to harm you. You have my word. Now, rest!'

With which, Elaine found herself drawn by a strong arm to lay her head against the broad shoulder beside her. It was an invitation too desirable to resist. Thankfully, she relaxed into the comforting embrace, and closed her eyes.

'You fool, Charles! What in the world possessed you to make such a promise?'

Charles crossed to the fireplace and rang the bell. The grate was empty, no fire being needed on a hot June day. But out of habit the Earl remained standing before it, resting his elbow on a mantelpiece of convenient height and relatively free of ornament, bar two Wedgwood vases and an aged bracket clock with an ebony veneer. This item little suited the elegance of the later Chippendale furnishings in the downstairs saloon, but since it had been in the family for near a century, sentiment kept it in a position of prominence.

The Earl turned to survey his sister, who had followed him in, leaving Meg to usher the newcomer upstairs along with his housekeeper, whom he had ordered to prepare suitable accommodation.

'I cannot imagine, Harriet,' he said with mild irony. 'Unless it had something to do with the distressing state of mind our guest appeared to be in.'

'You used not to allow yourself to be imposed upon,'

remarked his sister, moving to seat herself upon the long sofa that stood to one side of the French windows. Like the suite of matching chairs, it was gilt-framed, and upholstered in striped silk of faded straw, toning with the painted walls.

'But am I being imposed upon?'

'Good heavens, Charles, can you doubt it?'

'I fancy there is a good deal of doubt.' He threw up a hand as his sister opened her mouth to protest. 'I know, Harriet. It is the most unlikely story, and my suspicions were aroused as quickly as your own. Yet I find it hard to believe that her agitation was other than genuine.'

'Nonsense. Any competent actress might be as convincing.'

'And the wound to her head?'

'We don't know yet that there is a wound,' objected Harriet.

It echoed his own thought, but Charles did not say so. He still found it difficult to believe that the girl could have faked the injury, but this point of doubt would be eliminated shortly, since he was taking immediate steps for her relief. He was also loath to agree with his sister in any particular.

He was saved from answering by the entrance of Matthew Huntly, a thickset man in his late thirties, whose easy manners and light-hearted approach to life had long ago won Charles' friendship and affection.

'What's all this, m'boy?' demanded his brother-in-law without preamble, strolling to the fireplace and delivering a hearty buffet to Charles' back. 'Ain't there enough females about town that you must needs go picking up waifs and strays?'

'Don't you start, Matt,' said Charles wearily, turning from the newcomer to address his butler, who had followed Mr

Huntly into the room. 'Moffat, send someone to fetch Doctor Gorsty, if you please.'

'Certainly, my lord.'

'Ill, are you, m'boy?' asked Matt, throwing himself down into an armchair set to one side of the fireplace.

The Earl ignored the question, but Harriet turned on her brother-in-law. 'Good heavens, Matthew, don't be so simple! It is for the girl, of course.'

Charles found his attention drawn by the gentle cough of his butler. 'Yes, Moffat?'

'Mrs Tumby is placing the young lady in the blue bed-chamber, next door to that of Lady Margaret and Mr Huntly, my lord. It is by Lady Margaret's wish.'

'Yes, very well. Thank you. Have the doctor brought as quickly as possible, will you?'

The butler bowed and withdrew.

'Meg's playing nursemaid, is she?' mused Matt. 'Thought she came for a rest.'

It had been the excuse she had presented to Charles. Not that he had fallen for it! Indeed, he had protested with some vigour—to both sisters.

'You have perfectly good homes of your own. Why can you not stay in them? And if you have any thought of encouraging your numerous offspring to descend upon me,' he had added trenchantly, 'let me tell you that I have this moment conceived a violent antipathy towards my nieces and nephews.'

'Why in the world do you suppose I have escaped?' Meg had demanded. 'The twins are home from Eton, and if I am to survive the summer holidays, a respite was essential.'

'Won't they create the more mayhem for your absence?' he had asked hopefully.

'I dare say, but I shall not be there to see it,' she had said airily. 'And do not imagine that Matt's presence would curb them. You know he has no control over those rascals.'

Baulked, Charles had turned his attention to the elder of his interfering siblings.

'I know you wish me otherwise, Charles,' she had piped up before he could say a word, 'but this is my last opportunity. I will be bringing Priscilla out next year, and will have no leisure to attend to your affairs.'

'I must be grateful to Priscilla! I only wish Fanny was old enough to come out, and that would eliminate Meg as well.'

'The trouble with you, Charles,' Meg had put in, 'is that you are spoilt. You have been sought after for so many years that you have become cynical and bored.'

'Above all, bored,' Charles had agreed.

'What is more,' had pursued Meg unheeding, 'you are tired of being desired for your eligibility alone.'

'It is a pity that this intelligent reading of my state has no effect upon your insistence on trying to thrust a leg-shackle upon me.'

'We have no power to do so,' Harriet had responded snappily. 'But you are two and thirty, and to be shilly-shallying in this stupid way is ridiculous.'

It would seem, he thought drily, that Harriet's anxiety to see him wed did not extend to his falling victim to this supposed schemer, be she never so beautiful.

She was explosive in her condemnation of their sister. 'This is typical! Really, Meg is impossible!'

'Here!' protested Matt mildly. 'I don't say she ain't meddlesome, but that's going too far.'

'Is it, indeed? Will you say as much when you discover

that she has taken some romantical notion into her head? Before you know it, she will have espoused that female's cause, and will be badgering Charles to marry her!'

The female in question, at that precise moment, was conscious of no cause other than the desire to be free of an intolerable spasm of shivering.

Elaine had maintained a semblance of rationality, despite the hazy disorientation that afflicted her aching head. She had taken in vaguely the leafy drive leading to a considerable mansion of white stone. She had held up through a flurry of talk that had flown about her as her rescuer had lifted her down from the carriage, and helped her up a long flight of steps, across a pillared veranda, and into a substantial hall with a wide central staircase, which split into two at a convenient landing, and rose to a galleried upper floor.

Deprived of that strong supporting arm, Elaine had leaned instead on the matronly Meg and a stout female who had flanked her on the other side. She had climbed the stairs, obedient to insistent voices, and traversed a number of corridors before being led through a panelled door. She had taken in flashes of peacock blue, and then she had found herself sinking on to the softness of a bed.

'There, my dear, you have nothing further to worry about,' had come kindly from Meg. 'You are perfectly safe.'

Even as Elaine had opened her mouth to render thanks, such a trembling had started up within her that she had been obliged to grasp at a convenient post. She had been unable to speak or move for several moments, and even now, as she lay where the two women had almost forcibly placed her, she was unable to prevent the spasmodic tremors that attacked her.

'Shock, that's what it is,' pronounced Meg, wrapping the coverlet about Elaine's slim form. 'Poor thing, you must have been scared to death!'

Elaine was able only to offer a weak murmur of gratitude as her kind hostess, throwing off her hat, began to chafe the patient's hands and feet, having sent the housekeeper to fetch up a hot drink. A thick fog held her aching brain in thrall, and a sensation of intense fear was all that penetrated her consciousness.

But presently the hideous shivers began to subside, and Elaine sighed thankfully, her mind clearing a little, the pain subsiding to a dull ache. Murmurs above her turned into words.

'That is better, for you have a little colour returning. Poor dear, you were perfectly white! I hope Charles has not delayed in sending for Gorsty.'

'Gorsty?' Elaine repeated vaguely.

'The doctor. You will find him most sympathetic. He has been treating our family for years, you must know, for we were used to spend a deal of time here in the old days.'

Here? But where was here? 'What is this place?'

'It is Clevedon House,' answered Meg readily. 'Oh, dear, I dare say that means nothing to you. This is the second of the family estates, in Teddington.'

'Teddington?'

'On the river,' explained Meg. 'Close to Hampton Court? It is almost upon our doorstep, though the Royal Family are not in residence just now.'

'But the woods…it was a wild place.'

'Where we found you? They are part of Charles' property.'

Memory stirred, and Elaine blinked up at the plump features. 'You are his sister. What was his name?'

'Charles? He is the Earl of Wytham. Surely you must have heard of him?'

Elaine shook her head. 'I do not remember.'

Meg let out a laugh. 'How silly of me! Of course you do not. Now, do not tease yourself, my dear. Just relax until Gorsty comes.'

Only too glad to obey this behest, Elaine closed her eyes, half drifting into sleep. But she was stirred into consciousness again as she felt wetness passing over her face.

'Don't bestir yourself. I am only cleaning off the dirt. Will you not remove that gown, and let me help you into a négligé?'

Elaine was disinclined to make any effort, but she was required to do little more than shift conveniently, for the motherly Meg accomplished all, assisted by the housekeeper on her return with a steaming brew.

At length, Elaine found herself sitting up against a bank of pillows, dressed in a voluminous cotton bedgown all over lace, the worst of the ravages of her ordeal washed away. The tea was refreshing, and she sipped thirstily. Even the headache lessened. A comforting lethargy crept over her, and she was conscious of a reluctance to grapple with her difficult situation.

She could not help reflecting upon the circumstances of her hosts. She was glad to have fallen, in this extremity, into the hands of people of social distinction, for that would make it easier to assist her to find out her history. Meg, who had left her to rest while she discovered what was keeping the doctor, had assured her that they would do so.

Meg—and Harriet, was it?—did not live here, she had said. They were visiting their brother. Elaine could only be glad of it. She dreaded to think what she would have done had the Earl been here alone. He could not have brought her to his home, that was certain.

Oddly, she did not feel out of place in these opulent surroundings. The bedchamber was done out in a blue print to the wallpaper, with toning curtains hanging from the bedstead—a light affair japanned in white with a blue pattern—and drapes to the windows of a brilliant peacock hue. There was gilt to the overmantel and the mirror above it, and a thick patterned rug to the floor; the corner commode and a clothes press set against one wall were likewise japanned in white and blue. Her host was apparently a wealthy man. What were her circumstances that she could so readily slip into comfort here?

Restless, Elaine set down her cup, and rose a trifle shakily from the bed. The movement resurrected her headache, and she was obliged to grasp at the nearby clothes press. But in a moment or two, it receded a little, and she was able to cross to a window, and perch upon the fine stool with rolled ends, conveniently placed before it.

The view offered undulating country, dotted with other houses nestling in neighbouring estates, and a formal hedged garden below. She stared down at it, taking in the neat pattern of the paths, the variety of colour in the herbiage, the little fountain playing over a plinth into a crescent pond.

As she looked, the garden appeared to shift, taking on another shape. There was now a stern formality in the design, a scent of roses, the fountain a marble statue of a female form, spraying into a circular dip that overflowed again into a wide pool. For an instant only, Elaine felt she knew the place. Then the illusory image vanished, and the garden was alien once more. She closed her eyes, and a surge of emotion rose in her breast. A memory! Had it been real?

Chapter Two

Charles eyed the younger of his sisters, who had come down from the guest's chamber. To his own surprise, he found himself eager for news.

'How is she, Meg?'

'I would have put her to bed, but she would only lie upon the coverlet,' answered Lady Margaret in a tone of regret, perching on the arm of her husband's chair. 'Have you sent for the doctor?'

'I told Moffat to do so a short while ago. But you have not answered my question. Is she still as anxious?'

'Anxious? She is in shock, Charles. I have never seen anyone so white! And the poor girl could not stop shaking.'

'Then why have you left her?' demanded Charles, with unaccustomed sharpness, causing his brother-in-law to shoot a questioning glance at him. He could have cursed. What had made him do that?

'Of course I did not leave her while she was in that state,' said Meg, affronted. 'She is all right now. At least, she has regained some colour, and she seems a little calmer.'

'Seems!' came from Harriet in a scoffing undertone.

Meg cast her a frowning look, but turned back immediately to Charles. 'I managed to persuade her to take off her soiled gown, and don a négligé. And she drank the tea Tumby brought. I came down only to find out if you had sent for Gorsty.'

'I did so immediately. He is unlikely to have many calls upon his time on a Sunday, so I dare say he will be here directly.'

Even as he spoke, a clanging sounded from without, heralding an arrival at the front door. Meg jumped up.

'That must be Gorsty now.' She crossed to the door, pausing there to cast a mischievous glance back at her brother. 'She is uncommonly lovely, you know. I can't help feeling that this adventure has all the makings of a fairytale!'

'I knew it!' exploded Harriet, as the door closed behind her sister. 'She has already cast you for the role of the handsome prince, Charles.'

'An unlikely role, if I may say so,' uttered Matt, amused.

'An upstart nobody of whom none of us has ever heard!'

Charles was betrayed into a laugh. 'We have now. Don't concern yourself, Harriet. I am as unlikely to allow Meg to influence me as—'

'As you allow me,' finished his sister. 'At least I make no attempt to thrust you into matrimony with the most unsuitable females I can find.'

'No, I'll give you that, Harriet. You are steadfast in supporting Belinda.'

'Good heavens! Belinda will be mortified to discover this female in your house. What in the world are we to do?'

These remarks found no sympathy with Charles. He strolled with studied calm to the French windows, which had been left open to cool the room, and looked out upon the vast green lawns that stretched away from the side of the mansion. If Harriet supposed he thought himself in any way obliged to answer to that irritating female, she had much to learn of him! So little did he care for the opinion of Belinda Tarrington, that the thought of confounding her with the presence under his protection of a beautiful unknown was almost enough to reconcile him to Elaine's arrival. He turned.

'My actions have to do with no one but myself, my dear Harriet. I propose to do nothing.'

'You will be forced to do something,' returned his sister snappily, 'since you have brought her here. Besides, you cannot wish people to know that you were foolish enough to become the victim of such an absurd plot.'

'Plot?' echoed Matt, looking in a bewildered way upon his brother-in-law. 'What the deuce does she mean?'

Charles sighed. 'I fancy Harriet thinks the girl intentionally put herself in my way.'

'Oh? I thought Moffat said she had lost her memory.'

'So she claims,' Harriet said sceptically.

'Ah, now I see.'

An amused look was directed upon Charles, and a quizzical eyebrow raised.

'Well, what?'

'Is she as lovely as Meg says?' queried Matt.

'She looks like a China doll,' stated Harriet.

Charles conjured up the vision that had appeared before him in the woods. 'She is ethereal, rather. Fair, tall and very slim. With a pair of bow lips, delicate brows, and the bluest eyes I think I have ever seen.' He grinned. 'In fact, she is little short of a fairy princess.'

Matt burst out laughing, but his sister was positively glaring. Charles gave her his blandest look, as though he dared her to refute him.

'She sounds enchanting,' said his brother-in-law. 'I should think you better marry her as soon as may be!'

Shaken by her strange experience with the garden, Elaine was relieved when the doctor arrived. She accepted without complaint Meg's protests at finding her out of bed, and allowed herself to be driven back there to be fussed over by the businesslike Doctor Gorsty, a well-looking man of indeterminate years somewhere between fifty and sixty.

He sported a dark tie-wig, and was dressed in a sober suit of black, an ensemble that troubled Elaine with a faint ripple of unease. But there was nothing alarming in his enquiries of her condition, made with hands clasped behind his back, and a look of kindly sympathy in a pair of intelligent grey eyes. Shaking his head over her recital, he approached the bed, saying that he must check her over before making a diagnosis.

Elaine submitted with patience to his examination, lying quiescent under his hands as he explored her limbs for injury. She was still weak, and a resurgence of shivering swept over her from time to time.

'You are cold, ma'am,' said the doctor, observing it.

'Oh, this is nothing, Gorsty,' declared Meg. 'If you had seen the way she shook when first we brought her upstairs!'

'I am not surprised, Lady Margaret, for her limbs are yet chilled, and it is a very warm day. We must take care that you do not develop a fever, ma'am.'

Meg shrieked at the possibility, but Elaine merely requested what the doctor advised her to do.

'Remain in bed, and keep covered,' he said sternly. 'Drink plenty of liquid, and as much warm milk as you can swallow. A little of something more sustaining later in the day, perhaps. It is my belief that you have been exposed throughout the night, which is a very dangerous thing.'

Elaine stared up at him with dilated eyes. Under those bushes! But why? She could not have intended it. Was she so lost to all sense of safety as to remain in woodlands *all night*? Why had she not tried for a way out—sought for help?

She became aware of quivers attacking her frame once more, for the questions nagged, reawakening the headache that had almost died down, which coalesced into that stabbing point of pain at her head. The answer struck.

'I must have fallen unconscious,' she murmured, wincing at renewed discomfort. 'Else I would have found a way out.' One hand went to her head. 'The wound! I was bleeding.'

With a sense of shock, she realised that the doctor's fingers were already working among her curls. Was that why it had begun to hurt again? She saw his frowning features close above her, and quaked at what he might find.

'That is a nasty cut, ma'am,' Gorsty said, shifting back from the bed. 'You had it, I should think, from a sharp edge of stone.' He smiled reassurance. 'Which would readily account for the temporary absence of memory, you know.'

Elaine caught at the word. 'How temporary?'

The physician was rueful. 'Difficult to say, ma'am. These cases are never predictable. You will probably find that you at first recall snatches rather than whole events.'

Had that been a snatch—the vision of a garden that she knew? Elaine frowned over that flash of picture.

'The best thing you can do, ma'am, is to resist *trying* to remember.'

Had he read her thought? Should she mention the garden? But it had been so fleeting a thing. She was not even sure now whether it had happened. Perhaps she had imagined it.

'Leave well alone, ma'am, and it will likely come to you bit by bit.'

It was a daunting prospect, but Elaine was distracted as the doctor reverted to the subject of the cut.

'There is a trifle of swelling, so that it behoves me to wash the wound most thoroughly. We do not want to run the risk of infection.' He sought in his bag for a bottle of some liquid and a roll of lint. 'A cologne, ma'am. Thoroughly effective, I think you will find. It has been known to prevent gangrene in amputated limbs.'

'What a delightful thought!' exclaimed Meg. 'Really, Doctor Gorsty, must you say such things?'

He laughed. 'Now you know me, Lady Margaret. I like my patients to know what is being done to them.'

Elaine gave a little grimace. 'I must submit myself to your judgement, sir. Will it sting?'

'I fear so. But the effects rapidly wear off.' He proceeded to cleanse the wound, and Elaine hissed in a breath.

She could not judge whether the sharp sting of the solution increased her discomfort, for the doctor's swabbing motions, no matter how gentle, were almost unendurable. She could not forbear a groan or two, and Meg tutted in sympathy.

'It may well be,' mused the doctor, 'that the swelling is itself accountable for your loss of memory. We shall see what comes to you when it goes down.'

'Suppose nothing comes to me?' asked Elaine fretfully.

'You have already remembered your name, have you not?'

'I remembered a name. I do not know whether it is mine.'

'But you remembered it, that is the point. I have no doubt that you will find yourself remembering a good many other things.'

As she had remembered a garden? If she had done so. Elaine stared up at his jawline, for his eyes were on his work. The stinging had subsided, but his touch, deft and gentle though it was, had thoroughly inflamed the tenderness. Yet the twinges could not wholly hold her attention. Apprehension gnawed at her, and the thought crossed her mind that she had rather not remember. But that could not be true. Of course she wanted to know—who she was, what she had been doing in those woods. Yet the fear deepened, and she could not speak.

'There, that will serve.' The doctor stepped back, disposing of the bloodstained cloth. He met Elaine's eyes and smiled. 'Don't look so frightened, ma'am. You will remember—in time.'

'You don't think she should go back to the place where we found her, and take a look around?' suggested Meg suddenly.

Conscious of an inward shrinking, Elaine held her tongue. Why she should feel so much revulsion, she did not know. To her intense relief, the doctor vetoed the suggestion in no uncertain terms. Elaine breathed again. But what had she been doing there? That the answer must prove to be unpleasant, she was convinced. Because for no consideration in the world could she bear to go back!

To the annoyance of Charles, his sister Harriet resumed the argument when they met again at dinner. Meg had left the table for a space in order to deliver to Elaine's room a bowl of the sustaining white soup that formed the first course of the meal. Charles could wish that she had remained to deflect Harriet.

He was himself in two minds. Armed with the evidence of Gorsty, who had reported to him upon leaving the invalid, he was tempted to be convinced by Elaine. Only he had been hunted too many times, and in so many ingenious ways, to be sanguine.

'Suppose that it is a plot,' he said slowly, surveying Harriet, who was frowning at him even as she spooned her soup, 'how could the girl know that I would choose today to visit my own woods? I did not know myself until this morning.'

'Ha!' exclaimed Matt, with a conspiratorial wink. 'She must be in a string with Shawbury.'

Charles saw Harriet throw him a withering glance, but not much to his surprise, she did not deign to answer this pleasantry. That his secretary could be involved in a conspiracy against himself was ludicrous. His sister was looking nonplussed. Charles sipped at the broth and waited, conscious of a feeling of satisfaction. It was short-lived.

'She need not have known it,' said Harriet presently. 'Most likely it was an unexpected bonus to have come across you in person. She probably thought to have run into one of your forest keepers. You will not pretend that any one of them, given her story, would not have brought her to you.'

Disappointment entered Charles' breast, but he suppressed it. The notion was all too plausible. His keepers aside, anyone finding in or near his woods a female claiming to have lost her memory must inevitably have produced her for his inspection.

'I suppose that is true,' he agreed reluctantly, laying down his spoon.

'Y'know, Harriet,' Matt said, grinning as he helped himself to a refill from the steaming tureen, 'if ever you should tire of Penderyn and leave him, you could readily get a living at Bow Street.'

'How Meg can stand to live with you, Matthew, I shall never know!' said his sister-in-law, exasperated. She turned again to Charles. 'You know I am right, Charles. The whole thing is nothing more nor less than a hoax set up to entrap you. I wish you will send her packing.'

'I can hardly do that,' protested Charles.

'Especially if she is so very beautiful,' put in Matt irrepressibly.

'You could,' argued Harriet, ignoring this, 'had you not been fool enough to give your word to the girl.'

Charles turned on her. 'Harriet, I am neither so callous nor so gullible as you imagine. I admit to some doubt about Elaine's story but, hoax or not, I can scarce throw her out of the house in the apparent state she is in. Besides, where is she to go?'

'To wherever she came from,' said Harriet waspishly. 'And the sooner the better!'

'I am at one with you there, but since I don't know where that is—and nor, apparently, does she!—I am not in a position to send her back.'

'What do you propose to do then, house her here forever?'

Matt tutted. 'Couldn't do that without marrying her. Most improper.'

'Matt, do hold your tongue! I suppose I shall have to institute enquiries, Harriet.'

He was relieved to see his other sister walk in at this moment, and rang the handbell for the butler to produce the first remove. Her husband greeted Meg with a jocular request to note how he had been acting as her deputy in hustling his brother-in-law into matrimony.

'I can't think what you mean, my love,' she responded, seating herself in a chair beside him, 'but I know you too well to enquire. I have more important things to attend to.'

'Yes, and that is just the point,' argued Matt. 'Here have I been persuading Charles to—'

'Matt, do be quiet!'

Receiving a slap on the arm, Mr Huntly subsided. The entrance of Moffat and his minions, bearing a selection of viands for the second course, put an end to the conversation. Charles served himself from a dish of pigeons in scallop shells presented by a footman, and led the discussion into acceptable channels by enquiring whether Elaine had fancied the broth.

'She is drowsy, but I think she will eat a little,' said Meg, accepting a slice of a raised ham pie from her husband's hand. A mischievous smile was directed at her brother. 'She is very dutiful, Charles. She has been taking liquid all day, and has swallowed nearly all the warm milk I sent up just as Gorsty instructed.'

'Dutiful!' scoffed Harriet, refusing the pigeons in favour of white Scotch scollops. 'For all you know she threw it away.'

Charles refused to be drawn by Meg's sallies. 'There is no sign of fever?' he asked, oddly aware of anxiety as he added a portion of pickled kidney beans to his plate.

'No, thank the Lord. I think she is a degree warmer. Only she still complains of the headache.'

'If Gorsty's description of her wound is anything to go by,' Charles remarked, 'that is scarcely surprising.'

'No, indeed. I shall go up to her before I sleep, for Gorsty left a potion for her to swallow at night.'

'How long does Gorsty think it will be before she can leave?' demanded Harriet.

With her fork suspended halfway to her mouth, Meg stared across the table at her sister. 'Leave? She cannot leave, Harriet! Where is she to go?'

Charles took up his wine glass. 'My point exactly.'

'Have no fear, m'love,' said Matt, his eyes dancing as he chewed ham. 'Your sister has the keen mind of a Bow Street Runner, and she is determined to find Elaine out.'

Darkness had fallen…and Elaine was running. The terrain was unfamiliar, and she tripped several times, gasping for breath as she struggled up, fearful that the sounds behind her betokened pursuit. She could hear someone calling in the distance, and knew that the hoarse cries issuing from her own throat were dangerously giving her away.

Someone laid a hand upon her cheek.

'You are safe…hush now, you are quite safe.'

Her eyes flew open. A faint glow fell upon a face that was familiar. A painful sob escaped her.

'It is you.'

'Yes, it is I. There is nothing to fear.'

Her hand stole out from under the coverlet, and groped towards the presence of comfort. 'He almost caught me.'

Her fingers were taken in a warm clasp. 'But he did not succeed. You are safe.'

'Yes.'

'Go back to sleep.'

Obediently, Elaine closed her eyes again, and within a short time sleep had once more claimed her.

When she again awoke, to the rattle of curtain rings, she found herself in daylight as a pleasant-faced maid of middle years pulled back the hangings about her bed.

'Good morning, miss. Lady Margaret bade me wait upon you. My name is Frodsham. Will you allow me to tidy you? My lady has taken the liberty of ordering some breakfast to be sent up as soon as you are ready.'

For several moments, Elaine was unable to comprehend the sense of these remarks. But presently a dull ache at her head recalled to her mind her unfortunate circumstances. It remained, however, obstinately empty of any remembrance of her past. Except for that dream, if it was one.

While she submitted to the ministrations of Frodsham, she found she could readily recall the substance of it. Someone had chased her through the forest. A chill crept into her breast. How easily might that be truth! Could she indeed have escaped from a man of evil intent? But who could it have been? She was glad that the dream had not lasted. Thanks to the comforting voice, the hand caressing her cheek…

Her breath caught, the thought petering out. She knew the voice. She had seen his face dimly in some glow above her. *Bon Dieu!* What had the Earl of Wytham to do in her bed-chamber?

'Hold still, ma'am, if you please,' begged the maid, who was trying to comb her hair. 'I don't want to hurt you, and my mistress warned me to be careful of your wound.'

Elaine apologised, placing a hand against the jumping

breath below her bosom. Had it been part of the dream? It must have been. Lord Wytham would not have entered her room in the night. With his sisters in the house, too! It must be part of the wild imagination that had plagued her slumbers. Only she no longer knew the difference between the real and the imagined.

She was glad to be spared further thought by the entrance of Lady Margaret Huntly, bearing a tray and a beaming smile. She was today simply gowned in a figured lawn low-cut across her ample bosom, with sleeves gathered at the shoulder, and a lacy little mob cap perched atop her lustrous curls.

'I thought I would bring it myself,' she said, by way of explanation, moving towards the bed. 'Oh, you do look better! No, don't try to get up. I am determined that you shall remain in bed until Gorsty has seen you again. How do you feel? No fever, I do trust. Is your head as bad?'

Elaine sank into the pillows that Frodsham had banked up again behind her, and submitted to the investigatory hand upon her brow as a laden tray was placed across her knees.

'I feel less hazy,' she said, gazing in a daunted way upon the contents of the dish from which Meg was removing the cover. 'My head aches a little.'

'Did you sleep well?'

'Yes, thank you,' Elaine answered automatically. 'At least…'

She hesitated. Should she speak of that suspected visit made by her host? Caution won. Or perhaps she feared to be disbelieved. Meg's mind was elsewhere, in any event.

'Now, don't look at the food as if it must choke you! See, the seed cake is warm from the oven, so that the butter melts.

And the bread is fresh baked and very soft. Now have some tea.'

Elaine accepted the cup, and made some attempt to satisfy her anxious hostess by toying with the food. But her appetite was poor. She felt too fatigued to eat properly, although it must be many hours since she had done so. All she wanted was to lie quietly in bed.

But when at length Frodsham had removed the barely touched remains of the meal, and Lady Margaret was induced to leave her to rest, Elaine found that peace eluded her.

It was as if her life had begun only yesterday. Her whole acquaintance numbered those few inhabitants of this household whom she had met. Oh, yes, and the doctor. The entirety of her existence encompassed a walk in strange woods, a carriage ride and her sojourn in this bedchamber. The rest was a blank.

Unless she could count that flimsy glimpse of a garden? And the dream. Her heart beat faster, and fear swamped her. It must be true! Else she would not be subject to this quivering unrest. Who was he? What intent had he that caused her to run away from him? To run so hard that she fell somehow and hit her head with enough force to pound the very life from her brain!

For was she not as well lost with her memory gone, as if she had died out there in an alien place? Alien it must have been, for it belonged to Lord Wytham, with whom she had no acquaintance. Why there, in that particular place? How was it that the man who chased her had not found her lying there, with a gaping wound upon her head?

Almost without knowing it, her fingers crept to the place

and gingerly felt across the swelling. Had the lump reduced? It felt a degree less prominent, but Elaine could not trust her judgement, so shaken had she been yesterday. Was still, if the truth be told. If she could but sleep!

Before she could drive herself into a frenzy, the door opened to admit Meg, accompanied by the doctor. Elaine sighed with relief, and plied him with anxious questions.

'Have you known many cases such as mine? Do you indeed think that I will recover all my past? Pray give me some assurance that it may be soon!'

'Be calm, ma'am,' came the firm response. 'Nothing is to be gained by throwing yourself into a fever of apprehension.'

'Oh, but I have had such dreams!'

'Poor thing, why did you not tell me?' demanded Meg.

Elaine shook her head. 'I was afraid that it might be true. A man—chasing me through the woods.'

'Lord, that might well be true! What do you think, Gorsty?'

'I think that our patient would do better to rely upon her waking memories. Dreams, you know, have a way of dredging up our fears. You awoke in a strange wood, ma'am, in a condition of distress and injury, and with no memory of what had happened. It is natural for your fears to taunt you with horrid possibilities.'

Elaine shuddered. 'Then you think it was not a memory?'

His smile reassured her. 'Highly unlikely, in my opinion.'

Some of the desperation began to leave her. 'And what of my wound? I think it is a little less swollen.'

She endured while the doctor felt about the tenderness on her head. He expressed himself satisfied that the wound was healing, and agreed that the swelling had subsided a trifle.

'But we must not expect miracles,' he warned. 'You are

bound to feel it for some little time to come. I hear that your headache is yet with you.'

'Yes, but it is lessening,' Elaine told him.

'Nevertheless, we will take no chances. You have suffered a concussion, and your headache is a part of that. Rest is the only cure.'

He advised her to remain quietly in bed and, if she could not sleep, to occupy her mind with something other than her wayward memory. Elaine thanked him, and watched him leave in no little dudgeon.

Easy for him to say! How was she to occupy a mind that had so little information? She might read a book, perhaps, if Lady Margaret had one to hand. Did she enjoy reading? How strange to know oneself so little! But perhaps, since it was the first thing that had come to mind, she was used to spend time reading. Unbidden, a further thought struck her. She was used to reading in bed!

She could see it. *Bon Dieu*, she could see herself now! Sitting up in a four-poster, its curtains closed all but in the corner from where the candlelight fell upon the pages.

Rejoicing, Elaine captured the picture, treasuring its detail in the expanding image. The curtains were dark within the enclosed space, but she could see the faint brocaded pattern—red and gold? An elusive scent assailed her nostrils, as of musk, she thought. And beside her, warmth from the human form that slept at her side.

Like a slamming door, the memory shut out. Elaine sat bolt upright, eyes wide, the subsequent jolting pain a mere nothing compared with the hideous notion that had struck her. A pulse started up in her veins. Could she have been mistaken? Had she indeed lain in bed *with a man*?

* * *

Charles looked over the last of the letters that his secretary had written for him, and appended his signature.

'Is that everyone?'

'All whom I can think of at the moment, my lord,' answered Shawbury, carefully blotting the signature. He was a spare individual, several years the Earl's junior. He was dressed with neatness and propriety as befitted his calling, with a countrified frock of dark cloth over fawn linen breeches. His cravat was simply tied, and his dark hair was swept severely back, merely grazing his collar.

The Earl, by contrast, had on a mulberry coat over buckskins and topboots, and a baffling intricacy in the knot at his neckcloth.

'I will have them conveyed immediately, my lord,' said the secretary, gathering up the sheaf of letters and lightly bouncing it on the desk-top to shuffle it into shape.

Charles nodded, and rose from his chair. 'I doubt if it is of much use requesting my neighbours to use discretion, but I don't see what else I can do.'

'A most vexing occurrence, sir.'

'Most,' agreed Charles, and dismissed the young man who had for several years administered all the minutiae attending the business of running his estates.

Crossing to the window of the small room he had adopted for his study, Charles gazed upon the verdant slopes. It was the open vista of lawn which virtually surrounded Clevedon House that ever pulled him to spend the early summer here. With the exception of the back premises allotted to utilities such as the stables and the kitchen garden, and several small bowers devoted by the late Lady Wyndham to flower growing, the land had been left to verdure. As a boy, Charles had adopted hidden eyries within the intermittent islands of trees, and used the wide greens for games of quoits or battledore and shuttlecock with Meg; and the lure of the river had drawn him irresistibly down to the edge of the Thames. The cosy air of the place still gave him that holiday feeling, and it was with reluctance that he would in late July quit Teddington for the stately grandeur of his principal seat—where Shawbury would undoubtedly demand his attendance to business.

Today, however, the peaceful setting did little to assuage the vague feeling of dissatisfaction that had beset him these three days. He was irritated to find that the advent of Elaine had affected him to this extent.

Or was it due to Harriet's unceasing references to the girl's supposed plot that had, despite himself, fostered his own nagging doubts? They were aggravated by the complete lack of any enquiry from outside his gates. He had sent a message to his forest keepers to keep an eye out for anyone caught searching his woods, but no word had come from them. Whoever the girl was, she remained unsought. It was increasingly difficult not to be swayed by his sister's belief.

Yet Gorsty believed her loss of memory to be genuine. Not that Charles had expressed his sneaking suspicions to the doctor. But the man's concern was evident, and he had spoken of similar cases with which he'd had to do.

Charles could wish that Elaine might emerge from the seclusion of her bedchamber, so that he could judge further for himself. But Meg had told him at breakfast that, although Elaine was improving after a second full day of rest, she had said that she preferred to keep her room. Hardly the conduct to be expected of a female attempting to secure his interest! Unless she thought by this means to intrigue him?

If so, she was wonderfully successful, for he must confess himself very much intrigued. Chafed by his inability to speak to her—if only to try to uncover some clue to her identity— he had set in motion the only immediate means he could think of to find it out in some other way.

It seemed logical to start with the idea that Elaine had not come from any great distance. Therefore he had sent discreetly to his immediate neighbours to enquire. Perhaps one of them would recognise her description, or have heard of a young lady's disappearance.

It was indeed vexing, to use Shawbury's comment. For the moment he had begun the business of enquiry, it had come home to Charles that there was no possible way he could avoid becoming the subject of widespread talk. His world thrived on gossip, and this girl was already living in his house! Had she the faintest notion what interest she was going to arouse? With a face like that, too!

As though he had conjured her up by the image that had come into his mind, he saw Elaine herself stroll into view, heading slowly across the area of lawn that led to the river.

She had come out of her room after all. And at a moment when she was unchaperoned. Did she know it? Harriet had gone to visit a friend, and Meg had this morning insisted upon Matt driving her into the village of Twickenham, so that she might bespeak the services of a seamstress she knew to alter one or two of her own gowns to fit Elaine.

Charles had been struck suddenly by the awkwardness of

Elaine finding herself in possession of nothing but the clothes on her back. It had goaded him into irritated question.

'Why in the world do you not go into town and buy her some new gowns? Chalk them up to me.'

'I had best wait until she may choose for herself,' had decided his sister. 'Besides, she can scarce go into town to shop dressed in my bedgown!'

Undeniable. Only here was Elaine, dressed somehow—not in Meg's négligé, nor her own ruined garments. How had she managed it? And so conveniently, while the other women were out of the way!

Charles watched her for a moment, his gaze riveted upon the tall figure. He could see only her profile, for she was walking with bent head, looking pensive. She could not have known that the route down the side of the house would bring her within sight of his study. But she could have found it out. Any of the servants might have told her, upon enquiry, where he was, and how to reach the room.

Irritated by his own suspicion, Charles abruptly shifted from the window. On impulse, he left the study and headed for a side door that led out in the direction Elaine was walking, alongside a host of laurel magnolias, their huge white flowers much in evidence. She must have heard his approach, for she turned her head before he caught her up.

Her beauty struck him afresh. The image he had held of her sprang into life, but he was nevertheless unprepared for the impact of those bluest of eyes. Something gave in his chest. He fought the feeling, inwardly cursing its intensity.

Charles saw her check, and lifted a hand in greeting. 'I saw you from the window.'

She said nothing, only waiting for him to come up, polite

question in her face. She looked calm enough—which accorded little with the accounts Meg had given of her distressed state. Either she had rapidly adapted to her difficult circumstances, or she was of a remarkably cool temperament. Was her poise courageous, or suspect?

He smiled with practised ease. 'How do you do?'

'Better, I thank you.'

'Is the wound still paining you?'

'Only when it is touched.'

'And your headache?'

'It is very faint now.'

Charles paused. She was not precisely unfriendly, but there was a touch of constraint about her responses. It did not argue the case for Harriet! Was she shy of him?

'I am glad to see you up and about. A surprise, I admit. I was led to suppose that you would keep to your room today.'

Elaine looked away. 'I had intended it. Only I could not rest.' A fleeting smile caught at him. 'I thought a change of scene might help.'

So she was not as calm as he had supposed. His glance slid down to the gown of figured muslin that hung upon her in an ill-fitting manner. It was too short, showing kid boots beneath, yet overlarge for her slim form, and gaping at the bosom. Moreover, the style was too old for her. If she was bent upon attracting him, it was not the ideal garment in which to do so! Apparently she read the disapproval in his face, for a low laugh escaped her.

'Your sister would be wild with me for appearing in this.'

'Which sister? It must be Harriet's, for it is certainly too small for Meg.'

Elaine lifted the skirts and spread them. 'That is what I

thought. She said it was the smallest she could find, and that she would arrange something better. It is very kind of her. And kind of your other sister, too, to lend me this.'

Charles reflected with some satisfaction on the likely reaction of Harriet at having one of her gowns wrested from her to clothe the 'upstart'. That would teach her charity!

'I believe Meg has gone out for no other purpose,' he said. 'There is a local seamstress who will no doubt be able to make you fit to be seen.'

A ripple of distaste flitted across Elaine's face. 'I think I had rather not be seen.'

'Oh, I think you must reconcile yourself to some exposure,' Charles said drily. 'How are we otherwise to locate those persons who may have lost you?'

'Je ne voudrais pas qu'on me trouve!'

Charles' eyebrow arched. 'I beg your pardon?'

The blue eyes stared back at him in guileless enquiry. 'Yes, my lord?'

'You said something—in French, I fancy.'

That concentrated frown pulled her fair brows closer. 'Did I? I do not recall it—and I cannot speak French.'

If that was not genuine, then Elaine was a skilled actress! Charles toyed with the idea of pursuing the matter. She had used that language before. But true or not, Elaine would undoubtedly hold to it. If he understood her correctly, she had said that she did not wish to be found—an intriguing statement, which could fit either way.

'Have you yet recalled anything?' he asked instead. 'You are not, I trust, torturing yourself with trying to remember. I understood from Gorsty that this was not a suitable remedy.'

He was disconcerted to find that Elaine eyed him most oddly. And then she seemed to evade the question.

'He spoke to you of it? What else did he tell you?'

'Nothing that he has not told you, I fancy,' said Charles with a smile, deliberate reassurance in his tone.

Somewhat to his surprise, Elaine's gaze remained fixed upon his face. She was regarding him searchingly, as if she questioned his words.

'Why do you look at me so?' he asked without intent.

She did not answer immediately. The blue eyes did not waver from his face, but the expression within them changed. He was bound to admit that it did not accord with a female who sought to capture his interest!

The question, when it came, was so abrupt and sudden, that it shook him.

'Lord Wytham, were you in my room that first night?'

Charles let out a conscious laugh. Then he threw up a hand. 'Guilty!'

Elaine continued to stare at him, a spark of anger now lighting in the blue of her eyes.

'Pray don't glare at me!' he begged in rueful tones. 'There was nothing more in it than a desire to assure myself that all was well with you.' He sighed, for there was no diminution in the fierceness of her expression. 'Elaine, you cried out in no little distress, and I happened to be passing. I might have woken Meg, but it was very late and she had been long abed. So I entered and it was as I suspected. You were having a nightmare.' He saw the beginnings of relaxation in her features, and added gently, 'I did not think you would remember. You awoke only fleetingly.'

He did not add that she had, unconscious as she was, done

more to incline him away from Harriet's suspicions than she could possibly have done awake. The light from his candle had fallen upon her face, dazzling in its beauty despite the rippling effects of whatever had been disturbing her sleep. She had looked movingly innocent, and he had been haunted by the trouble in her eyes as they had briefly opened to his call. It had taken some effort to harden himself against her.

Elaine's gaze broke from his at last, and she put a hand to her forehead. 'I did dream. I remembered the dream, and thought you had been part of it.'

'I am sorry to have added to your confusions.'

She sighed. 'It is immaterial. Doctor Gorsty says I should disregard anything that I do not remember waking, and you could not belong to my past.'

But had she some idea of his belonging in her future? 'Have you remembered anything waking?'

She hesitated a moment before facing him. 'There was a garden. The first day I came here. I was looking from the window, and I thought I saw a garden.'

'You did,' said Charles flatly. 'There is a formal garden immediately below that window.'

Impatience flitted across her face. 'Yes, but it was not that. The image of your garden altered as I looked at it—or I thought it did. It was for an instant only. But I thought there had been a garden like it…somewhere in my life.'

She ended on a wistful note that caught at Charles' sympathy. He suppressed the feeling, concentrating instead upon what she had said. It was so slight a thing. Could she not have thought of something more convincing?

'Is that all?'

Her gaze shifted away. Too quickly—her features all too

conscious. Evidently she realised that she must do better than that. Movement caught his eye and he looked down. The slender fingers at her side were clenched. She was tense. Well might she be! True or false, she trod a perilous path.

'Have you recalled nothing more?' he asked.

Elaine gave him a fleeting glance. Instinct urged her to trust him, but there was a quality in some of his utterances that both puzzled and troubled her. She had been startled by his sudden appearance—and a touch dismayed. She had concealed it, trying to appear calm. His features had been instantly familiar, though she had not remembered the fall of chestnut locks whose wilful curl defied order. Coupled with the hazel eyes, there was a startling attraction. His expression was bland, yet she noted an inflexibility about that firm jawline, a touch of unremembered hardness to his eyes. She had recalled only kindness, and wondered if her desperate state that day had made her stupidly blind. Perhaps Lord Wytham's generosity was forced upon him?

How then to answer his question, when she had lost all impulse to confide in him? Besides, she could not speak of that other memory—if it was one. What was he to think if she told him that a man had figured in a vision of a bed? Only the logical conclusion. But she wore no ring. A fact that had occasioned her a troubled night. And if she was a married woman, how had she come to this sorry pass?

'There is nothing more,' she said, keeping her gaze averted.

'Well, it is early days,' came the light response.

'Easy for you to say!' uttered Elaine, goaded into retort. She caught herself up. 'I beg your pardon, sir. You have done me a great service, and I should not have spoken to you so.'

Charles had been conscious of a ruffle in his temper, but this frank apology disarmed him. 'Think nothing of it. It would be astonishing if your mood were not a trifle uncertain.'

She smiled, and the sudden light in her countenance took his breath away. 'I have not yet thanked you properly, Lord Wytham. I only hope I may not trespass upon your hospitality and kindness for too long.'

It was a moment or two before Charles recovered himself. If that had been meant for an attack direct, it had hit with unerring aim! She was all too convincing. He summoned up the practised look of bored indifference that had for so long stood him in good stead against female wiles.

'I am at your service for as long as the business may take, ma'am.'

Puzzlement spread across her face. Or was it dismay? She turned from him and began to stroll on—aimlessly, he was persuaded, for she was heading directly for a clutch of laburnum bushes without seeming to notice. Her tone was politeness itself.

'You have a charming property here.'

'Yes, don't I?' he returned, on the same note of faint cynicism. 'Not, I hasten to add, the largest of my various estates.'

'No?'

Was there even interest in the one word? If she knew it already, why should there be? He took her gently by the arm for a moment, skirting the laburnum.

'Wytham is much more extensive. It is situated in Buckinghamshire, near Hedgerley Dean. I don't know if you are familiar with that area?'

There was a frown in the glance she cast at him. 'How should I be? I don't know which areas I may be familiar with.'

'I was forgetting that. Well then, let us see if I can jog your memory. You will have noticed that I am as yet unmarried—to the disgust of my sisters.' Another quick look came his way. Really, if this was an act, she was most accomplished!

'Need you marry?' she asked, her tone almost as bland as his own. 'Have you no heir?'

'Oh, yes. Harriet will have it that he covets my estates. In fact, Rob is devoted to politics and would think poorly of giving up his ministerial responsibilities in order to run mine.' It occurred to him that his cousin, should this adventure come to his ears, would be loud in condemnation. 'Besides, he has already been elevated to the peerage, and will no doubt rise further in his own right. Thus it behoves me to marry, you understand. A fact so well known in the world that it is not uncommon for females to look for unusual ways to secure my interest.'

It was a moment or two before Elaine took in the significance of this. The oddities of some of his earlier remarks fell into place, as did the discomposing change in his attitude. Unless she had misread the tenor of his speech? She halted, and stared at her host's face, indignation gathering in her breast. He paused, too, watching her, his expression unreadable. But that hardness at his eyes was pronounced.

Disappointment flooded her. A vague recollection of some earlier reference hovered at the back of her mind. That day in the woods, when they had found her. There had been snatches of dialogue that had made no sense in her hazy state. At the moment when she had learned his identity, was it?

Their import had some meaning now, if she had not mistaken him.

Hasty words rose to her tongue. 'If I understand you correctly, sir, I can only say I am astonished that you have not ejected me from your house!'

'Now why should I do that?' queried his lordship in a bland tone that threw Elaine into further disorder.

She had misread him! Or had she? She stared searchingly into his face, but no vestige of his thoughts could be discerned there. He looked at ease, his expression merely enquiring. Had she read suspicion where it did not exist? But there was falsity in his manner. Elaine could not trust it, and was unable to keep a slight tremor out of her voice.

'Let us hope that you are not long troubled by these importunities, my lord.'

With which, she turned abruptly from him, and moved with swift steps towards the house, beset by an overwhelming desire to weep.

Chapter Three

All the way to her chamber, Elaine was conscious of a bursting feeling in her chest that threatened every second to overcome her. At each step, the conviction grew upon her that she had not mistaken the Earl's meaning. He believed her to be involved in an elaborate plot to entrap him! Entering the room, she closed the door and leaned against it, her eyes pricking.

How could he think it? She had supposed him so very kind—her rescuer! How gently had he treated her that first day. And in the night—it had been no dream, for he admitted as much—he had been drawn by some distressing signal of hers to come into her room to investigate. Could he do these things, and yet harbour such ungenerous suspicions?

A sob escaped her, and she ran to the uncurtained bed, sinking down upon its cushioned softness and grasping one of the japanned posts—just as she had done that first day, gripped by those hideous tremors. Had not Meg told him of them? Did he suppose her to have conjured them from thin air? Oh, cruel! What monster was she imagined to be, who could suffer these good people to fuss over her without true cause?

Meg, whose care and concern had been all in all to Elaine in these first days. Was she supposed to have taken advantage of that matron's sincere compassion? It was unbelievable that anyone could think it. What, was she alleged to have put herself voluntarily into a situation of extreme distress and danger? All for the purpose of creating—what had he said?—some unusual way to attract his interest!

Anger blazed in her breast, and Elaine dashed the tears away with a savage hand.

'You, my lord Wytham,' she uttered aloud, 'must be possessed of an uncommon degree of conceit!'

What was she to do? She could not stay here, prey to his insinuations and distrust. Yet how could she go? Where could she go? She had no means at her disposal—no past to guide her. It would be the height of folly to leave the protection of this house. She had no choice but to remain. All she had on her back was a borrowed gown.

She sniffed, and searched unavailingly for a handkerchief in the pocket of Lady Harriet's figured muslin. Her eye caught upon the extremely unflattering line of its set across her bosom, and an involuntary laugh escaped her. She must have been simple indeed, had she any thought of attracting his lordship attired in such a fashion!

Rising from the bed, she shook out the folds of muslin, and crossed to the pier-glass set opposite the bed. She looked like a scarecrow. It was no fault of the gown, although its style was not to her taste. Was she ever thus gaunt? Apart from the way the muslin hung so slackly, there were shadows in her face. She leaned towards the mirror in critical examination. Her eyes were red, but that was to be expected. Was her complexion always so pale?

She stared at her face. How was it that she knew her own features? And the cut of her fair locks. Ought she to have been wearing a cap? Her unadorned head felt distinctly out of place. Did that mean that she was indeed married?

A pulse rippled in her veins, and her heart began to beat uncomfortably loud, thumping in her chest. Why? Why should that thought affect her so? It must be false! But if he was not her husband, then *who was that man*?

Would she might find the image again so that she could try to see his face, but it obstinately refused to appear. She had tried over and again these two days, but in vain. A comment of Lord Wytham's came to her. Doctor Gorsty had said that she should not try. Easy to say! But then, Lord Wytham did not believe that she had any memory to recover.

Yet there was one matter for satisfaction. If she was discovered to be wed, it would acquit her of this infamous design attributed to her by her host. Which presupposed that his investigations would prove successful.

Had he set about it? A scrap of conversation came back. He had said she was welcome to stay for as long as it took. Did that mean he had begun? If so, what had he done? She must suppose that he was as anxious to be rid of her unwelcome presence as she was now to be gone.

An image of his face came into her mind—as she first had seen him. The strength in it, to which she had instinctively responded, readily throwing herself upon his mercy. Had she imagined his welcome? Or was it distress of mind that caused her to see something that was not even there? Guilt began to invade her. Should she not give his lordship the benefit of the doubt? And if he had truly made an effort to locate her history, she must at least be grateful for that.

The thought caused her to turn for the door. She must know! She would find him again, and ask.

Traversing the galleried upper floor, Elaine headed for the stairs. Lord Wytham must have come in, for he had said that he had seen her from a window. Likely he had returned to whatever occupation she had unwittingly interrupted.

She had wandered around the left side of the house. Her glance encompassed the doors to that side of the wide hall as she came down the central staircase. There were three, and she picked at random the middle one.

It opened into a sunny saloon, done out in straw and gilt, with painted walls and a number of plush striped furnishings. Elaine halted on the threshold, realising that the room was occupied—and not by the Earl. She began to retreat, but was checked by a voice she recognised.

'Don't go!' said Lady Harriet.

Hesitating, Elaine looked across at the woman. She was seated facing the door, upon a chair that flanked the central fireplace. Her face was familiar, but the smile that curved her thin mouth looked oddly out of place.

'I would like you to meet a friend of mine,' she said, wafting a hand in the direction of a long sofa situated to one side of the open French windows.

The female indicated was the epitome of sophistication. She was fairly young, attired in an elegant white muslin gown, augmented by an overdress of lemon-coloured net, braided at the edges, and a flowered bonnet of green-dyed straw nicely complemented the golden curls beneath.

Elaine felt immediately conscious, and turned her eyes upon her host's sister. 'Pray excuse me, ma'am. I am not dressed for company.'

The woman's brows rose, and she gave an arch simper. 'Considering that is my gown you have on, I might be pardoned if I took exception to that remark.'

A slight feeling of resentment entered Elaine's breast, but she responded with deliberate calm. 'It is kind of you to lend it me, ma'am, but I am loath to show myself since the gown does not fit me.'

From the sofa came a trill of metallic laughter. 'An understatement! What were you about, my dear Harriet?'

'It was not me, but Meg,' said the other snappily. She was herself attired in a spotted muslin gown of similar cut, but crossed over at the bosom. 'At least it is better than if she had been drowned in one of Meg's gowns.'

Elaine took a step into the room. 'Indeed, ma'am, I am glad of it, for I have nothing else to wear.'

She was relieved to see Lady Harriet look mollified, and a smile more gracious than the earlier one was bent upon her.

'I am happy to have been of service,' she said formally. 'But do please come in and meet Miss Tarrington. Belinda, this is the girl I was telling you about—Elaine, we think.'

Unable to find a way to excuse herself that would not entail outright rudeness, Elaine perforce crossed the room and took the hand held out to her. Miss Tarrington did not rise, and despite the fact that she had to look up to greet Elaine, she did so with an air of arrogance.

'I am extremely interested to meet you. What an adventure!' She patted the seat beside her. 'Come, sit by me, and tell me all about it.'

It was the last thing Elaine desired to do, but she knew not how to extract herself without giving offence. Not only was she a guest in this house, but it had been made apparent that she was here on sufferance. This woman, for all she knew, was a female of distinction. She seated herself upon the lengthy sofa, at a slight remove.

'Now then, I wish to hear every last detail.'

Elaine looked at her, amazed. The woman spoke as if she sought the latest tidbit of gossip! Was she supposed to be an object of pity, or of curiosity?

'I do not know what you would have me tell you, ma'am. I know little beyond the circumstances of my own waking, and my discovery by Lord Wytham and his sisters.'

'Oh, tush, that is nothing to the purpose!' exclaimed the other. 'Harriet has already told me all that. But I cannot conceive how you must have felt in such a situation.'

It argued an insensitive mind. Before Elaine could think how to answer, Lady Harriet broke in.

'Elaine was obviously distressed. She behaved, you know, just as one would expect. She appeared disoriented, a little dizzy. Indeed, she quite fainted away, and Charles was obliged to carry her to the carriage.'

'How very romantic!' tittered Miss Tarrington. 'I declare, it is enough to make one jealous!'

At a loss how to respond to such remarks, Elaine remained silent, observing the visitor. Miss Tarrington was too thin in the face to be pretty, and she had an unfortunate trick of looking down a rather long nose. Her smile was superior, her pale eyes a trifle hard, and a jagged quality in her voice tended to grate on Elaine's nerves.

'I understand that your gown was torn and dirty,' she was

saying in a tone of almost ghoulish delight. 'Were you lying out in the bushes all night?'

'It seems so.'

'And you were actually wounded, I hear.'

'Yes,' agreed Elaine shortly.

'How in the world did that happen?'

Elaine could not help a tart response. 'If I knew that, I doubt I should still be staying in Lord Wytham's house.'

From behind her, came the voice of the man himself, acid in quality. 'In which, my dear Belinda, she ought to be safe from the morbid curiosity of the vulgar!'

Miss Tarrington jumped almost as violently as did Elaine. The visitor squeaked in protest, leaping from the sofa and turning to face his lordship who was entering through the French windows. A shriek of girlish laughter escaped her. She tripped up to the Earl and delivered a playful slap upon the mulberry sleeve of his coat with her closed fan.

'How dare you startle me so, wretched creature! No, and I will not bear your strictures, Charles. Vulgar, indeed!'

Since this indignant protest was accompanied by a flirtatious batting at the lady's eyes and a shrill giggle that went straight through Elaine's skull, she was in no danger of supposing Miss Tarrington to have been seriously offended.

Elaine was obliged to fight a flurry of nerves and a rapid pulse that had succeeded the shock of Lord Wytham's unexpected entry. She was glad to be spared any involvement in the conversation as Lady Harriet fired up in defence.

'Really, Charles, how could you? If Belinda is intrigued by Elaine's story, it is not to be wondered at.'

'Intrigued?' Miss Tarrington floated to the fireplace, clasping her hands together, and, to Elaine's secret dismay, the visitor's glance turned once more upon her. Was that rapt look in the pale eyes to be trusted?

'I declare, Harriet, I am far more than intrigued! I think it is vastly exciting. Do you not, Charles?'

The appeal was coquettish, the eyelids fluttering as Miss Tarrington made play with her fan. Although the Earl moved towards her, Elaine did not think that his response was other than polite. Indeed, his voice was decidedly flat.

'It is not the adjective I should have used, Belinda.'

Miss Tarrington wafted her fan, directing an arch look up at him. 'Oh, you need not say so! I know you too well to suppose that you would appreciate the romance of it.'

'If you suppose there is anything romantic in finding oneself suddenly bereft of all vestige of memory,' said his lordship, 'then your imagination must be singularly lacking.'

His tone struck Elaine as distinctly unamiable. What did he mean by it, when he had already given her to understand that he did not believe in her condition?

'Charles, how can you?' protested Lady Harriet.

A trill of laughter escaped Miss Tarrington's lips. 'Oh, don't concern yourself, Harriet. If I have not by this time accustomed myself to being criticised by your brother, then it must be quite my own fault.'

'I wonder, then, at your continuing to visit my house.'

'But we are such old friends, Charles. I am used to your ways. You will not frighten me away.'

It seemed to Elaine that the boot was on the other leg. Lord Wytham shifted to the far side of the fireplace. Beating a retreat? The visitor hesitated, and then swooped down upon the sofa again, placing herself all too close to Elaine.

'Indeed, Charles is right. You must be very distressed, poor dear Elaine. May I call you Elaine?'

'I believe you must, since I have no other name.'

'And you are not even sure of that one, I understand.'

'Unfortunately, no.'

Elaine could have wished that the female had chosen rather to converse more with Lord Wytham, for a certain penetrating steel to the pale eyes made her uncomfortable. The woman glanced again at his lordship, and smiled sweetly.

'You may scold, Charles, but you must confess that it is an extraordinary situation.' Her gaze returned to Elaine, who could not help feeling this was all done to gain the Earl's approval. 'You poor soul! Have you no recollection whatsoever of anything?'

'I am afraid I have not.'

'Extraordinary.'

Lady Harriet interrupted this. 'Obviously you don't recognise her, Belinda.'

'Oh, not at all. I could not have forgotten a face like this!' A flashing glance was cast at Elaine. She felt as though it sliced her. 'So beautiful, Charles, and in distress! Now do you see why I thought it romantic?'

A sinking feeling crept over Elaine as the Earl's bland gaze turned on her. She read scorn in his eye.

'My dear Belinda, I have been cast for the role of knight errant by so many damsels that I am inured to the lure of romance—however dazzling the fair victim might be.'

Elaine felt sick, but for pride's sake, she kept her gaze steady upon his until she caught, in the periphery of her vision, the look of triumph in the face of the woman at her side. Glancing quickly at her, she saw it veiled with a spurious expression of regret.

'I only wish I might have been of help to you in this, Charles, but sadly, it is not to be.'

'Do I understand that it was in hopes of placing Elaine that you talked of this matter to Belinda?' said Lord Wytham to his sister. The tone was sharp, drawing Elaine's glance.

Lady Harriet fidgeted with her skirts. 'It was always possible, Charles. I met Belinda at Lady Lilleshall's, and it seemed—well, I thought...'

She faded out, and there was a short silence. Elaine's distress began to give way to puzzlement. What was the man at? First he all but repulsed this Belinda; then he spoke in that alienating way, reviving her belief in his suspicion; and now he appeared to be angry with his sister for speaking of the matter. If he wanted to be rid of her, why should he care?

Miss Tarrington spoke up brightly, turning to Elaine. 'Such a shame that I have not seen you before. No doubt I would have recognised you, had you moved in the first circle of society, Elaine.'

For a moment, the studied offensiveness of this remark did not strike her, although she felt the hostility that lay beneath the sweetness. With a feeling of slight surprise, she gathered the import of what had been said. She heard a faint cough, and saw Lady Harriet staring hard at her visitor. It was without effect.

'What a pity poor Horry died last year! He must certainly have nosed out your background.'

'Horry?'

'The author Horace Walpole,' explained the Earl. 'But more famous for knowing all the scandal. He was a neighbour.'

'Strawberry Hill is but a mile or two from here,' added Miss Tarrington, in a voice of superior kindness. 'Horry knew simply everyone. Still, I am sure I must know everyone who is anyone—by sight at least.'

'So does Lord Wytham, I should imagine,' Elaine pointed out. 'But he does not know me either.'

'Where would be the sport if he did?' trilled Miss Tarrington. 'Or the point, if it comes to that.'

A faint bewilderment threw Elaine for an instant. She frowned slightly. 'The point?'

The eyes that met hers were of a sudden sharp. With malice? Elaine became aware of a shift of atmosphere in the saloon. As if the air were charged. In another ensuing silence, she looked at Lady Harriet and found her cheeks suffused with colour. As of instinct, Elaine's glance flew to the Earl's. The hazel eyes had narrowed, and the glint therein was startling. A pulse abruptly leapt into life at Elaine's bosom, as a series of recognitions popped in her head.

Lady Harriet shared the Earl's suspicions, had communicated them to this female, and Lord Wytham was furious. Then what was this Miss Tarrington to him?

'Elle désire être sa femme.'

'Oh, you speak French?'

Elaine turned quickly to the woman. 'I beg your pardon?'

'You were saying something in French.'

Instantly the puzzlement was back. Elaine frowned. 'I do not understand you.'

Miss Tarrington let out a laugh. 'My dear Elaine, it is I who did not understand you. You spoke with such a perfect accent, and in a very murmur. Perhaps you would care to repeat it for me?'

Blank with amazement, Elaine turned helplessly towards Lord Wytham. Suspicious he might be, but he had supported her earlier, and was thus the only potential ally in the room.

'What does she mean?'

To her relief, he came to her rescue. 'Don't tease her, Belinda. Elaine is not always mistress of her own utterances.'

He threw her a smile of reassurance, and Elaine felt her heart bump uncomfortably. There was no sign of his earlier anger in his face, nor of that blandness that hid so much— even, if it existed, his suspicion of her. A haze of bewilderment seized her. Had she imagined it all?

'You must understand that Elaine's ordeal has left her in some degree of confusion. It is not merely a matter of being unknown to others. She is quite unknown to herself, which must be very uncomfortable indeed. The last thing she needs is to be plagued with disconcerting statements.'

'But I only—'

'Well, don't!' said his lordship, quite gently. 'Harriet told you in order to discover whether you might have some knowledge of Elaine. Obviously you don't, and there's an end. I trust we may find someone who has seen her before.'

'Oh, you are bound to,' uttered Miss Tarrington airily. 'We all have about our estates those lesser circles where the ordinary local gentry may be found. Rest assured that someone will have seen Elaine somewhere.'

'Or it may all come back to her,' suggested Lady Harriet, with a sugary smile. 'I have heard of such cases. A sudden shock will often do the trick.'

'In that case,' put in the Earl, 'we shall have to think of some way of administering a series of shocks to you, Elaine. I wonder I had not thought of it for myself.'

The metallic giggle grated in Elaine's ear. 'Charles, you are dreadful! I should think she had been shocked enough.'

'I agree with you, Belinda,' he said, moving to the door. 'Insults are invariably shocking.'

With which, he walked out of the room, without a word either of farewell or apology. It was left to Lady Harriet to fill the breach.

'Really, Charles is abominable! What in the world can he mean by such behaviour? I must beg you to disregard it, Belinda. He has had much to vex him lately.'

Elaine found herself the recipient of a venomous look that accompanied this remark, and the little trill of laughter that issued from the lips of the female seated beside her quite set her teeth on edge.

'Dear Harriet, you need not make excuses for him. I hope I know Charles well enough to make allowances myself.'

But Elaine had seen her face of chagrin at the instant that Lord Wytham had left the room. It was obvious that Miss Tarrington was a pretender to the position of the Countess of Wytham, and she was put out to find Elaine living in the Earl's house. It did not seem that his lordship favoured her. Elaine began to think that perhaps there was some justification for an attitude of suspicion towards herself.

'What was that insufferable creature doing here?' demanded Meg, entering the parlour not five minutes after the Tarrington woman had been ushered out by Lady Harriet.

Elaine had not realised how tense she had become during the late contretemps, but as the door had closed, she had sunk back against the cushioned seat, expelling a long breath of relief. She felt unequal to withstand Meg's exuberance.

'Elaine, you are up! Where is Charles? I thought he had been in here. Why in the world are you wearing that dreadful gown of Harriet's? Oh, don't tell me you appeared before Belinda dressed like that?'

Elaine lifted helpless hands against the barrage of questions, and had to laugh. 'What would you like me to answer first?'

'Oh, my dear, forgive me!' Meg rushed across the room and dropped into the sofa beside her. 'Never mind me! How are you feeling?'

'Well enough, I thank you,' answered Elaine, and stopped, staring enquiringly at the gentleman who had followed Meg into the room. He was of middle years, and looked to be good humoured, with a pleasant face and dark hair cropped short. But he was staring at Elaine, his jaw dropping comically, and warmth crept into her cheeks.

Meg laughed out. 'Matt is obviously smitten! My husband, you know, Matthew Huntly. You must not pay the slightest attention to anything he says, for he is for ever cutting jokes. The thing is to ignore him completely. I always do.'

Elaine's eyes widened, and she knew not what to say. Mr Huntly bowed, his face creasing into an engaging grin.

'I was given a word picture of you, m'dear, but I can tell you it was barely adequate.' He glanced down at her person and the grin widened. 'Despite that ragtag you have on! What a fortunate thing m'wife engaged that seamstress.'

'Yes, indeed,' enthused Meg. 'She will be here tomorrow morning, and will have you sorted out in a trice. But tell me at once, Elaine. What did Harriet mean by bringing that wretch here, and how did you come to meet her?'

Elaine omitted any mention of her earlier unsettling meeting with the Earl, saying only that she wanted to find out what his lordship might have done to discover her history.

'Only I had no opportunity to ask him, for I mistakenly came into this room and found Lady Harriet in here with her visitor. I believe she wanted to find out whether Miss Tarrington had ever met me.'

Mr Huntly, who had taken his seat in a chair opposite, let out a guffaw. 'The devil she did! There now, m'love. Didn't I tell you Harriet was determined to play at detection?'

'Play at meddling, you mean,' said Meg irately. 'I'll warrant you she has told Belinda precisely how matters stand!'

Mr Huntly coughed in a meaningful way, and frowned at his wife. Elaine glanced at Meg, and found that lady looking a touch discomfited. Before she had time to wonder at it, the door opened to admit Lady Harriet.

'Harriet!' exploded Meg at once. 'How could you bring that creature here? And don't think I do not know what you would be at!'

'Be quiet, Meg!' snapped her sister.

Elaine caught the significant glance that was cast at her. She was conscious only of a rise of weariness. It was not difficult to divine the cause of these veiled allusions. That there had been much family discussion about her was evident. Meg, she guessed, was her champion, but she wondered if Mr Huntly shared the Earl's suspicions. Her heart sank, and she rose from the sofa.

'Forgive me, but I find myself tired out already. I think I will go and lie down.'

Retreating to her bedchamber, Elaine resolved to remain

there. No one could suppose her to be attempting to entrap his lordship if she did not appear in his sight!

Restless, Elaine wandered along the upper corridors towards the back of Clevedon House. She would have gone outside but for the drizzle that had succeeded yesterday's heat. It had rained heavily in the night and she had slept little. Which, after the snatch of conversation she had overheard last night, was scarcely surprising.

Owing to the exertions of Mrs Droxford, the diligent seamstress whose services had been bespoken by Meg on her behalf, Elaine had been induced to surprise her hosts with an appearance at the dinner table. Mrs Droxford had made over an evening gown of gauze over a rose petticoat, with long sleeves and a low-cut bosom that had been augmented with a lace frill in deference to Elaine's supposedly single state. When she had tried it, the finished gown had so raised Elaine's spirits that she had forgotten her resolve to stay aloof and ventured forth, despite having told Meg that she would eat in her room.

This happy state of mind had lasted only as long as it had taken her to arrive at the dining-room door to the right of the grand staircase. Her fingers had turned the handle, but as she had begun to push the door open, Meg's voice had floated clearly from behind it, and she had frozen at her words.

'It is your fault that she will not come out of her room, Harriet. Yours, too, Charles, for allowing Harriet to persuade you into disbelieving Elaine's story!'

'I don't yet know what I believe,' had come from the Earl.

'It is no surprise that you are taken in, Meg. Charles has at least the sense to express some doubt.'

That had been Lady Harriet's mocking tones. Then Lord Wytham had taken the matter up again.

'It is of no use to look like that, Meg. You know I have been hunted by every possible means.'

'True,' had interpolated a new voice. Later, she had realised it had been Mr Huntly. 'I've seen females at it. Charles is bound to be wary.'

'Yes, indeed. But really, Charles, not *this*.'

'Why not this?'

Elaine had missed the next few remarks, for her heart had been thumping unbearably hard, and she had found herself breathless with upset. All she had wanted was to escape, but she must have made some slight sound, for even as she had moved with the intention to close the door with stealth, it had been pulled open from within. Elaine had found herself looking into the face of Moffat, the butler, as all discussion within the room had instantly ceased.

She had stood poised upon the threshold, in an agony of indecision, as four startled and conscious faces had looked towards her from under two huge chandeliers that brightened the centre of the room above the table.

Then Meg had risen, moving swiftly to the door, a glib and voluble welcome upon her lips. Elaine had been swept to the long oaken table, finding that the gentlemen had risen, and in the flurry of creating a place for her, it had been possible to fall into the welcome deliverance of pretence.

Elaine had accepted with a slight smile the Earl's compliment upon her improved appearance, and had feigned amusement at Mr Huntly's remarking upon the made-over gown never having looked so well. But by the time Elaine had been served with a dish of buttered crab for the first course, discomfort had made itself felt, reigning throughout dinner.

Conversation had been stilted, and Lord Wytham all too bland. Meg had clearly been suppressing a good deal of spleen, and had cast unloving glances at her sister throughout the meal, adopting a pointedly caressing manner towards Elaine. Lady Harriet had been markedly silent, her features pinched and set. Only Mr Huntly had appeared unaffected, except for the occasional frowning glance of concern cast at his wife.

Elaine had wished fervently that she had not been tempted to come down to have all her unhappy doubts irrefutably confirmed. Her distress had been acute, and the worse for a consciousness of being the cause of dissension within the family group. If only there was an alternative to accepting the unwilling hospitality of the Earl of Wytham! But until such offered, she would keep out of everyone's way.

She had taken her breakfast on a tray in her room, and allowed herself to be hustled into another of Meg's gowns, which the indefatigable Mrs Droxford had found time to alter down last night. Lady Margaret, said the maid, sent her apologies, for she expected to be out for most of the day. Relieved, Elaine had donned the round gown of white muslin, pleased both with its fit and its simplicity, and had sat down to await the expected visit of the doctor.

But this had passed without incident.

'The wound is healing well, ma'am, and there is little more I can do for you. Do not hesitate to send for me, however, should you feel the slightest need. Or—' and he had smiled understandingly '—should the deficiencies of your memory prove too distressful.'

Elaine had been more distressed by the matter of her host's unkind suppositions, and the doctor could not help her there. She had tried to settle after his departure, but had found herself weary of the limited surroundings of her bed-chamber. Thus she found herself hunting distraction in an agitated meander about Clevedon House.

In a bid to avoid encountering any member of the family, she kept to the upper floors. There were paintings upon the papered walls, and ornaments enough set into every niche to furnish interest. Her wanderings around the corridors brought her up to a third floor, and thence to the gallery that ran around the main front staircase. Looking over it, she saw the wide hall far below, and two potted palms either side the stairs that she had not before noticed.

There was no one about, and she wandered along the gallery with one hand on the polished wood bannister rail.

The doors that she passed were closed, so she could not accuse herself of spying. Yet at one corner was a door un-latched. Moving to shut it, she went to grasp the handle, but it slipped away from her and swung further open.

Feeling absurdly guilty, Elaine moved a little into the room, and realised that she must have reached one of the bays at the front of the house. It was a small room, bare-walled and almost empty, but for a couple of trunks to one side, a straight-backed chair from which the seat stuffing was protruding, and an odd-shaped structure covered with a dust sheet. Evidently she had stumbled upon a disused room now kept for storage.

She was about to leave when something about the concealed object stayed her. Elaine stared at it, a hint of recognition hovering in her mind. Almost without meaning to, she crossed to grasp the sheet that covered it, dragging it slowly off.

Mesmerised, Elaine gazed at the harp. A picture broke into her mind: fingers on the harp strings, plucking in rhythm; beyond them—an expression of tenderness in the eyes, and upon the lips a dreamy smile—the face of a man.

A sob caught in Elaine's throat. The sheet fell from her hand, and she reached out, grasping the frame. But for that support, she would have fallen. In a second, the image was gone, and all she could see were her own trembling hands, clutching tightly at the gilded wood.

What had that been? Whom had it been? Could it have been *that man*? A feeling of intense sadness overcame her, and she knew she did not want to remember.

Her legs felt weak. Letting go of the harp, she staggered to the damaged chair, and sank into it, her eyes riveted upon the fatal instrument. Here was something at last! Only she could not bear to explore it. The very question of whose face it might be threw her into acute panic. As for whose fingers were playing, the answer was obvious.

She lifted her hands and turned them, examining the curling fingers. Had it been these very fingers plucking at the strings? There was one way to find out!

In anxious haste, she got up and crossed to the harp. Her fingers shook as she reached for the strings with one hand. She ran her fingers across them, producing a ripple of sound. But that was not how it was done! She drew the chair closer and sat again, setting her knees either side the harp. She tipped it into position, and drew an unsteady breath. Flexing her fingers, she placed them on the strings.

The strains of music reached the Earl as he headed towards the stairs from his personal apartments on the first floor. He had just changed his clothes, having come in with his brother-in-law from a morning ride cut short by the rain. Pausing at the top of the central stairway, he listened intently.

The sound was faint and came from above. It was a sound he had not heard for many years in his own house, but he recognised it instantly. Who in the world could be playing up there—and in so intermittent a fashion? For there was little continuity in what he heard. A series of notes, and then a pause. A repetition which stopped abruptly. Then something quite other, breaking off in mid-note.

A possibility entered his mind. Could it be? There was no one else in this house likely to take up the harp. Intrigued, Charles moved swiftly to the staircase at the other end of the gallery, and ran lightly up two flights. Following the broken sounds, he took a few quick strides which brought him to the corner of the mansion. He checked in the doorway to the little room in the bay.

It was indeed Elaine! Had it been instinct that told him so? Her features were tight with concentration, a frown between her brows, as she struggled for the sequence she sought to remember. That she was at home with the instrument was evident, for her fingers plucked the strings with practised movements, pulling away as each note was struck. It was only the melody that escaped her.

For several moments, Charles was able to watch her undetected. She looked much younger—and all too innocent!—in a gown of white that seemed moulded to her slim form, and fell in graceful folds that revealed a shapely leg beneath. It was with mixed feelings that Charles' eyes played over the contours of her face. From where had she come, with that exquisite countenance? Such enchantment in the angelic blue of her eyes! If he had not such a rooted distaste for trickery, he might readily succumb to her wiles— if impostor she was.

Harriet, of course, had no such doubts. He was furious with her for dragging Belinda into the equation. Yet his reaction had been mild compared to Meg's when she had discovered that their sister had blurted out their suspicions to Belinda.

'How perfectly birdwitted you are, Harriet!' Meg had exploded. 'Don't you know that the whole neighbourhood will be apprised of the matter before the day is out?'

'True,' had agreed Matt. 'Regular gabster, that girl.'

Charles could not acquit himself of complicity in the business, however. For he had allowed Belinda to goad him into defending his position. And that after he had tried to throw dust in her eyes by supporting Elaine's story! Not, he admitted ruefully, that this had been his object at the time. The case was that Belinda's trite observations had irritated him beyond endurance. If Elaine was genuine, the stupid female's remarks had been insensitive in the extreme.

He had been uneasy on the following day, awaiting Meg's predicted descent upon them of the gossipmongers. They had not come. But neither had Elaine emerged from her seclusion, and his sisters had again fallen into dispute—just as Elaine had walked in upon them as they dined.

Had she heard them? If so, she had been remarkably cool. Which had demonstrated, Harriet had insisted—when Elaine had retired and argument had broken out again over tea in the saloon—that it suited Elaine better to pretend to be ignorant of suspicion.

Charles was by no means convinced. Her manner towards

himself had been distinctly unalluring. Indeed, he had been nettled by her adroit ability to slide out of his attempts to engage her in conversation. She had answered Matt with more friendliness! And Meg had revived his sense of grievance.

'There is nothing for it, Charles,' she had insisted, 'I will do the rounds tomorrow and spread the story myself.'

He had frowned heavily. 'I dislike having my hand forced. I could have wished to await answers from my neighbours.'

'Whose wives would likely have leaked the story,' had said Harriet waspishly, to his further irritation.

It had been Matt who had cut in before Charles had an opportunity to express himself further on the subject. 'No point in speculating. All water under the bridge now. What we need is a campaign.'

'Just so,' had agreed Charles. 'What do you mean to say to people, Meg? The most irritating part of the business is that I will be held to distrust Elaine.'

'Whose fault is that?' had demanded Meg, glaring at their sister. 'And it is true!'

'Stop it, Meg!'

Glad once again of Matt's intervention, Charles had controlled his temper. 'True or not, she is in my care. To allow people to suppose that I don't believe her story would be the height of impropriety.'

'What do you expect Meg to do?' had demanded Harriet. 'She can hardly mention it without people immediately guessing at the truth.'

'It is not the truth!' Charles had snapped. Then he had checked himself. 'Because I am suspicious, it does not mean that I am convinced. Indeed, quite otherwise.'

Meg had applauded this, and in the end they had been agreed that she should not speak of his distrust unless anyone mentioned it to her.

'And then I shall say that Belinda mistook you. Even if people don't believe it, they must at least harbour doubt. Everyone knows that Belinda hears what she wants to hear.'

But Charles had not been entirely satisfied. 'If Belinda speaks of the matter to you, Harriet, you must say that you were misinformed.'

'Good heavens, why should I?'

'Harriet, you owe it to Charles,' urged Meg.

'I am offering you no choice, Harriet,' he had said, deliberately cold. 'If you wish to remain here, those are the terms.'

Meg had visibly brightened. 'By all means, let her go. Elaine does not need more than one chaperon, and I can adequately fill that role.'

It had been, Charles realised, too much to hope for. Harriet had capitulated, saying that she knew what would happen if she left Meg to her own devices. He could only hope his sister's mission would prove fruitful, serving at least to counter the worst outcome of the inevitable rumour-mongering.

He became aware that Elaine's fingers had stilled. Her head turned, and a tiny gasp escaped the bow lips. Her hands flattened against the strings, cutting off their vibrations.

'Did I startle you? Pray don't stop.'

She returned the harp to its upright position and withdrew her fingers, clasping her hands in her lap. 'I should not have started.'

'Why not?' He said it lightly, shifting into the room. 'This was my mother's instrument. No one has played it for years.'

Elaine looked away from him. 'I cannot be said to have been playing it.'

'Oh, come. You may be rusty, but it is obvious that you have talent.'

She frowned at the harp. 'I cannot remember enough.'

'Could it be that you are trying too hard?'

The blue eyes came around to his again. 'It could be that I was never very good.'

Charles smiled. 'I don't believe that.'

The clouded eyes remained upon his. 'It is all of a piece. Is there anything that you do believe?'

So she had overheard them! He felt immediately guilty, and crushed it. But how to respond? He hesitated, and saw her glance shift away. A faint colour rose in the pale cheeks.

'I beg your pardon. I should not have—I did not mean to speak of it.'

Grimness settled into his chest. 'Perhaps it is as well.'

Her gaze returned to his. 'Is it?'

Was that hurt in her eyes? He did not reply for a moment, instead moving to the far window so that he need not meet the blue gaze. Again the guilt rose. Why should he feel it? He had every reason to be wary. Yet her upset reproached him. If she was innocent, she had a right to be upset. He turned.

'We have made you uncomfortable, I fancy. I am sorry for that at least.'

'But not for your suspicions.' Abruptly she rose from the chair, heading for the door.

An involuntary surge of feeling shot through Charles. Without thought, he crossed the room and caught her by the arm.

Chapter Four

Elaine checked, looking round at him. The expression in her eyes threw Charles into speech.

'Don't look like that, I beg of you! I am truly sorry for your suffering.'

'How can you be, when you don't believe in it?'

An unaccountable shaft of irritation struck him, and he released her abruptly. 'I have not said that I don't believe in your condition, Elaine.'

She turned to face him. 'What, then? Do you think the wound was self-inflicted? Did I take a stone and hit myself on the head? Or do you suppose Doctor Gorsty to be in my confidence? Perhaps I have paid him to keep silent!'

'No, that is an absurdity, but—'

'But what, my lord?' Elaine demanded despairingly. 'How have you settled it amongst you? I acquit Meg, for she championed me, and I cannot suppose her kindness to be feigned. But I would be glad to know how you, and Lady Harriet—and your precious Miss Tarrington!—may suppose a female could subject herself to the indignities of my circumstances only for the motive which you attribute to me.'

Her words might have reproved him—she made enough sense!—but they had the opposite effect. He was chagrined beyond words, and his response came unbidden.

'We will leave Miss Tarrington out of this discussion, if you please.'

'I have no wish to talk of her, my lord.'

'I am equally unanswerable for my sister's views.'

'But not for your own!'

Elaine turned abruptly from him, and swept back to the chair by the harp. She was at once furious, and ashamed at having lost her temper. She sat down, and without thought, stretched her fingers to the instrument, pulling it towards her. But she plucked the strings with no real idea of what she did, heedless of the sounds that echoed round the room.

She should not have spoken out, she had no right. Now she would have to beg his pardon—and she could not! A riot of distress engaged her bosom, and her thoughts were all chaos. She closed her eyes, and laid her forehead against the frame, her fingers coming to rest.

'Elaine?'

It was gently said, and she pulled quickly upright, her eyes fixed upon the harp even as she spoke.

'Pay no heed to me! You have been generous—I should have remained silent. Had it not been for what I heard last night, I should not have… Forgive me, pray!'

'Elaine, for God's sake!' came from his lordship in explosive accents.

She looked at him, and found the hazel eyes half-rueful, half-exasperated. 'My lord?'

'I wish you will not be so absurd!' he uttered rapidly. 'Say what you wish to, only cease this oppressive gratitude! It is no more than anyone might have done.'

'Except that you are not anyone,' said Elaine, before she could stop herself. 'And therein lies the difficulty.'

Charles paused for a moment. This was getting them nowhere. Now that the murder was out, he could hardly leave the discussion where it was. Something had to be said. He felt impelled to defend himself. He shifted to the window and spoke without looking at her.

'If I am cynical, Elaine, I have good reason. I have been an object of unremitting pursuit for the last dozen years.'

'Well, you are uncommonly eligible, are you not?' said Elaine bitterly. 'You hinted as much to me the other day. But I am forgetting. I knew it already, did I not? Else I had not concocted this elaborate scheme to trap you into matrimony.'

Her sarcasm irritated Charles, but at the back of his mind came the obstinate supposition that she would be bound to take that tone if she were acting a part. He turned to face her.

'It seems ridiculous to you? I fancy it is not so far-fetched. I do not wish to sound like a coxcomb, Elaine, but I have had females literally swoon at my feet in the open street. If you don't believe me, Matt will bear me out. He was present on one occasion.'

Elaine continued to regard him with mockery in her eyes. 'I must remember to ask him.'

'You don't believe me, I see that. There is more. I have been tricked into accepting false invitations, and found myself tête-à-tête in situations of alarming intimacy. I have even been waylaid in a bedchamber by a debutante intent upon getting herself compromised by me.'

Elaine was secretly aghast. She could not doubt him. Why should he make up such a tale? Yet her resentment at being herself accused was undiminished. She knew little of herself, but it galled her to be coupled with women of this description. She could not keep the tartness from her voice.

'Do you seek to convince me of my own guilt?'

Charles bit back a sharp retort. It was natural enough that she should be angry and bitter, but he was determined that she should recognise his reasoning.

'What I am trying to convey to you is that my experience has moulded me. There is no end to the wiles of women. Not that I suppose these efforts to be provoked by anything other than my riches and my title.'

'Yet you are not precisely unhandsome.'

Which was true, for he looked excessively attractive, the rich colour of his untamed locks enhanced perhaps by the forest green coat he had chosen to wear.

'That hardly enters the equation,' said Charles, a trifle embarrassed. 'But, yes, I had hoped to convince you that it is not concentrated vanity that makes me suspicious.'

Elaine sighed, and stared up at him, a sense of hopelessness damping down the bitter hurt. 'Very well, I am convinced. I have nothing to offer in return—' She stopped, remembering suddenly the bed, and the man who lay beside her. 'But there is something!'

Light had entered her face, and Charles found himself holding his breath. If she could indeed prove herself!

'I did not speak of it before, for the memory—'

'You have recalled something?'

'I might have told you when first we spoke of it, but I could not—then.' She met his eyes and, half-unknowing, her fingers sought for the strings of the harp. 'Just now—before you came in—there was something more, and I think...'

The image stole back into her mind and her voice died. The man's face, with that dreamy look, watching her so intently. She closed her eyes, a breath of anguish caught in her throat.

'*Mais, c'est encore lui!* Was it to me that he listened?'

Her fingers moved, began to pluck at the strings. From somewhere inside herself, the whole air resurfaced. A delicate, poignant little tune.

Charles listened in silence, captured by the haunting sounds, and the tears that escaped from beneath Elaine's closed eyelids to sparkle on her cheek. Warmth cascaded into his chest, and he was obliged to fight an impulse to catch her up and hold her in a comforting embrace.

There was no vestige of suspicion in his head. He could no more have persuaded himself that she was acting than he could have walked away. And he could swear she had no notion of having spoken in French.

It was a short little piece, and it ended all too quickly. Elaine sat with yet closed eyes, her hands quieting the strings as the last vibrating note died away.

'Bravo!' said Charles involuntarily.

Her eyes flew open, and she jumped. She had forgotten that he was there! What in the world had come over her? She had played—what? Already the melody was drifting away.

'That was delightful,' said the Earl, a quality of warmth in his voice. 'But why were you weeping?'

Elaine stared at him, and became aware that there was a haze about her eyes. One finger darted up, and she discovered the wetness on her cheeks. She wiped it away, and found that Lord Wytham was holding out a handkerchief. She sniffed and shook her head.

'I thank you, but there is no need.'

Charles frowned as he pocketed the handkerchief. 'You did not know that you were crying, did you?'

It was true, but she was chary of saying so. He was so very distrustful that she felt it hopelessly inadequate to answer either way. If she confirmed it, would he not think she was trying to draw his sympathy? She prevaricated.

'It is a sad piece, is it not? Perhaps that is why.'

Charles felt himself again moved by the wistful note. Had there been a memory involved? 'Of what were you thinking?'

'A man's face,' Elaine answered unguardedly.

An odd pang smote Charles. 'What man?'

It did not occur to her to prevaricate. 'I think he might have been my husband.'

It was only by a supreme effort of will that Elaine managed to maintain a façade of calm. Somehow she succeeded in coping with the endless stream of questions that emanated from the three visitors perched upon the sofa in Lord Wytham's saloon.

She had foolishly allowed Meg to persuade her to make an appearance in church on Sunday. Since then, Clevedon House had turned into a hive of buzzing comment and speculation as, one after the other, the local acquaintances of the family arrived to inspect her and probe the mystery of her background. She felt like an exhibit in a museum. It was hard indeed to maintain an air of calm, but she was determined to appear as collected as she could, answering every impertinent question or observation with cool detachment.

'But can you not even recall who your parents are?'

'I regret that I cannot, ma'am,' she stated, for what seemed the fiftieth time.

'How strange it must be to have forgotten everything about one's life!' The woman gave a loud laugh. 'One can scarcely imagine it.'

Elaine was spared answering this by the intervention of Meg. 'Don't try, Lady Kilpeck. More to the point is that it is evident that none of you can help us with placing Elaine.'

'No, indeed,' agreed the woman, sadly shaking her head.

Her companions, who had been introduced to Elaine as the lady's daughter and an aunt who resided with the family, gravely nodded their agreement.

'I only wish I might have done so,' pursued Lady Kilpeck, with a pitying look at Elaine. 'It must be most uncomfortable for you, poor dear.'

A practised smile was all the answer Elaine felt able to give. She would rather have avoided these confrontations, but it had become imperative to find some clue to her identity— ever since the Earl had admitted his suspicions.

It might have been supposed that the matter being laid open between them would have made for ease of communication. But if he regarded her with suspicion, then so must she regard anything he said to her. And it had become oppressive to be dependent upon his generosity. This on top of the sense of alienation from everything that ought to be familiar. Did Lord Wytham understand how isolated she was? She was more than ever grateful to Meg, for the withdrawal of her host's sympathy had left her curiously bereft.

As a consequence, she had felt unable to address him beyond the commonplace. Indeed, she had studiously avoided his company these several days while the world was busily subjecting her to its scrutiny. It had not been difficult, for his lordship was apparently eschewing these encounters, and it was his sisters who generally played host.

'Well, that's that,' announced Meg, as the ladies were ushered out. 'They were the last of the neighbouring families. I am afraid we have drawn a blank, Elaine.'

'If you anticipated otherwise, my dear sister,' said Lady Harriet from the window seat from where she had been quietly observing the visit, 'I can only say that I did not.'

Elaine suppressed the rising choler. She must not allow the female's antipathy to upset her. It was difficult not to feel resentful, for it had been made abundantly clear that it was Lady Harriet who had fostered the Earl's doubts.

Meg ignored her sister's remark. 'It is very curious, I find. I made sure someone would have known something of you. Surely you must have been missed by now! I cannot believe that no one has made any attempt to recover you.'

'Perhaps they do not wish to recover me.'

'And perhaps,' put in Harriet, rising from her seat with a twitch of her muslin skirts, and moving to the fireplace, '*they*—if they exist, which I take leave to doubt—know very well indeed where you are.'

Elaine compressed her lips, but Meg was wrathful. 'Harriet, don't be so unkind! Whatever you believe, it is hateful of you to be taunting poor Elaine in this fashion.'

'I cannot endure to hear these speculations,' retorted her sister, 'when I am convinced that Elaine could leave this house tomorrow and return to wherever she came from.'

'But what basis have you for it, Harriet?' demanded Meg. 'Do you suppose Gorsty is fool enough to have been duped were she faking? I wish you might tell him so!'

'Pray, Meg, leave it!' begged Elaine. 'There is nothing you can say to dissuade Lady Harriet from her opinion.'

'But it is so stupid!'

Elaine fidgeted with the muslin of the plain made-over gown she still wore by day. 'Perhaps it is not, Meg.'

She sustained a narrow look from Lady Harriet, but Meg fairly gaped at her. 'What in the world do you mean?'

Elaine shrugged helplessly. 'I have been thinking about it all. You are not the only one to wonder at the lack of any vestige of recognition from these people roundabout. Perhaps it is just as Lady Harriet suspects. For all I know, I was involved in a bid to gain Lord Wytham's interest. If I was, though, I do not now know it.'

There was silence for a moment. A derisive snort from Lady Harriet broke it. 'Oh, very clever!'

Elaine looked at her, bewildered. 'Why is it clever?'

From the doorway behind her, the Earl spoke. 'Harriet thinks it a neat attempt to turn the tables on us, I fancy.'

She turned about in her chair, a riffle of discomfort running through her, and found him entering, with his brother-in-law just behind him peering over his shoulder. She wished he would not make these unexpected appearances! It was decidedly unsettling. She clasped her hands together to hide the unsteadiness of her fingers.

Meg took up the cudgels again as her husband, clad in his habitual country garb of a fawn frock-coat over buckskins, followed his brother-in-law in and perched on the arm of her chair, which was adjacent to Elaine's.

'Really, Harriet, you are abominable! The poor girl can say nothing without you making an issue of it. Charles, I beg you will not pursue such a ridiculous thought!'

Lord Wytham had strolled past to stand before the mantel. He arched an eyebrow. 'Do you think it ridiculous, Elaine?'

She eyed him warily. 'If I answer, you will find a way to turn it against me.'

'No, that is your province—at least, according to Harriet.' Charles looked at his sister as he spoke, and was gratified to see a spot of colour enter her cheek.

She gave him one scorching glance, and swung away, seating herself in a chair farthest from the fireplace. Charles leaned one arm along the mantelshelf. His glance encompassed his family, and then settled upon Meg.

'I came to tell you that my own efforts have met with no success, and to discuss with you all what next we might do.'

'Don't look at me!' Meg returned crossly. 'If you had not absented yourself these three days from the saloon, you would know that we have been no more successful.'

Charles had not meant to single Meg out. He had merely looked to her to avoid Elaine, for he had no wish to discompose her further. She was calm enough on the surface, but her eyes betrayed her—and troubled his conscience. He regretted having taken the family into his confidence, for once Harriet realised that Elaine knew herself to be under suspicion, she had thrown off all restraint. Most of all, he was sorry he had mentioned Elaine's supposition of being married. Harriet had mocked it.

'Depend upon it, brother, she said it only to put you off your guard. It is only too convenient for her, this alleged loss of memory. With a little ingenuity—of which we know her to be possessed—she may turn anything to good account.'

Charles had not wanted to believe it. Indeed, he had been driven to offer in refutation the moving sight of Elaine weeping as she played the harp. Harriet had only responded that she had never doubted the girl to be an accomplished actress. Meg's furious rodomontade had done nothing to assuage the revival of his suspicions.

A part of him wanted to believe Elaine innocent—that part in particular which had reacted in so foolish a manner to the notion that she might be wed. He had surprised in himself a sensation of shock, followed instantly by a feeling far too akin to jealousy for his comfort. He was obliged to acknowledge a dangerous tendency to warm to Elaine. It must be the combination of her beauty and her sorry situation—a fatally attractive mix! Which, were it deliberate and he a little less wary, must certainly have captured his fancy.

Harriet thus planted her seeds in fruitful soil. An obstinate devil in his head would keep returning him to her insistent remembrance that Elaine wore no ring upon her finger. Which statement proved nothing, and was besides unaccountably irritating. There had been but one remedy. He had avoided Elaine as far as possible, allowing his sisters to play host to the stream of visitors. Only now did it occur to him that Elaine had made no attempt to come in his way, which did not accord with the picture of a scheming adventuress.

He realised that they were all looking at him enquiringly. 'I beg your pardon. I was thinking.'

'Charles,' asked Meg, 'have you heard from everyone to whom you wrote?'

He nodded. 'The last of the letters came in this morning.' He turned to find the blue eyes upon him. 'No one claims you, Elaine. Worse, no one has heard of you. No one knows of any female going missing in these parts.'

'The natural conclusion then,' said Matt in a bracing tone, 'is that she is not from these parts.'

'Oh, well said, my love!' exclaimed Meg.

'I had not overlooked that possibility,' agreed Charles. 'I believe we must look further afield. I propose to put an advertisement in the *Gazette*.'

Elaine was conscious of a quiver in her voice. 'And if there is no response?'

'We will cross that bridge when we come to it—if we come to it.'

'And meanwhile…'

She faded out, unable to bear the thought of the hideous days stretching ahead with no knowledge of those that had gone before. Days, moreover, during which she must endure the scorn of Lady Harriet, and the unabated suspicions of her host.

'Meanwhile, we had better gown you more suitably,' said Meg brightly, rustling the petticoats of her own figured lawn. 'We will go to town tomorrow, if you should care for it.'

'But I have no money.'

'Don't let that worry you,' said Charles.

Elaine met his eyes. 'I have no wish to be further beholden to you, my lord.'

'I fancy you have no choice in the matter.'

A well of distress rose up to choke her, and she looked quickly away. His voice, on a softer note, came again.

'Don't despair, Elaine. You may yet recover your memories, and then you will no longer be beholden.'

'I wish I might! Something—anything. *Mais, je n'ai rien!* We know that I play the harp. Beyond that, all I have is a garden and a man's face. *Alors, c'est lui qui était dans mon lit, comme je pensais.* Yet how am I to know that? Why have I remembered nothing more?'

'What did she say?' came from Harriet in a shocked tone. 'Someone was in her bed?'

Elaine turned to her. 'I beg your pardon?'

'You spoke in French again,' explained Meg.

'I don't speak French.'

There was a silence. Elaine frowned, looking from one to the other. What ailed them all? Meg was looking decidedly troubled. She saw Mr Huntly raise his brows at the Earl, who was himself as bland as ever.

'Oh, this is too much!' Harriet cried. 'Are we expected to allow this nonsense indefinitely? You have spoken in French not once, but many times, Elaine. You are either fluent in the language, or it is a device intended to support your story.'

A pulse began to beat in Elaine's bosom, turning rapidly to a thud that hammered at her breast. Her head started to ache, and she looked instinctively towards the Earl. She could barely speak for the tremble at her lip.

'Is—is that true?'

His voice was even. 'It is true that you have several times spoken in French.'

'But I don't remember! I don't know any French!'

'Charles, stop!' uttered Meg, rising quickly.

Charles held up a hand. 'Wait, Meg! If there is something to be discovered here, then let us pursue it. We cannot be forever shielding Elaine. That is to take from her all hope of recovery.'

The thumping at her breast was subsiding. Elaine put her fingers to her brow, pressing at the temple where a dull ache had settled. Why should she react in this way? All for some nonsense about language?

'I do not know any French,' she repeated distinctly. 'If you ask me to speak it, I cannot conceive of one single word.'

'Don't try!'

'Meg!'

'Charles, what do you imagine you may achieve by this? Did not Gorsty say that she should not try to remember?'

Elaine made an effort to look at her champion. 'Believe me, Meg, if I could grasp at anything at all, I would. But this talk of French is nonsensical! I have no loss of memory in the present. I know precisely what has happened since I woke up that horrid day. Why should I forget it if I had been speaking in French?'

'There is no answer to that,' said Charles flatly, 'but you have certainly spoken French several times, and each time you have not remembered doing so. Don't you see, Elaine? There must be something in it.'

'Not necessarily.'

'Be quiet, Harriet!' snapped Meg. 'I wish you will leave her be, Charles. You are only confusing her further.'

Elaine sighed. 'If you all say it is so, then it must be so. *Mais, je ne me souviens pas d'un seul mot de Francais!*'

Slowly Elaine became aware of restraint in their faces. Her heart skipped a beat, and she glanced wildly round, her eyes settling on the Earl. 'Did I just do it again?'

His face was answer enough. Elaine gave a despairing cry, and sank her head into her hands.

The expedition was intended to cheer Elaine. That, and the obvious necessity to acquire at least a modicum of the necessities of a female wardrobe. Meg had ransacked the attic boxes for her mother's disused garments in order to find those indispensable items of a lady's toilette that changed little according to fashion.

'Mama's figure scarcely altered with the years,' Meg had averred, 'and she tended to the spare. Moreover, she was tall like you.'

Elaine had been able to make use also of a pair of slipper sandals that were only a shade tight. But the gowns of yesteryear would not do in these days when waists had risen below the bosom, and the muslins and lawns that draped the feminine form bore no resemblance to those heavily corseted dimities and brocades.

'And you cannot be forever appearing in the two gowns my dear Droxford made over,' said Meg decidedly.

Elaine was in agreement. Nor could she expect her kind benefactress to give up more gowns to be altered. On the whole, though she felt the obligation keenly, it was better to allow Lord Wytham to foot the bills—which she might repay whenever she was restored to her rightful milieu.

It had begun to seem that this might never happen. Moreover, Elaine was no longer so sure that she wished for a recovery to a past which hinted at misery and pain. She could not think of the face of the man who had watched her playing without a contraction at her heart. And the whole sorry business with the French tongue had left her with so much confusion and distress of mind, that a headache had since been her most constant companion.

But today she determined to throw off her tense mood and gratify Meg with a show of enjoyment. She owed her that much.

This resolve almost deserted her when the Earl unexpectedly joined the party, saying that he had business in town and would travel down with them. Meg greeted this decision with acclaim.

'That is excellent, Charles! I knew it was no use asking Matt to escort us. Besides, he has gone off to the Anglers, and I dare say will not be seen again until dinner. I had rather a gentleman came, too. Not that the journey is anything, and I do not contemplate any mishap, but you never know.'

'I am sure Parr and my coachman would prove capable of dealing with any emergency, Meg. But if Elaine does not object to my company—'

'How should I, my lord?' Elaine interposed hastily. 'It is your carriage, and you are paying for my costume.'

'True, but I thought you looked daunted when I said I should join you,' said the Earl frankly.

Elaine held his eyes. 'You were mistaken.'

Charles smiled, and Elaine felt a flutter at her bosom. 'Then let us cry friends for the day. I will engage to suspect you of no other design than to enjoy the delights of shopping. You may have lost your memory, but I refuse to believe that any young lady can have forgotten how to do that!'

Meg cried out upon him, but Elaine was unable to keep from laughing. The cloudy eyes lit, and Charles was conscious of a swelling of warmth. She really was breathtaking!

Settled in one of the forward seats, his back to the horses, and his long legs in well-fitting buckskins negligently crossed, Charles allowed himself the indulgence of surveying her from under the brim of his hat. The seamstress had mended her black spencer, which she wore over Meg's gown, and she had on her boots and a riding hat that he thought might have belonged to his mother. It was not an ideal ensemble, but she wore it with aplomb. Besides, Charles was more interested in watching her face.

She looked to be more relaxed than she had been lately, if a trifle preoccupied. He had jested about the prospect of making her purchases, but it seemed to him that she indulged Meg with a half-hearted response to an enthusiastic discussion of what might be needed to make a respectable showing.

'For we are bound to be invited to a series of engagements now that people have met you. You cannot wear the same garments day after day.'

'No, I suppose not,' was all Elaine could find to say.

And when Meg further enumerated the number of gowns she considered indispensable to the circumstances, Charles was almost inclined to believe that Elaine was not even listening.

'I will be guided by you,' she said. Which might have referred to anything!

It was only when they reached the capital that Elaine's attention appeared to be caught. She began to look about her and take notice as the carriage penetrated into the busy quarter of the town, which was as noisy as ever, despite the current absence of the fashionables.

The sights and sounds that grew into a tumult were enough to distract Elaine from the thoughts that had been revolving in her head throughout the journey. She had been more aware of Lord Wytham watching her, than she had been of Meg's discourse. She had felt both fidgety and conscious. Several times she was tempted to stare back at him, and would have done, had she not been convinced that such a challenge would only serve to increase his convictions. It really was very difficult to concentrate, with those hazel eyes fixed upon one's face! What did he mean by it? She wished he had not chosen to accompany them, if he meant thus to embarrass her.

But London forced her concentration. The jostling horses; jarveys hailing one another with greetings or a curse; the sound of the carriage wheels clanging on stone; vendors crying their wares; the babble of voices rising and falling, and the constantly changing patterns created by the vast press of humanity going about their affairs. It was bewildering to see the hurry and bustle of clerks, and a barrel of a man lounging against a wall catching a clip at an urchin speeding by too close. Here and there she caught a glimpse of a scarlet coat, and once a porter and a liveried servant in hot argument. Then there were the incessant cries of beggars. It was abnormally loud, but it felt uncannily familiar.

'I have been here before, I think,' she said tensely.

'You might well have been,' agreed Meg. 'Though I would have thought that if it was so, someone must have known you.'

'Perhaps it was some other city,' suggested the Earl.

Elaine looked at his face, across which was a dappling of shadows cast by the moving outside world. 'But are there cities much like this? I had thought none were as big.'

'No, but they might be quite as noisy in parts.'

'That is very true,' Meg chimed in. 'I know that the only time I went to Bath, I was deafened by the racket. And I was supposed to be taking the cure!'

Elaine's mind froze. She muttered it. 'Bath!'

A movement beside her brought her eyes round to Meg, who was looking eager. 'Does it ring a bell? Oh, Elaine! Is it possible you were there?'

'I don't know.' She felt lightheaded all at once. 'It may be so.'

'But what were you doing so far from home?'

'Home!' The oddest conviction came to her, and she reached out unconsciously for Meg's hand, clutching it tightly. 'I have no home!'

'Now you haven't, no,' said Meg, 'but you must have had one once.'

'A very long time ago.'

'Oh, nonsense! Why, you cannot be much above twenty— if that. It cannot be so long.'

'Yes, but I think it is.' Only half conscious of gripping the hand she held, she bit back a welling desire to weep.

Charles had not spoken, but he was moved for all that. No thought of duplicity entered his head, and his words came from an uncontrollable urge to reassure her.

'Elaine, don't think of it any more. Come, don't upset yourself. Look, we are entering the better part of town.'

Meg ably seconded his efforts. 'Charles is right. We shall soon be in Bond Street, and you may lose yourself in the joy of selecting gowns.'

Elaine did her best to comply, for she could not endure to draw the Earl's cynical look. He had said he would not judge her today, but there was no depending on that. Besides, she did not wish to spoil Meg's obvious pleasure in bringing her to town. But the sensation of being upon the point of discovering something remained with her.

Lord Wytham left them at the door of the fashionable modiste patronised by Meg. 'Not overly dear, for Matt's fortune is not immense, but most elegant and fashionable. Indeed, this very habit I have on is one of hers.' She was wearing the riding-dress in which Elaine had first seen her, which was certainly well cut.

Elaine entered the portals with no feeling either of awe or surprise, although the salon was luxurious, decorated with potted palms and turned pillars painted in gold. Samples of the designs of Madame Honorine were set tastefully in alcoves, and a bevy of assistants scurried in and out of a green baize door at the back. Elaine felt completely at home.

Before long, she and Meg had entered into interested negotiation with Honorine. Only after she had been bundled in and out of a number of gowns did it come home to Elaine that she was conversing with the modiste in fluent French.

She stopped in mid-sentence, gazing at Meg as the thud of her heartbeat started up. She fought for calm, and knew from Meg's expression that she had not been mistaken.

'How long have I been doing that?' she managed to ask.

Meg grimaced. 'Almost from the first moment that you began to talk to her.'

Elaine pressed one hand to her bosom in a vain attempt to still the tumult there, her glance shifting to that of the modiste, who was looking at her in a good deal of surprise. She ought to excuse herself somehow, but—she had not the words! She tried to think of the appropriate French phrase, but nothing came into her head.

To her relief, Meg suddenly began talking to Honorine in rapid English, going over the different gowns that had been tried. Elaine affected to be examining herself in the long pier-glass, although in reality she saw nothing but a willowy cloud of white.

It took some little while for the sensations in her bosom to subside. She was grateful to Meg for taking up the modiste's attention. At length she was able to resume the business for which she had come, reverting for the purpose—all too consciously!—to English. She ignored as best she might the odd looks cast upon her by Honorine, and made her choices almost at random, and with no enjoyment.

As they left the shop at last, Elaine could not have said, had she been asked, which gowns reposed in the bandboxes that an assistant was bestowing in the carriage with the assistance of Lord Wytham's groom.

'Fortunately,' said Meg, once they were safely installed inside, 'I remembered those you liked. I could see you were too overset to think properly. Lord knows what Honorine thought!'

'She must have thought me mad,' Elaine offered, low-toned. 'Indeed, I feel quite unhinged. Meg, once I realised what I was about, I could not remember a word. Not one word!'

'Now don't, for the Lord's sake, get into a stew!' pleaded Meg. 'Only wait until we are at the Nag's Head, where we may discuss the matter over luncheon.'

'So that Lord Wytham may convince himself that it was nothing but an act,' said Elaine bitterly.

It had been agreed that the Earl would meet them at this convenient inn so that they might all partake of refreshment before beginning the journey home.

'He won't do that,' Meg soothed. 'Recollect that you were with me, and I need no convincing. What would have been the point?'

Elaine let out a mirthless laugh. 'Do you think your brother will not find a way to argue that?'

'Harriet might have done, but Charles will not, you may

be sure. Believe me, I know my brother.' She dropped her voice to a conspiratorial level. 'If you wish to know what I truly think, Elaine, it is that Charles is fighting against his own inclination. He would much rather believe in you!'

The notion, to Elaine's consternation, caused a flutter in her breast. Was she growing susceptible to the Earl? She could not deny his personal attributes, and he had a certain charm—when he chose to exert it. There was a power of soothing that worked upon her. Add to that his eligibility, and Elaine could well understand what drove females to attempt to storm his defences. But if she was married, she must not allow herself to become attached to any man. Least of all one who already had reason to suppose her to be in pursuit of him.

By the time the carriage drove into the yard of the Nag's Head, however, her mind was once again haunted by the episode at the modiste.

Ushered into a wainscoted private parlour on an upper floor of the aged inn, Elaine could not help a slight rise of apprehension when they found the Earl to be already in occupation. A waiter was setting the centre table with a selection of viands bespoken by his lordship, and the ladies were invited to be seated.

A good ham was offered—of which his lordship partook liberally—along with some potted beef and pickled red cabbage. Meg opted for the beef, and chose a cheesecake from a variety of sweet dishes which flanked the meats. Elaine accepted a small helping of the savoury items, and a slice of plum cake. As soon as they had been served, Charles dismissed the waiter and poured wine for the ladies.

The moment they were alone, Meg lost no time in apprising her brother of what had occurred at Honorine's.

'Interesting,' was his comment, as he gave Elaine his blandest look and quaffed the ale he preferred at this hour.

Her apprehension gave way to annoyance. 'I knew you would not believe it!'

'Have I said so?'

'Elaine, don't be silly!' protested Meg, with her mouth full of beef. 'We will get nowhere if you mean to take up that attitude.'

Elaine sighed, and took up her fork. 'Forgive me, my lord. I am so overset that I scarce know what I am doing.'

Charles refilled his tankard from the jug and began upon his repast. He was not in the least inclined to disbelieve the story. The odd phrase here and there might be done for effect. But to hold a fluent conversation in French with a stranger, and then pretend to no recollection of it? He fancied that would be beyond the talents of the most accomplished actress.

'That is what is interesting, Elaine. You don't know that you are doing it. Speaking French, I mean.'

Elaine relaxed a little. 'It is evident that I slip into it automatically, without knowing it. Indeed, I can never now be sure whether I am speaking in English or French. How can I, when I do not recognise that I have done so?'

'But it did register with you, Elaine, on this occasion,' Meg pointed out, eyeing an almond and orange tart with a predatory eye.

'Perhaps because I was conversing wholly in that language? I only wish I could remember what we talked about!'

'That is nothing to the purpose,' said Charles soothingly. 'Why tease yourself over details? More to the point, what

conclusion may we come to over this? It springs forcibly to
the mind that you are French in origin.'

Elaine stared at him, prey to a growing hollow in her
chest. 'I never thought of that.'

'How should you, when you knew nothing of the matter?'
tutted Meg. Her features brightened. 'But I believe Charles
has something. Frenchwomen have unerring taste in fashion,
and you selected those gowns as if you had known all along
just what the current fashion is.'

'Which might as well mean,' said Elaine dully, pushing
aside the remains of beef upon her plate, 'as your brother will
tell you, that I was perfectly aware of it.'

'True,' agreed Charles drily, helping himself to more of
the ham. 'But let us leave that. Because you speak the
language, it does not automatically follow that you are
French. You could have learned to speak it with fluency.'

'Not unless she had spent some time in France,' argued
Meg, succumbing to the lure of the tart.

'You may be right, Meg. But since she is fluent in both
languages, either might be her mother tongue. That is not
what I am driving at.'

'Well, say what you are driving at!'

Charles ignored his sister. There was deliberation in his
tone. 'What strikes me is that if Elaine were French, it might
account for the total lack of knowledge of her that we have
so far encountered.'

Meg chewed meditatively on the pastry. 'But that would
mean that she had only recently come from France, which
in the current climate is most unlikely. Besides, she has no
trace of an accent.'

'Accents can be eliminated. It only takes practice.'

Elaine began to feel faintly nauseous, and laid down the cake that she had only just picked up. There was more to Lord Wytham's suppositions than he was revealing. She eyed him, and that arch of his eyebrow became accentuated.

'You look most distrustful, Elaine.'

'What is it you are really saying?' she challenged.

'Oh, Charles!' groaned Meg. 'You gave your word!'

'I am not accusing,' he protested. 'I am merely toying with a hypothesis.'

'Which is?'

The blue eyes were steady on his and he recognised apprehension. It cut at something within him. Yet he might as well say it. If they were to get to the bottom of all this, there was no point in shying away from unpalatable notions.

'Consider the facts. No one knows you apparently. Therefore, either you come from a set of people of whom none of our acquaintance has ever heard, unlikely as this seems.'

'Is that not what Miss Tarrington suggested?' said Elaine, trying to keep a bitter note out of her voice.

'Something of the sort,' he agreed dismissively. He had no desire to reawaken the hurts that came from that quarter. 'Or if not that, it may be that you have no claim to gentility, and might fairly be described as an adventuress.'

'Charles, how dare you say so?'

'Let him say it, Meg. How do I know whether it is not the truth? Please continue, my lord.'

Charles regarded her for a moment, affecting to sip at his ale. She appeared collected, but her eyes, wearing that haunted look, gave her away. And renewed that uncomfortable reaction inside himself.

'That explanation,' he resumed in a carefully neutral tone, 'might encompass your being French.'

'You mean that I am a *bourgeoise* attempting to gain entry to a higher sphere.'

'It is one conclusion.'

'I don't believe it!' exploded Meg.

'Neither do I,' agreed Charles unexpectedly.

A faint tattoo started up inside Elaine, and the sick feeling reawakened. Her voice shook, and she pushed away her plate. 'Why do you say that?'

His eyes did not waver from her face. 'There is that in your bearing, in your lack of consciousness in society, that speaks all too clearly the careless assurance of class.' His voice softened. 'No, Elaine, you are not a *bourgeoise*.'

'I knew it!' said Meg with satisfaction.

'Then what am I, Charles?' Elaine asked shakily, unknowing that she used his name.

'There are fewer now, of course, for though France is England's present enemy, there is a modicum of stability in that country. But you might well have come over during the Terror.' Charles leaned forward across the table. 'I think, Elaine, that you may be an *émigrée*.'

She stared at him, a curious numbness blanketing her mind. There was no penetrating thought. Only a whispered echo of that one word, over and over. *émigrée*. She did not know that she murmured, words straight from her soul.

'Otherwise, I would be dead.'

The realisation of what she had said hit her a second later. There came a buzzing in her ears, and her bones turned to water.

Chapter Five

'Charles, she is going to faint!'

The next few moments passed for Elaine like a dream. Vaguely she heard the rapid voices.

'Catch her, for the Lord's sake!'

'I have her, never fear.'

She felt herself lifted, helpless to aid whoever it was who sought to right her from the odd position in which she found herself.

'Her head! Hold her head!'

'Do stop fussing, Meg. I have her safe.'

Her head was cradled, and a strong arm held her to rest against comforting support. A warm and cosy place.

'I think I have some smelling salts in my reticule.'

'A little water is all that is needed. She has not quite gone, I fancy.'

Even as the sense of this came clear to her, the mists that wreathed her brain were shifting. She opened her eyes to find the Earl's hazel orbs looking into hers, close—and concerned.

'That is better. Here, drink a little of this.'

She felt the cool of glass at her lips and obediently sipped.

'She is very white. Take my salts for her, Charles!'

Her nostrils were assailed by a bittersweet aroma. The nausea rose again, and Elaine pulled her face sharply back, bringing up a feeble hand to waft the thing away.

'I said she did not need it. Here, take it away!'

Once again the glass was put to her lips and she was bidden to drink. The water helped, and she was presently able to keep her balance.

'Are you able to sit without aid?' Charles asked, removing his supporting shoulder, but keeping firm hands upon her to prevent her from falling again.

Elaine nodded. 'I shall be well in a moment.'

Charles removed his hands, but hovered where he was for the time. Her collapse had secretly shocked him, but he had not allowed himself to feel it until now.

Meg busied herself with pouring tea. 'Drink this, poor thing. There is nothing like tea when you have been faint. Shall I sugar it well? I know you prefer it unsweetened, but for shock, you know, sugar is most efficacious.'

Elaine opted to drink it as usual, and it revived her so well that the Earl felt confident enough to leave her and resume his seat. He picked up his tankard and drank off the ale, wondering if Elaine would remember what had caused her to swoon. For his part, now that his own discomfort was subsiding and he was once more able to think rationally, her reaction was conclusive. His scepticism had sustained a severe jolting.

The dream was disturbingly real. Even as he caressed the warm flesh, teased with his mouth the golden areola, and ran his hot gaze over the parted lips that breathed his name in wanton supplication, Charles knew it could not be happening. Her voice in his ear became harsh.

'Charles! Charles, wake up!'

His eyes flew open. The face looked grotesque in the shadows cast by the candle flame held close to his head.

'Meg?'

'You must get up. It is Elaine. She is not in her bed!'

Bleary, Charles struggled out of the dream. Elaine? Warmth tugged at his loins, and he groaned. Confound his unruly mind! Almost he turned his head, convinced for one split second that she lay beside him, naked and open to his questing hands. But that could not be!

The remnants of sleep began to leave him, and the sense of Meg's words shot him through with shock. He threw off the covers.

'Have you looked for her?'

His sister hastily stepped back out of the way as he got to his feet, hunting for his bedgown left carelessly upon the chair by the window.

'I have checked only this floor,' Meg answered in a hushed tone of suppressed anxiety. 'I sent Matt to look downstairs, so that I might call you at once.'

Charles found the robe and hastily dragged it on, thrusting his feet into a pair of slippers, the implications of Meg's message striking havoc within him as the hazy recollection of his unwary dream hovered stealthily at the back of his mind.

'Hurry, Charles! Lord knows what may have happened!'

He shifted to the chest of drawers and seized the candelabrum that always rested there, taking a taper from the silver box beside it. 'Give me a light from your candle.'

He applied the lit taper to the set of candles, his head busying with possibilities as he came mentally alert. Meg gave voice to his own thought.

'Can she have left the house, do you think?'

'And gone where?' he demanded, as if he answered himself.

'There is that.'

Charles wasted no more words, but trod swiftly to the door and went out into the galleried corridor, peering over the bannisters into the darkness of the hall below. He knew that Meg closely followed him as he made for the stairs. Light flickered in one of the doorways.

'Matt, is that you?' he called.

The light shifted, moving towards the stairs. 'She's in the saloon,' announced his brother-in-law's voice in a penetrating whisper. 'Softly, m'boy, for I think she's sleepwalking.'

'Oh, no!' came from Meg behind Charles.

He hurried down the stairs, coming to rest beside Matt's sturdy form, which was likewise encased in a bedgown over his long nightshirt. The stronger light from Charles' candles encompassed the faces of the other two in a pool at the bottom of the stairs as he paused there.

'She did not see you, then?' he asked his brother-in-law.

'Doubt it. She didn't turn towards me.'

'What is she doing?' asked Meg, her plump features anxious under the frilled nightcap.

'Muttering. Pacing up and down, and muttering.'

'In French?'

'Half and half,' said Matt.

Charles turned and made for the saloon door.

'Take care!' warned Meg.

He paid no heed. He might have anticipated some such development after today. He should have sent for Gorsty! He beckoned to Matt, and held out his candelabrum.

'Hold this!'

Matt relieved him of it, and obedient to his signal, prevented Meg from crowding him. Taking hold of the handle, Charles cautiously opened the saloon door.

The place was not in total darkness, for the drapes were open at the French windows—had been dragged back by a hasty hand. One had caught upon the gilded back of the sofa, another was open halfway. In the silvered beams that made shadows of the furnishings in the room, a figure shifted to and fro.

Elaine was in her nightshift and barefoot, her face pale in the glow of night, the short hair forming an untidy halo about her head. Her restless fingers kneaded at her own arms huddled tight across her bosom. Her breath was short, and from her lips issued a series of staccato utterances, so low as to be incomprehensible. But it was clear from the timbre of the words that she switched from French to English and back again.

That she had come to this! Guilt swept through Charles, as though by his determined suspicions he had worsened her condition. Was she sleepwalking? Should he approach her? His glance flicked to the curtains. Their unruly treatment argued rather a mind disturbed than asleep. And if she slept still, why open them at all? It was said that sleepwalkers could see in the dark.

'What is she doing?' came in a whisper from Meg.

'See for yourself,' Charles returned, and opened the door wide, his eyes on Elaine.

The sudden access of light caught her attention, and she turned towards the door with a frightened gasp.

'Don't be afraid!' Charles said quickly, walking towards her. 'It is only I, Charles. What is the matter? Why are you wandering about in this manner?'

He reached her, and she extended her hands towards him. He took them in an automatic clasp, and discovered them to be chilled.

'Good God, you are ice cold!' He turned to his sister, who had followed him into the room. 'Get her a wrapper of some kind, Meg. She will catch her death!'

Without thinking, he closed with Elaine, and drew her into his arms, rubbing her back with vigorous strokes.

'You little fool!' he scolded. 'What in the world made you come down thus unprotected?'

A shaky whisper reached him. 'I dreamed…it was horrible. And then, when I was on the stairs, I saw it again.'

'Saw what?' came from Meg behind him.

Charles released Elaine and turned sharply, blinking in the sudden light. 'I thought I asked you—'

'I have sent Matt,' she interrupted, holding up the silver candleholder which she had taken from her spouse. 'Lord, Elaine, you look dreadful!'

Looking back quickly, Charles saw in the brighter glow that Elaine's features were ravaged and shadowed. He stripped off his own bedgown and wrapped it about Elaine's shoulders, guiding her to the long sofa, and flinging off the curtain that was caught there.

'Come, sit down and tell us what it is you saw.'

She sat, huddling into herself. 'It was horrible! He lost his footing and fell his length, tossing over himself again, bereft of control. Like a doll of rags.'

Charles sat beside her. 'Who fell? Who is it you saw?'

Elaine did not seem to hear the question. 'Horrible!' she repeated, beginning to shiver. 'An accident…tumbling down the stairs.'

'Who?' insisted Charles, possessing himself of her hand and holding it strongly. 'Who fell down the stairs?'

She turned frenzied eyes upon him. 'I do not know. But after…I saw that face again—the one I saw before. *Il est mort.*'

'What, dead?' gasped Meg, who was standing close by, holding up the candelabrum.

Its light cast shadows on the white features, enhancing her beauty in a haunting image that wrought upon Charles' senses. He had to force himself to concentrate.

'Which face do you mean?' he asked, with deliberate calm. 'The man you spoke of when you were playing the harp?'

Elaine nodded, shuddering. 'A dead face. He broke his neck. *C'est la même chose.* All, all…dead. Dead at the neck.'

Charles exchanged a horrified glance with his sister. This was what came of airing his confounded theory! Was it all to do with the one man, or was she referring to some poor soul beheaded by that monstrous French invention that had all but denuded that country of its noble population? There was no way of telling what was truth, and what might have been a dream.

'I think we should send for Gorsty,' said Meg worriedly.

'So that he may tell me that these are memories?' cried Elaine, throwing a hand over her eyes. 'If this is what is there, I do not want to remember!'

'Elaine, listen to me!'

She dropped her hand and glanced wildly round. Charles

took her by the shoulders and pulled her about to face him. She seemed to realise his presence, and stilled.

'Elaine, if these are returning memories, there is no need to fear them. Whatever griefs may have been involved, you have already experienced them. It is all in the past.'

'Easy for you to say!' she uttered frantically.

'Yes, I know. It is hard to be given only a glimpse of the tale. But each glimpse must open the picture wider. You cannot hide forever in a fog of forgetfulness.'

Her lip quivered. 'Is that what I am doing? Hiding?'

'Perhaps. The mind plays strange tricks.'

'Tricks,' she repeated dully. 'Like the tricks I have played upon you.'

Charles let her go and drew away, irrationally irritated. The reminder was alienating, and he had to quell an impulse to react with a violent display of… He checked the realisation at its source. Confound it, where were his thoughts tending? He could not seize Elaine in his arms and demonstrate how very wrong was her distrust of him! Besides, it would be highly inappropriate. Had she not borne enough?

He rose, and the stiffness of his voice in no way expressed his true feelings. 'I think you should go to bed.'

Clucking agreement, Meg bustled a resistless Elaine out of the saloon, and met her husband coming down the stairs with one of her wrappers. Meg waved it away, saying that she would return her brother's garment to him presently.

Charles watched them go, torn by conflicting emotions. He was disgusted with the base urges that afflicted him. It must be that his idiotic dreams had overset the balance of his judgement. Yet he was conscious of a strong desire to know more of Elaine's sketchy history. Which was mad! Why should he care? He could only wish for a speedy resolution from the means of enquiry he had put in hand today. Fervently did he long to be able to wash his hands of the whole concern!

'Did you find out what happened?'

Charles turned to find his brother-in-law beside him. 'It seems she has recalled some distressing memories. A man in her life was evidently killed falling down some stairs.'

He hardly heard Matt's astonished comments, for one phrase he had spoken echoed oddly in his head. *A man in her life.*

'In any event,' said his brother-in-law, eyeing him with an expression of wry humour that Charles found distinctly disturbing, 'it is evident that you believe in these recollections. Or have I misread you?'

'I don't know what I believe,' he responded flatly. 'But if you are trying to probe the question of whether I thought this whole night's adventure an act, then I can confidently say that I did not.'

'Ha! That won't please Harriet.'

He was not best pleased himself, Charles decided. While he suspected Elaine to be scheming, he was a good deal safer. Believing in her made him infinitely more vulnerable.

It was all Elaine could do to maintain a façade of calm while the doctor's hands probed in her hair from behind the chair. Meg had acted the tyrant, flatly refusing to allow her to get up before Doctor Gorsty had seen her. But Elaine had not the patience to remain in bed, and her kind hostess had relented, instead producing a charming wrapper of green silk from her mother's aged store and insisting that the patient donned it.

'I cannot think why I never thought of it before. Not that I suppose you would have put it on last night, as distracted as you were.'

Elaine felt no less distracted now! She was edgy from lack of sleep, and the riddle rode restlessly round and round in her mind. She was impatient of the doctor's insistence on examining her wound again. It was near two weeks since her mishap and she felt its tenderness but little. It was the least of her troubles!

'The swelling is very little evident,' said Doctor Gorsty at last, pulling away. He came around to the front of the chair and stood before the empty grate.

Elaine eyed him broodingly. 'I remember you told me that my memory would return when the swelling went down.'

The doctor smiled, a twinkle in his eye. 'I said it was possible. And, if I understood Lady Margaret correctly, you have indeed begun to recover something of it.'

She shuddered. 'Too much of it for my liking.'

'How is that?'

Rising from her chair by the fireplace, Elaine shifted to the window, the silk wrapper swishing with the movement. 'I think there is a man—who died.'

'Yes?'

She turned her head. 'Are you not going to ask me who he is?'

'If you knew that, you would not need my services.'

Elaine looked away, beset anew by the bewildering shock of her discovery. 'When I first saw him, I thought he had been my husband. Now I am not sure.' She swallowed, her throat dry. How could she say it? But she must let out her fears to someone! She forced herself to the words. 'I remembered a man—in my bed. But I did not see his face.'

A hollow feeling entered her breast, and she whirled, moving swiftly back to the chair. She perched there, looking up at Gorsty, her hands fisted in her lap.

'I could not speak of this to my hosts. But you are a doctor—to whom else can I turn, if not to you?'

'Rest easy, ma'am. Your confidence is safe with me,' Gorsty assured her.

She held her breath, eyeing the doctor warily. What might he think of her? Then she caught the kindness in his eyes, and out it came, laden with distress.

'What if I am a loose woman, sir?'

His brows rose. 'Rather than a married one?'

Elaine held out her left hand, the fingers splayed. 'Where is my ring?'

He made no reply and she rose again from the chair, pacing away from him. 'Perhaps I am an adventuress. Lord Wytham will have it that I am an émigrée. I fainted on that thought, you see. It seems that I speak French without knowing it.' Turning, she faced the doctor again. 'Suppose then, Doctor Gorsty, that my birth is genteel, if not noble. How have I come to this—to be lost alone in a strange forest? Why have I no protector? I cannot speak with certainty of this man whose face I have seen.' She drew a painful breath. 'But what of the man in my bed?'

The doctor's eyes showed compassion, but he shook his head. 'I have no answers for you, ma'am. This is all conjecture. Only tell me the substance of your memories.'

Elaine sighed wearily, and shifted again to the window. 'They have little substance. There was a garden, similar to the one down there, below this room. That I saw the very first day, though I said nothing of it to you. I found the harp, and was drawn to play it, so that the memories came. There was a face that watched me. His face—the dead man. It may be he who fell down the stairs.' A spasm caught at her chest, and she thrust the memory away. 'But I cannot be any more sure of that than I am of the identity of the man who slept at my side as I read a book in bed.' She turned back to Gorsty. 'The rest consists only of feelings and fears.'

'And so you have decided that you do not wish to recall any more of it?' suggested the doctor gently.

'Did Meg tell you that?'

She received an indirect answer. 'I gather you said something of the sort when you were found wandering in the night.' He came to her, and taking one hand, pressed it. 'I have only one piece of advice for you.'

Elaine eyed him. 'And that is?'

'Do not allow the reactions that jog your memory to agitate you.'

'Easy for you to say!'

A broad smile creased the doctor's face as he released her. 'It is always easy to be the adviser. Yet I beg you will attempt it, ma'am. The more you fight against the memories, the more difficult it will be to recall it all. When something occurs to you, try to relax and allow the thoughts to come.'

Elaine gave a weak laugh. 'Sound advice, undoubtedly. I will do my poor best.'

'More than that I do not ask. I will advise your companions not to question you. That is prone to bring on your fears. Instead, let them pamper you a little! An atmosphere of calm is what is called for, and you should certainly rest more. Lady

Margaret spoke of a number of upcoming engagements, but I suggest that you do not indulge in any but the most desultory entertainments.'

It was a programme that found favour with Elaine. She welcomed anything that kept her from public scrutiny. Particularly now, for she had discovered that it was worse to have a little to draw upon than nothing at all.

She thought Meg might not be as enthusiastic of the scheme, and was surprised when that lady entered wholeheartedly into the spirit of the doctor's request.

'I have instructed Tumby to have this upstairs parlour prepared for you,' she said, ushering Elaine into a pretty little chamber at the back of the house on the first floor.

The room was decorated in the Adam style, with delicate reliefs in garlands of flowers and palm leaves over a pastel ground of blue. A set of Hepplewhite chairs, of mahogany, with heart-shaped backs and tapering legs, were placed strategically about, and a couple of half-moon sideboards sat either side of the white moulded fireplace. In the deep bay of the window reposed an elegant day-bed, set so that its occupant might enjoy the view of the orchards and the rising hills beyond.

Several landscapes adorned the walls, and one portrait of a female, whose striking resemblance to Meg and Lord Wytham made her identity almost certain.

'This was our mother's personal sitting-room,' Meg explained. 'Charles had her portrait put in here after she died. He had the harp removed. She used to play here always. But you see that I have had it restored to its old place.'

Turning with her hostess, Elaine saw with a rise of mixed emotions that the harp was set in one corner, with a stool already placed conveniently before it. Her heart sank. She was by no means sure that she wanted to play it again. And what would Lord Wytham say? Had he approved these changes?

A sudden thought struck her, and she looked at Meg with a new interest. Was this a genuine effort to comply with the doctor's request? Could she not have found some other room? There was a significance in using her mother's old room that begged the question hovering in Elaine's mind. Was it possible that Meg was matchmaking?

'Why do you look at me so?'

Elaine started. 'Forgive me, I was thinking.' She affected to examine the view from the window. 'It is a charming room. I hope your brother does not mind my using it.'

'Why should he?' countered Meg.

Elaine glanced at her. 'Did you ask him?'

A mischievous look entered the matron's face. 'Let me give you a morsel of advice about Charles, my dear. The best way to deal with him is to present him with a fait accompli. If you had been a schemer, you could not have done better than to do just what you did. He is too much the gentleman to have abandoned you to your fate.'

Elaine turned sharply away. 'We do not yet know that I am not a schemer.'

'Lord, I do! But I shall say nothing on that score. I have promised Gorsty not to speculate.' She bustled to the day-bed, and rearranged the cushions there. 'Now do you make yourself comfortable, Elaine, and rest as you were ordered. Don't fear to be lonely, for we shall all visit you. Indeed, I dare say this room will become the centre of our lives again, as it was when Mama was alive.'

* * *

Elaine had some doubt whether a lonely sojourn in the pretty parlour would serve to settle her mind. As it was, she had little opportunity to find out, for her privacy was invaded within an hour of her returning there after luncheon. Lady Harriet not only came herself to inspect the new arrangements, she brought Belinda Tarrington with her.

'You are not to stay long,' warned Meg, following them in.

As she greeted them, Elaine found herself the recipient of a covert rolling of Meg's eyes from behind the pair. Belinda launched into voluble appreciation of Elaine's improved appearance in one of the new gowns. It was of the ubiquitous white muslin, but augmented by a pale blue overgown, with delicate little sleeves. It had not the extravagance of Miss Tarrington's spotted lawn, with an elaborate arrangement of pleating and trimming to the bodice, and Elaine felt the admiration to be suspect. The visitor moved swiftly on to exclaiming over the reappearance of the harp, which she claimed to remember from visits during her childhood, calling Lady Harriet's attention to the decorative cherubs at its base.

'I was always used to love to run my fingers over them. Did not you, Harriet?'

Under cover of this, Meg whispered a hasty apology. 'Forgive me, my dear, but I could not stop them. I could kill Harriet! She might have waited for Belinda to leave, for of course the wretched creature would come.'

There was no opportunity for Elaine to reply, for Miss Tarrington claimed her attention, with a sugary smile that did nothing to soften the patronising tone of her brittle voice.

'And what is this I hear, my dear Elaine? That you are a positive maestro with the instrument!'

A laugh was surprised out of Elaine. 'If that is what you heard, I can only say that you have been misinformed. Indeed, I cannot think who could have said such a thing of me, for only Lord Wytham has heard me play, and I am very sure he did not.'

That trilling laugh fell upon the air, and Elaine all but winced. 'Charles? No, indeed. I think it was Matthew. Yes, I am positive it was Matthew.'

Meg snorted. 'Then you should have known better than to believe him, Belinda. You know his funning way.'

Miss Tarrington opened eyes wide with innocence. 'Is it then an exaggeration? But you do play?'

'Apparently,' Elaine agreed. Anticipating the coming demand from a predatory look in the creature's eye, she added hastily, 'But I do not recall the skill. What I have played has been accidentally remembered.'

'Or conveniently,' murmured Lady Harriet.

'Harriet!' came warningly from Meg.

'Tush, you need not fear me, Meg!' chimed in Belinda. 'Harriet has explained it all. I should be the last to wish to expose poor dear Elaine to horrid rumour. And it is by no means proven that she is on the catch for Charles, now is it?'

Elaine was more scornful than angry. Common courtesy was evidently not a quality known to Miss Tarrington. Meg was predictably up in arms.

'So this is how you keep your word, Harriet! Well, I am sorry to disappoint you, Belinda, but my sister is behind the times. It so happens—'

'Meg, pray don't!' cut in Elaine, fearing that her

champion's temper would lead her to unfold what had so far been found out to these most undesirable ears.

'I was only going to—'

'We need not burden Miss Tarrington with details which can be of no possible interest to her,' Elaine pursued meaningly.

She saw realisation pop in Meg's eyes, and was satisfied. With a social grace that she did not know she possessed, Elaine instantly covered the lapse.

'I cannot imagine why we are all standing about in this stupid way. Why do you not take a seat, Miss Tarrington?'

Without waiting for a reply, she guided the female to a chair, and herself moved to the day-bed, pointedly sinking down into an attitude of ease that she hoped would make it look unlikely that she would easily get up again.

'You are not slow to take up the role of hostess, I see,' remarked Lady Harriet, moving to a chair next to the visitor.

'Why should she be?' demanded Meg belligerently, stomping purposefully across to a chair and carrying it to the head of Elaine's day-bed. 'I gave her the place for her own use.'

'You gave it to her? And what of Charles, pray? Is he content to see our mother's place taken up by a usurper?'

'Oh, do stop talking like some play-actress, Harriet! Usurper, indeed!'

Lady Harriet regarded her sister narrowly. 'You did not ask him, did you?'

Delighted laughter cooed out of Belinda Tarrington. 'I declare, how I long to see his face! My poor dear Elaine, I do trust he will not turn you out.'

Elaine received one of Lady Harriet's dagger looks. 'Of

course he will not, Belinda. Meg has relied upon Charles' ingrained gentlemanly instincts.'

Meg looked as if she would explode. Elaine quickly broke in. 'May we talk of something else?'

'An excellent idea,' said Meg pointedly, glaring at her sister. 'Elaine is not supposed to be agitated. Gorsty wants her to rest, and you are not helping.'

'Dear Harriet, do not be provoking a quarrel,' said Miss Tarrington sweetly. 'I came here only to discover how poor dear Elaine is getting on.'

Poor dear Elaine summoned a smile which she trusted was every bit as insincere as the one now being bent upon her! In the ensuing silence, she had time to wonder how Lord Wytham bore with the importunities of this female. He had made his lack of interest plain enough, but Miss Tarrington appeared to be impervious to the pointed snubs that had been dealt her on the last occasion. She was not very intelligent, Elaine concluded. That, or her ambition was stronger than her sensitivity.

She was trying to think of something innocuous to say, when she was forestalled.

'It seems a little pointless your having caused the harp to be brought down here, Meg,' observed Lady Harriet in a waspish tone, 'if Elaine is not going to play it.'

'She may, when she is alone,' countered Meg.

Elaine sighed inwardly. Hostilities between the sisters, it appeared, had not been abandoned.

'Oh, tush, where would be the point?' came with Miss Tarrington's metallic laugh. 'If she is going to play at all, she must have an audience. Why must we poor females acquire these accomplishments, if we are not to show them off?'

'To gentlemen, you mean?' said Lady Harriet. 'To what purpose? Matthew has no ear for music, and Charles has complained more than once of boredom in being obliged to listen to accomplished females twanging away.'

Meg visibly bridled. 'Matt is extremely fond of music, I will have you know. At least,' she amended, 'he listens to Fanny with pleasure. As for Charles, it was he who mentioned how beautifully Elaine played.'

'Then of course she should play for him!' declared Miss Tarrington with an enthusiasm that Elaine must suppose to be feigned. 'Indeed, I beg you will play, dear Elaine, for I quite long to hear you.'

Elaine could not imagine why. Unless Belinda wished to find out whether she represented any sort of competition?

'Do you play an instrument, Miss Tarrington?' she asked on impulse.

There was no mistaking the malice in the woman's eyes. 'As it happens, yes. I play both the pianoforte and the harp. But of course I was taught by Italian masters.'

'Of course!' muttered Meg in a tone meant only for Elaine's ears.

'Then you must be very good indeed,' Elaine said coolly, refusing to be intimidated. 'Do you sing, too?'

'Naturally.'

'Italian masters again?' queried Meg innocently.

'Happily, yes.'

'You were fortunate. *Je n'avais que le maître de l'école.* It was a seminary in Bath.' Hearing a sharp intake of breath from Meg, Elaine abruptly realised what she had said. 'Bath! Did I not mention Bath once?'

'I mentioned it,' Meg agreed eagerly. 'But it did seem to

ring a bell with you. There, now. Did not Gorsty say that this would happen.' She turned fiercely to the others. 'Not a word, either of you! You must not interfere at all.'

Elaine glanced at Miss Tarrington, and saw bewilderment in the thin face. But Lady Harriet was looking sceptical. No doubt she supposed that it had been done for effect. Or that it had been a slip which Elaine was trying to retrieve.

She turned back to Meg, and found her expression of expectancy so ridiculous that she broke into laughter.

'You look like a dog waiting for a bone, Meg! I am so sorry, but I am afraid it has already gone.'

'How unexpected!' said Lady Harriet.

To Elaine's surprise, Belinda seemed disappointed. She had quite lost her air of superiority. For the first time, her words had a ring of sincerity.

'Oh, were you about to find a memory? What a pity that you have lost it! Were you at school in Bath, then?'

'No questions!' snapped Meg.

Elaine felt abruptly sorry for the visitor. Impelled, she tried to soften the response. 'Doctor Gorsty has advised that my memory will respond better to being allowed to flow naturally. Questions are likely to dam it up, he thinks. As happens, I have found,' she added ruefully, 'whenever I realise that I have remembered something.'

Miss Tarrington was staring at her in a bemused sort of way. Elaine frowned. 'What is the matter?'

'It is true, then!' she said blankly. 'You have indeed lost your memory.'

'Of course she has!' exploded Meg.

'But I thought—Harriet said...' Belinda faded out,

glanced once at Lady Harriet, whose cheeks were flying two spots of colour, and back to Elaine. 'Does Charles know?'

There was a short silence. Elaine knew not how to explain the complexities of the Earl's involvement. Moreover, she was uncertain of his belief in her, although she suspected that his scepticism had been eroded by recent events. It showed in his manner towards her, which had been gentler of late.

What difference could this make to Belinda Tarrington? Would she find it more or less of a barrier to her own ambitions? Elaine prevaricated.

'I am not privy to his lordship's thoughts on the matter. I don't think anyone is.'

From the corner of her eye, she saw Meg's mouth open and quickly frowned her down. Frantic to change the subject, she said the first thing that came into her head.

'Miss Tarrington, why do not you indulge us with a little music?'

Unexpectedly, Lady Harriet encouraged this. 'Yes, do, Belinda. I am sure we should all enjoy hearing the touch of a real maestro.'

Meg looked daggers at her sister, but Elaine reached out and lightly clasped her arm to silence her, smiling at Belinda.

'It would be a pity if neither of us played the harp, since Meg has been to the trouble of having it fetched down. And if Lord Wytham should happen to come in…'

She allowed the words to trail away, confident that Miss Tarrington would far rather she was herself discovered at the harp by his lordship than her supposed rival. As Belinda graciously consented and moved towards the instrument, Elaine wondered that the female should consider her a threat. Had it been put into her head by Lady Harriet?

But it was madness to suppose that the Earl could be so lost to all sense of his position as to contemplate matrimony with a female who had not even a name to her credit, let alone a background! Besides, it must be obvious to the meanest intelligence that he was indifferent to her. The only interest he had shown—beyond common compassion—was in his wish to discover whether she was an impostor. If Miss Tarrington had eyes, she had only to look!

Realising that the visitor had begun to play, she forced herself to concentrate. There was indeed a sureness of touch. Belinda had mastery over the instrument. The rendition of the piece—a somewhat complex and demanding one—was technically expert. Something was lacking, however. Elaine wanted to be charitable, but it was difficult to reach any other conclusion than that the piece was rendered with very little feeling.

Miss Tarrington finished with a flourish, and looked up for applause. Elaine clapped with more enthusiasm than she felt, and it was only after she had added a word of praise to Lady Harriet's effusive compliments that she saw that Mr Huntly had entered the room during the recital.

'Ah, that wasn't you playing, Elaine,' he said on a jovial note. 'Surprised me as I came down the corridor. Didn't think you'd be as sure-footed as that, from what Charles told us.'

'Sure-fingered you mean, my love,' interposed Meg before Elaine could say anything. 'And if I remember rightly, Charles was impressed with Elaine's playing.'

'No, he wasn't,' argued Matt, crossing the room to perch on the window-sill near his wife's chair. 'Said she was fumbling for the notes. What he did say,' he added, turning a grin upon Elaine, 'was that your playing had depth. *Poignant* was the word he used. Remember it distinctly.'

A look of chagrin stole across Miss Tarrington's face, and Elaine felt an uncontrollable urge to compensate her.

'You have misunderstood, Mr Huntly. He can only have been alluding to the fact that I wept as I played. I had no idea of it at the time, and I cannot now recall the tune.'

'Ah! Tied up with a memory, was it? That explains it.'

To Elaine's consternation, the chagrin of the visitor deepened, and it was in her most metallic tone that Belinda spoke, rising from the stool before the harp.

'It must have been most touching.'

'Won't you play again?' Elaine said, a faint feeling of desperation assailing her.

'No, no, no!' came from Matt. 'Your turn, Elaine.'

'I could not hope to impress after Miss Tarrington's expertise.' Why had Mr Huntly to do this? The last thing she wanted was to play in front of this female and Lady Harriet. As well ask to be insulted! 'Besides, I am not even sure that I can play to order.'

'Try!'

'Matt, what are you about?' demanded Meg *sotto voce*.

Elaine did not hear the reply, for Meg's husband leaned to her, murmuring. Ignoring them, she looked at the other sister.

'Lady Harriet, I appeal to you. Persuade Miss Tarrington to play something else.'

But Belinda was evidently determined to be generous. Before Harriet could open her mouth, she advanced towards Elaine and seized her hands.

'Matthew is right. Come along! I simply must hear you

play. Never mind it if you fumble. I am sure we will all make allowances.'

The patronising note was back. Wishing that they would all go away, Elaine allowed herself to be pulled to her feet. Talking all the time, Miss Tarrington marched her to the stool and pushed her into it, standing over her like a gaoler.

Elaine was conscious of a slight feeling of trepidation as she drew the harp towards her and positioned it comfortably. God forbid she should be plagued with the memory of that face in this company! She reached for the strings, and rippled her fingers across them. Aware of the female standing sentinel at her side, she plucked notes at random, improvising desperately as she searched her mind for some vestige of a tune. Any tune—only to get this over with.

An echo of a voice came to her. 'Perhaps you should not try to remember.' Had Charles said that? It was the doctor's advice. But this was not a hunt for a memory. She was trying to revive a lost skill. Unknowing, she closed her eyes.

Like a dream, she found herself instantaneously in a different room. A vast saloon, all gilt and splendour. At a distance sat a number of shadowy forms. She could not see their faces. A name resurfaced.

'St Vigians. I know this place. *C'est le château.*'

She picked out notes, and pictures floated through her mind. Vast halls. Paintings that covered half a wall. A huge stone stairway and a grand arched entrance. The garden! Here was where it fitted—somewhere in this great expanse of land. A long avenue, peopled by marble statues at intervals down its length, and ending in a fountain. As if she turned, she beheld the frontage of the palatial building. Massive and wide, with turreted towers at its sides. Château de St Vigians.

'And this was home.'

Her fingers splayed into the strings, jangling them out of control. Pain, sharp and jagged, thrust into her chest. She could not breathe. There were voices suddenly—urgent and shrill. But Elaine's attention held on the heavy sound emitting through her lips, and the laboured drag of her chest as she fought to regain her wind.

Chapter Six

Presently the pain subsided. Elaine coughed, drew a shuddering breath, and panted into life again. Or so it felt.

She was being held, and a murmuring in her ear began to penetrate, forming words.

'Steady, now, steady. Don't try to move. I have you safe.'

Then she was helpless, swung up into a powerful embrace. A moment passed, and she was lying down, her head brought to rest upon cushions.

'I am so—sorry,' she gasped. 'Forgive me—pray.'

'Hush!'

The commanding tone at last had familiarity. Elaine forced open her eyes. They fell upon the Earl's features.

'Charles! How—came you here?'

'Don't tease yourself over that.'

But Elaine was insufficiently mistress of herself to heed this injunction. With a vague notion of having interfered in something, she uttered a disjointed protest.

'Belinda…you must not. She will not like it.'

Lord Wytham had no reply to make to this. Vaguely troubled, Elaine tried again.

'Charles, it will not do. Tell her I did not mean it.'

Once again, no reply was forthcoming. Elaine gave it up. If he would not see the danger, what was she to do? Could he not understand that Belinda was jealous of his attentions to her? He was watching her with that bland expression.

'You hide so much,' she said involuntarily.

He frowned. 'I do?'

That moved him, Elaine thought with satisfaction. 'You think I do not see it, but I know that a great deal goes on behind that face.'

A grin broke across it. 'Anyone would suppose you had been drinking, Elaine.'

Charles cherished the smile she gave. He had entered upon a scene of chaos. Belinda excitedly babbling, with Meg holding her by the arm and hissing furiously. Harriet emitting snorts of derision, held back by a bemused-looking Matt. And all the while, Elaine groping for air in their midst!

Taking in the situation in one raking glance, he had commanded Matt to remove the women instantly, and thrust rudely aside both Meg and Belinda, who were crowding the victim without being of the least use. He had caught Elaine as she began to cough, and carried her to the day-bed. Oblivious to what was going on elsewhere in the room, it was only when he was sure that Elaine was recovering fast that he glanced back to find that his brother-in-law had not failed him.

He was disinclined to pay any heed to Elaine's disjointed utterances. Had she been in her senses, he would have informed her pithily just how little Belinda's possible emotions meant to him. Elaine was not to know for how many years he had been laid siege to from that quarter. He had successfully ignored the proprietary air Belinda adopted towards him. If she persisted in a hopeless cause, it was on her own head.

He spoke briskly. 'I had better let the others back in now. I am sure they will not have gone away.'

She blinked up at him. 'You sent them out?'

'It seemed preferable. Neither Belinda nor Harriet could keep from exclamations, and Meg was too apt to fuss. I am mindful of Gorsty's instructions, you see. You were obviously in the grip of a memory, and nothing is to be allowed to interfere with that. Remember?'

He rose to go, but was stayed by Elaine's hand grasping at his own. Warmth spread through him at this evidence of trust. But there was a hint of panic in her eyes.

'Wait!'

'What is it?'

She drew a breath, and he saw a determined look come into her face. 'Help me to sit up, if you please. I do not want to be found like this.'

'Why not? You look charmingly.'

He was smiling, and Elaine's pulse pattered into life. This would not do. Her voice sharpened. 'Pray do not be absurd! I will not be discovered half-fainting upon the couch.'

Charles arched an eyebrow, but refrained from further comment. She did indeed look entrancing, her eyes glowing bluer than ever in the enhancement of that colour in her gown.

He leaned down to her, but hesitated. 'Do you feel light-headed still?'

She gestured impatiently. 'I am well, Charles. Pray help me!'

Thus abjured, he drew her to a sitting posture, waiting until she had dropped her feet to the floor before he let her go. Then he went to open the door. Somewhat to his relief, Harriet and Belinda had withdrawn. Only Matt and Meg remained.

'How is she? Lord, what a turn you gave us, Elaine!'

Leaving his sister to cluck over the sufferer, Charles looked at his brother-in-law. 'How did you manage it?'

Matt grinned. 'Nothing to do with me, m'boy. Silly female went off in a huff the moment I ejected her. Harriet ran after her with a mouthful of apologies.'

From the other end of the room, Meg spoke up. 'Don't believe him, Charles. Belinda went off because Matt was praising Elaine's playing to the skies. I have never known him to be so tactless.'

'Tactical, you mean,' said her husband, winking at Charles. 'Knew it would rankle. I'd already told her that you thought the world of Elaine's playing.'

'Which was quite untrue,' put in Elaine, recalling the passage of arms that had earlier occurred.

'How do you know?' demanded Charles quizzically. 'You were not present when I spoke of it to Matt.'

Elaine eyed him. What did this betoken? Was it to tease her? Never had he treated her with so much ease of manner. He was meeting her gaze with that arching brow, question in his face. She was conscious of warmth in her cheeks, and her heart did an unrhythmic dance.

'How suspicious you look, Elaine!'

'Have I not reason?'

Glancing round, she caught Meg exchanging a mischievous glance with her husband. Her heart skipped a beat.

Surely Mr Huntly could not be party to Meg's antics? Did not Lord Wytham see what was in the wind? Unless she was mistaken. She looked away.

'I am glad you are come, Charles,' said Meg, moving to clasp her brother by the arm. 'Are you wild with me for settling Elaine in Mama's room? Harriet made sure you would object to it, but I—'

'You, Meg,' he interrupted without ceremony, 'thought the best way to ensure my agreement was to do it first and tell me afterwards.'

Elaine's glance flew back. Though she was disclaiming in no little dudgeon, it was exactly what Meg had stated. And Lady Harriet's comment had agreed with the outcome. It was evident that, much as they understood their brother, he was one jump ahead of his sisters. It cannot have escaped his notice that Meg was doing her best to throw them together.

Her champion's next words served to underline this thought, to Elaine's instant dismay.

'I told Elaine that we would all visit her, and I beg you will not be slow to come yourself, Charles. We cannot have her upset by Harriet and that cat of a female she insists on throwing in your way.'

Aghast, Elaine cast a frantic look at the Earl. 'Pray pay no heed to your sister, my lord! I have no need of visitors, and I will not suffer you to dance attendance upon me. I am sure you have far more pressing calls upon your time, and I would not be the means of keeping you from them.'

A most charming smile was bent upon her. 'On the contrary, I am quite at leisure. There is so little business to be attended to here at Teddington that I can rely upon Shawbury implicitly. I will visit you with pleasure.'

'You will do no such thing! You mean only to be sarcastic and I will not be so used!'

'Elaine, don't be silly!' Meg said, laughing. 'How can you suppose anything of the sort? Don't you know that Charles has changed his mind about you?'

An uneven pulsing started up in Elaine's veins. She stared at the Earl, but his expression was too bland to be read. She did not know how bitter was her voice.

'I don't believe it.'

'Can't say I blame her there,' put in Matt. 'What's more, I'm not sure I agree with you, m'love. Has Charles said as much to you? Only told me that he didn't know what to think any longer.'

'Pray don't hesitate to speak for me, either of you!'

'We would not, Charles, if you spoke for yourself,' Meg told him, unabashed. 'You must have been wishing to visit Elaine, for you came in here quite uninvited.'

'I was not aware that an invitation was needed,' he responded ironically. 'However, I came for a sufficient purpose.'

He looked at Elaine and recognised the alienating withdrawal in her features. His reaction was involuntary, and all idea of caution went out of his head.

'My advertisement in the *Gazette* has yielded some response.'

Elaine's face drained of colour, and shock was in her eyes. Instant remorse assailed him. She was unfit to have news of this nature flung at her so abruptly. Yet he could not prevent the thought that she was afraid of what he might have found out. Fear of the unknown—or of being exposed?

'Lord above, Charles!' exploded Meg. 'Why could you not have said so before?'

'In the heat of subsequent events, I rather forgot about it,' he confessed, his eyes on Elaine.

'How could you forget something so important?' demanded his sister crossly.

Elaine's unruly pulses had shot into high gear. She felt sick with dread, and was barely able to get the words out. 'What have you found out?'

Charles delved into his pocket and brought out some papers. 'See for yourself.'

He came to the day-bed and handed three letters to Elaine. She almost dropped them in her feverish haste, but managed to unfold one with fingers that fumbled, the open paper quivering in her grasp as she ran her eyes rapidly down the sheet.

With one accord, Meg and Matt moved to the head of the day-bed and read over her shoulder. Meg was the first to respond.

'But this is nothing to the purpose! Why, this man claims a missing person, but the description does not fit Elaine in the very least.'

Elaine let the sheet slip from her fingers, and it drifted to the floor. The Earl picked it up as Elaine thrust hastily at the broken seal on the next, tearing it open. Bemusedly, she read a missive of much the same content, and handed it to Meg without a word. Her eyes flickered up at the Earl's face, only to encounter his habitually enigmatic expression. The flurry of panic gave way to burgeoning resentment.

He knew this! He knew there was nothing here. Yet he had neither prepared her, nor said anything to mitigate her eager grasping at these straws. He had meant to test her, to see by her reaction if she was lying. Oh, it was ill done of him!

With a great deal less expectation, she perused the third sheet. It was from a lady in Yorkshire, offering to take the stray female off the Earl's hands for the purpose of employing her as a companion. Elaine made no resistance when Meg snatched the sheet from her fingers. She sank back against the rolled end of the day-bed, and regarded the Earl.

Charles met the accusation in the blue eyes and was conscious of distaste for his own tactics. It was not how he had planned it. He had meant to state that the advertisement appeared to be a failure. But Meg and Matt must needs meddle, and he so much disliked coercion, however wellmeant.

'But there is nothing here at all,' Meg commented in a bemused tone.

'No, I had never much hope of the advertisement proving useful. There were a number of letters, all expressing much the same sort of thing.'

Matt handed Charles the papers which he had taken from Meg to read over again. 'What do you mean to do now, m'boy?'

'I have already done it.'

He was still watching Elaine's face, and her expression altered. 'What do you mean?'

'I have passed the whole affair to Bow Street. I went there on the day we travelled together to London.'

For a moment, Elaine did not take this in. But Matt's sudden laughing comment enlightened her.

'Aha! So you had no faith in Harriet's detection.'

'As it happens, Matt, it was your funning that put the idea into my head.'

'But will it answer?' asked Meg anxiously.

'I fancy so. I have given them what little we have to go on, adding to it when Elaine has remembered more.'

Elaine stared at him. 'You have set a Bow Street Runner on to my trail? Why did you not tell me?'

'You were in enough upset. I could not know how such news would affect you.'

'You mean that you supposed I might take fright at the thought of being found out!'

He was obliged to bite down on a stinging retort. He had given her cause, but her attitude irked him none the less. 'Had that been the case, I would have told you. Were you guilty of deception, you would undoubtedly have abandoned the game.'

'And run away? I wish I might!'

Meg began to exclaim in protest, but Charles held up a hand to silence her. Driven by feelings he could not ignore, he took a chair near the day-bed, and reached for Elaine's hands. They lay slackly in his, but to his secret relief, she did not try to pull away.

'Elaine, don't fret so! Sooner or later, the whole truth will out.'

'Your truth—or mine?'

Charles set his jaw, but the forlorn hurt in the clouded orbs disarmed him. An impulse at his chest dictated his words. 'I am talking of your past, from wherever it comes. Until it does so, you can do nothing but accept the situation. Gorsty was right. Rest is what you need—and no disputes!'

Elaine lay back upon the cushions placed in the front of the small boat, watching above her the sun dappling through the leaves. She had protested the invitation, for it had certainly been forced upon the Earl by Meg.

'Nonsense!' had said that matron when Elaine had demurred. 'It is a perfect day for it, and I know Charles will be delighted to take you.'

Now she could not be sorry that she had been overborne. The motion was strangely relaxing, the flowing waters either side engendering a sense of tranquillity. She felt suspended in a vacuum, where the enemy—for so had thought become—did not exist.

Stripped to his shirtsleeves, Charles rowed at a lazy pace, regarding the play of light upon the dreamy softness of her face. His blood stirred. There was enchantment in her beauty. And sensuality in the slender curves, accentuated where the soft white muslin draped about her limbs. Confound this modern fashion—alluring almost beyond endurance!

It had not been brotherly affection that had made him yield to Meg. The idyllic vision that had sprung from her suggestion had been irresistible. To be thus isolated—and Elaine his prisoner.

Wherever it was he had started, he was now so thoroughly enmeshed that he knew not how to unravel himself. He had been intrigued from the first—despite himself. She had begun by enlisting his sympathy, and pulled him somehow into this intensity of need that demanded an end to the enigma of her background. He had as well have said the enigma of Elaine herself!

She was often so cool in manner that he was apt to forget her distresses. That straight look which she dealt him from time to time was unnerving. Had he not cultivated his own social mask over the years—essential in his position, prey as he was to every matchmaker in town!—he must have crumbled before that look, just as Elaine crumbled under the extremes of her unfortunate condition. She was so self-possessed at times. Yet she could go to pieces in a minute. It was, to say the least, unsettling. Had she tried, she could not have plotted so successful an assault upon his defences.

He had thought himself inviolate. To find his armour pierced, and from so uncertain a source, was an experience at once novel and alarming. He recognised its danger, but felt powerless to arm himself anew.

Her very distance, as she lay there with such seeming serenity, began to irritate him. Her gaze had moved from the trees. She was trailing the tips of her fingers in the water, her eyes following the broken patterns that she made. A faint smile curved her lips. Charles felt an almost overwhelming compulsion to kiss them.

Confound it! What, had he successfully evaded myriad traps, only to fall victim to a female who came to him with no character and no name? He would conquer this! Besides, if her slight memories were anything to go by, Elaine's affections had long been engaged elsewhere. The remembrance of her probable wedded state brought him up short. Was he mad, to be indulging in these sorts of reflections when Elaine was depending upon his aid and comfort?

'What are you thinking about?' he asked, more to distract himself than anything else.

Elaine started. The misted gaze lingered upon his face before she answered. In the silence, three swans glided serenely past, eyeing the occupants of the small boat with royal disdain.

'I am not thinking,' Elaine said at last. 'That is why I am at peace.'

'I am glad of it,' Charles said. Not that he believed it for a moment. She had been miles away. It had taken her some time to find that excuse. Her eyes were upon him still. He arched an eyebrow. 'What?'

Elaine spoke the thought in her mind. 'It strikes me that in all our dealings, we talk only of me. Tell me something of yourself, Charles.'

He looked taken aback. 'What would you wish to know?'

Her mood was so tranquil that it seemed nothing could shatter it. The sun glanced off the chestnut locks that were dishevelled from effort. Endearingly so. She dared the question.

'Why have you never married?'

Charles gave a short laugh. 'Is it not obvious?'

'Not if you had been French. Do not they arrange marriages in England for persons of your rank?'

Suddenly alert, Charles answered with caution. Was she aware that she was speaking as if she knew her background?

'It is usual. But my father died before I was quite of age, and my mother was sickly.' He grinned. 'However, my sisters have expended much effort on the task.'

'Fruitlessly, it would seem.'

'Quite so.'

Elaine continued to search his face. 'You might have married for love. Were you never in love?'

The question pierced a nerve, but he managed a self-conscious laugh. 'With the most unsuitable females only.'

'It is one of the advantages of England,' Elaine continued, her tone dreamy, as though she was not fully aware of what she said, 'that one can marry for love. Otherwise, I dare say I should have been betrothed to some man of rank. I would scarce have known him perhaps. I might have been happy.'

Had she then married—for love? The thought caused a hollow feeling to rise up in his chest. Suppressing it, he searched his mind for some innocuous comment that would not throw her back into forgetfulness. Nothing came to him save the urgent questions born of his own desires. He was relieved when she relapsed into silence.

Had she been all the time in some half-waking state where the veils that tortured her mind were lifted? She had not been thinking, she had said. But thought, when it encompassed all that was one's life, was unconscious. What Elaine meant by thinking was the fretting conjectures that only increased her frustration. If he could but get her talking again!

'Elaine?'

'*Oui?*'

She had drifted into French. Now what was he to do? Inspiration failed him. And this intimate situation was all too dangerous. He lifted the oars from the water.

'I am going to turn the boat. It is time we started back.'

A shadow crossed her face. 'Already? I could stay forever on this river. There are no demons here.'

'Demons?'

'Of the mind.'

Her eyes dimmed as they stared at him, and a faraway look entered there. Charles held his breath, unmoving. The oars dripped, and a hazy odour of honeysuckle drifted in the quiet air. Her voice was hushed, at odds with the haunting intensity of her words.

'They began long years ago. I used to wish that *Grand-père* had not sent me here, that I might not have been spared. Had I been one of them, my pain would have been soon over. When I knew they had gone...*toute la famille*...I dreamed of it night after night. I saw them in my sleep. Slaughtered, one for one. *Maman*; my brothers, cousins, *tante et oncle*. Others of our name. *Même Grandpère*—despite his age, they cut off his head. They had no mercy. They took them all. And in their place, they gave me demons.'

Her voice ceased. She lay deathly still, a trickle of moisture unheeded at each eye. Charles could not move. He had no words. The compression at his heart took from him all power of will. If this was what she must remember, then confound all memory! Was she aware of having spilled this poignant history? Her entire family victim to the guillotine! And Elaine left to suffer these griefs alone. Small wonder she had retreated from such horrors.

But this must be some time in the past. It was near ten years since the terrible events across the Channel had been set in train. Elaine's family might have been killed at any time within some four years during which the Terror had lasted. What was the more recent background? That which encompassed the face of an unknown man—whom she might have loved, and who might have died from a fall down stairs.

'Are we not going to go further?'

Charles started, loosing the oars so that they splashed into the water. Elaine flinched from the spray, pulling herself up. She laughed, brushing at the wet as she cast a reproachful eye at him.

'Why, thank you, Charles. I was feeling somewhat warm, but there was no need to give me a bath!'

The change was totally disorienting. 'Forgive me!' he uttered, shaken. 'My attention wandered—you startled me.'

'Evidently.'

He received the enchantment of her smile, and his breath

caught. A riot of questions ran through his head. She knew nothing of it! Was it possible? Could she have said all that and been unaware? Or had he been tricked? If so, she was marvellously successful. Confound it, he would not believe it was artifice! Yet how engaging had been that interlude. He was—had been!—ready to give his all, could he but rid her of those demons that tormented her soul. If indeed they existed. It was not an impossible tale. Lord knew how many unfortunates had been destroyed by the ruling regime in France!

Yet, despite all—even the emotive wrenching that she drew from him more and more—a part of his mind could not keep from one cynical notion. It would have been hard to find a more moving method of letting him think her the offspring of aristocrats.

Doubt raged in his mind, fostered by the impact upon him of her aspect as she spoke, even more than her words.

'Charles, what is the matter?'

A faint furrow creased between her brows as she looked at him. With an effort, Charles pulled himself together. His habitual practised social ease had deserted him. He could only hope that long habit would rescue him. At least to a semblance of normality.

'Nothing is the matter. I was—only wondering whether we should go on. Do you wish to?'

Elaine shifted her limbs, stretching luxuriously. 'I have had a delightful rest. But I will not keep you longer. I know well that it was Meg's doing that you brought me.'

She was completely back in the present—with no memory of any of it. Or was she indulging in triumph at having caught him so fully in her snare? Confound it, he did not want to doubt her! She was too lovely—and he was already too much involved.

'It has been a pleasant interlude, Charles,' she said, and there was gratitude in her smile.

'The pleasure was all mine,' Charles answered, with more haste than grace.

He saw puzzlement creep into her eyes, and knew he had failed to hide his disquiet. Cursing inwardly, he turned the craft, heading for home.

Elaine was unaccountably nervous. She could not doubt but that Lord Wytham was a competent driver. Mr Huntly had said that he handled a phaeton and four with an ease of control that must command admiration. But from the moment she saw the equipages waiting upon the drive, a coil of alarm settled in her stomach.

The landaulet, an elegant carriage with a crest upon the panel, must be the vehicle in which she first came to Clevedon House. It was, on this warm fifth day of July, open to the elements with its hood down, as it had been that first day. Her glance travelled to the team of horses. They were standing quietly under the charge of a groom at the leader's head, while his lordship's coachman settled himself on the box.

In front of the larger carriage stood the phaeton. Harnessed to it were four resty bays, who tossed their manes and shifted gravel with impatience. It took two grooms to hold them while the Earl looked them over.

Ice crawled down Elaine's back, and she wished she had not agreed to this expedition—nor to Meg's unsubtle arrangements for the party's occupation of the carriages. Did they need two carriages? Harriet was not to be of the party.

'You will never get Charles to travel in a landaulet when he can drive himself,' had said Matt when she ventured to ask.

Must he also drive Elaine?

'You will get there quicker, and have a smoother ride. Charles' phaeton is so well sprung.' Thus Meg.

Elaine was not fooled for a moment. She was astonished that Charles had agreed to so blatant a ploy. And she did not wish to be alone with him. There had been, in her memory of the row on the river on Monday last, an oddity in his behaviour that dismayed her. The gentleness that she had grown used to from him had felt almost forced. His manner had been—yes, charged. As if he laboured under strong emotion. Had he regretted allowing Meg to persuade him to take her boating?

In any event, she had no real desire to watch a Review of Volunteers at Wimbledon. But Meg had been adamant for, 'The King is to be there, you know, and all the world will follow. Besides, it will do you good to get out.'

She had been hustled into her old black velvet spencer over the white muslin, for the wind could bite against the swift passage of a phaeton. Elaine had discarded her old boots in favour of the new blue and white striped shoes that had been purchased through Honorine, which matched the ribbons adorning a pretty cabriolet bonnet of black velvet that she had purposely acquired to go with the spencer.

Despite the boost to her spirits of this pleasing attire, Elaine felt a craven wish to cry off. Only it would be churlish to do so when they were on the point of setting out.

Dismay engulfed her nevertheless as the Earl gave her his hand and she was obliged to climb up into the phaeton. She bit her lip, settled her petticoats, and gripped the side of the carriage the instant Charles turned away.

He jumped up and took the reins, and Elaine could not but be glad that his positively plunging horses took all his attention for the first few moments of the journey.

'I have not had them out this age,' he said presently, by way of explanation. 'They are used to be very active daily when I am in London.'

'You do not use them in the country?' Elaine made the effort to ask, her eyes on the sleek backs and powerful haunches of the beasts.

'I more often ride. Parr takes them out for exercise, but they like to work as a team.'

From behind, the groom tutted. 'I would've given them a run yesterday, me lord, only I thought they'd best stay fresh. It's a fair way for them to Wimbledon, and you won't wish to change.'

'You did quite right, Parr.'

Elaine caught his glance as Charles spoke, and tried to quiet her tension. With little success apparently.

'Do you fear that I may overturn you? Don't concern yourself. I have been handling this team for several years. They know better than to play tricks upon me.'

She hardly heard him. The very mention of overturning caused a resurgence of icy dread. Why should she be so much afraid? She must have been many times in a carriage.

'You seem *distraite*, Elaine.'

She glanced quickly at the Earl and saw him only in profile under the brim of his beaver hat, rakishly tilted, for his concentration was upon the road ahead. What to say? She had been sharing all such thoughts with him recently. But she was wary since the incident upon the river, and was, besides, acutely conscious of the presence of his groom. Damping down her fears, she attempted to pass it off.

'A little. It is a new experience to be venturing forth.'

'And you are nervous?'

'A trifle.'

To her relief, the Earl appeared to accept this. He drew in his horses and slowed the pace a little.

'Is that better?'

It was undoubtedly better. But Elaine had not said that it was the speed which was making her nervous. It was uncanny that Lord Wytham had divined as much. She examined his profile with suspicion.

'How did you know it was that?'

A grin flashed in her direction. 'You have been hanging on for dear life ever since we started!'

Abruptly conscious, Elaine looked down, and found not only that her left hand was glued to the side of the phaeton, but the other clung to the seat. With a gesture of distaste, she let go, straightening the hand and flexing the fingers.

'I would have slowed down earlier,' said Charles in an apologetic tone, 'only with the bays so fresh, it would have been useless. They would have been unruly to the end.'

'Will they be content now to proceed at this pace?'

'Oh, yes. Once they have had the edge taken off them, they are as docile as you please.'

Relief swept through Elaine, and the knot in her stomach began to loosen. 'Thank you,' she said with gratitude. 'I do not know why I should have been so fearful of accident.'

Even as she spoke, an image flashed through her mind: horses plunging behind the glass, a violent swerve that threw her hard against the other passenger and back again into the open doorway. There was a confusion of whirling sky and shouts. Then blackness.

'*Accident.*' Hardly knowing what she did, Elaine gripped Charles' arm. 'Stop! Oh, pray stop the carriage!'

The Earl glanced before and behind. They were in the middle of open country, and the road was clear. In a moment, despite the hampering clutch upon his arm, he had brought his horses to a standstill. Parr did not need his command to leap down and run to the bays' heads. When they were safely in charge, Charles looped the reins over the clip, and turned to Elaine.

She was shaking, her features set, staring straight ahead. Removing her fingers from his arm, he held them in one gloved hand, and grasped her shoulder with the other.

'Steady!'

The blue eyes came waveringly up to his face. Her free hand clutched at the lapel of his white drab driving coat.

'Tell me,' he coaxed.

'An accident, Charles! I was thrown from a coach doorway. I must have lost consciousness. Don't you see? That must be how I hit my head.'

'What did you see just then?'

'The horses. They were out of control. The carriage swerved. I was thrown to one side—there was someone there, I don't know who. And then, I fell out of the door! The sky—trees—and then nothing.'

Charles did not speak for a moment. This was all too plausibly the origin of her unhappy situation. He despised himself for the nagging doubt that instantly attacked him. Why should he suppose her an actress of remarkable skill rather than believe her? Had there been one single instance of error? Not the veriest slip of the tongue. It was his ingrained defences at work.

'At least we now know why you were nervous of the horses,' he said lightly.

A faint laugh escaped her, and she relaxed her grip on his coat, sinking back into the seat. 'Yes, it would explain it.'

'Come, this is encouraging, Elaine. You are closing in on that elusive memory of yours.'

His tone was much more what Elaine had been used to hear from him—until the day on the river. Her sense of relaxation deepened. With it, came a feeling of intimacy. Before she could control the impulse, Elaine's voice slipped into a confidential murmur.

'I trust your groom may not overhear us for a moment, Charles.'

He looked a little taken aback. 'Why, what is it?'

She eyed him, wariness returning. Why had she begun on this? She could not think how to change direction. She would have to go on. She drew a breath and took the plunge.

'It was not only the horses.'

Charles frowned. 'What else, then?'

'I have wanted to say this for some days.' She glanced away and back again, and found him watching her gravely. 'I know you have been suspicious of me—perhaps you are still. But please believe that these determined efforts of Meg's to throw us together have not been of my making.'

'No, I know they have not,' he answered, aware of his own stiffening. Could he sustain a discussion of this kind?

'It would have suited me better had you not acquiesced in these schemes,' Elaine said.

His reaction was uncontrollable and swift. Withdrawing from her, he shifted back. 'Would it?'

Elaine gazed at him in dismay. What ailed him now? Why speak with such hardness in his tone?

'Of course it would,' she returned, an involuntary protest in her voice. 'It goes against everything you have ever said to me. You cannot wish for these intimacies!'

'Nor you, evidently.' Unable to help an acid note, Charles added, 'I gather you take no pleasure in my company.'

She blinked, aware of a constriction in her throat. 'It—it is not that, Charles. For one thing, I may be married—indeed, I am almost sure of it.'

'A convenient assumption.'

A spark of anger lit in her breast. 'What in the world makes you say such a thing? I am going by my feelings, and—'

'Pray don't speak to me of your feelings, Elaine, for beyond your own troubled enquiries, you have none! You have made that abundantly plain.'

The words cut, and Elaine could only gasp at the sudden access of bitterness in his tone.

'Have you run mad? What have I done that you should speak thus to me?'

But Charles had heard the echo of his own words with a sense of shock. Some madness had indeed possessed him! 'I beg your pardon,' he said quickly. 'I didn't mean it.'

Elaine's indignation could not be so easily assuaged. *'Je ne comprends pas!* Why, Charles? Why did you say it? If I am self-absorbed—'

'It is no matter for wonder,' he interrupted in a rapid and staccato fashion. 'Forget I said anything.'

She only wished she might, but she was too hurt—yes, too bewildered—to allow it to pass. Her gloved fingers fidgeted with the rough blanket that Meg had insisted should be laid across her knees.

'I cannot forget it,' she said frankly. 'But I think it will be better if we converse no further on the subject. Or indeed on any other!'

'I thank you,' Charles responded curtly. 'That will suit me very well.'

Before another word could be exchanged, the Earl had called to his groom. In a state of upset almost worse than the tension she had earlier experienced, Elaine watched him take the reins again. Then the team was away, and all opportunity to re-establish communication had disappeared.

Confused, Elaine tried to recapture the sequence of the conversation. How had they arrived at such a point? What ailed Charles to be pokering up in that fashion? He had never done so before. And then to veer wildly from those horrid accusations to that cool apology!

There had been no explanation offered. Why should he treat her so? What had she done to merit that acidity from him? Conscious of a desire to weep, Elaine fought to contain it. It dawned on her gradually that his words were entirely inapposite. Though she had tried not to do so, she was apt to enjoy his company. And as for her feelings—they were all too tender.

The realisation shocked her. Where were her thoughts leading? She must not like him! Every vestige of common sense militated against it. Aside from a distaste of proving to be as bad as Lady Harriet thought her, she could not afford to like him. She was not free! Nor had he the freedom to be disposed to any sort of fondness for her. He could not so abuse his position.

The memory of his words belied her. Freedom or no, there had been in them a suppressed violence of passion. As though he believed her indifferent—and resented it. What could that mean but that he had begun to cherish a fondness for her?

Warmth cascaded into the secret hollows of her bosom. She turned her gaze firmly upon the passing scenery to one side, fearful of letting him see her unrest. Acutely conscious of his nearness, of his strong hands on the reins, and of the smouldering drag of emotion that emanated from him, Elaine sat breathless with shock.

Then she had not mistaken it that day on the river! Was it these sensations she had picked up, and not recognised? Had he, despite his own alienating suspicion, succumbed to the magnet that she had been steadfastly ignoring on her own account? Her heart thumped painfully suddenly, and she found herself clutching at the seat below her. In fear, but this time of a different nature. For she knew—without proof, without memory, but she knew it!—that the torrent she had unleashed within herself was a betrayal of another man.

Meg's prophecy proved correct, for the rise above Wimbledon Common was packed with carriages, and teeming with pedestrians all the way down to the plain. The corps being reviewed, as a well-informed Matt kindly explained to Elaine, was the London and Westminster Light Volunteers under the command of Colonel Herries.

In watching the various manouevres undertaken under the eye of his Majesty by six troops of cavalry, and a further three of marching infantrymen, Elaine forgot her preoccupations for a while. The surge of scarlet and white, moving with precision and steadiness, could not but draw her admiration at first. And a stir of excitement must be felt at each flash of steel, every glint of the sun upon highly polished brass.

But the exercises palled after a time, and Elaine was relieved when Matt left her in the landaulet with Meg and went off to gain a closer vantage point. Yet, deprived of his guiding words, she was dismayed to find her mind reverting to that quarrel in the Earl's phaeton.

As for Charles, immediately upon discovering the landaulet and edging his own carriage next to it, he had hastened out of her company, seizing with alacrity—as it appeared to Elaine—upon his brother-in-law to replace him, explaining briefly that he had been an army officer in his youth.

'Matt, why don't you give Elaine the benefit of your experience?'

Then he had walked quickly away, and vanished into the crowd. Elaine had not known whether to be affronted or relieved. But now, with nothing to claim her attention but the drone of Meg's chattering friends, she was all too open to reflection. The image that had caused her to cry out for the carriage to be stopped slid into her mind, adding nothing to her comfort. She wished now that she had cried off!

Meg and her acquaintances paid little heed to the Review. The real business of the day was apparently to see and be seen. In her present mood, the inane chatter became at length too irksome to be borne. She sought for an adequate excuse.

'I think I will stretch my legs for a little, Meg.'

Her champion gave her a narrow glance, but made no

demur beyond an admonition not to stray too far from the carriages. How might Meg react if she knew the substance of Elaine's thoughts, and the reason for her jangling nerves?

She was glad that there had been no opportunity for private discussion, for the memory of the accident was at present too inextricably bound up with the breach between herself and Charles, and Elaine did not think she could recount the one without touching upon the other. To have Meg gloat upon the success of her tactics would be unbearable!

She gave place in the carriage to one of Meg's intimates, and turned away with the intention of finding some quiet spot where she might think in peace. But no sooner had she threaded her way through the throng to a little distance from the carriage than she was accosted by Belinda Tarrington.

'Elaine, how delightful to see you out and about! Those stripes are very dashing. Do come and talk with me.'

Without waiting for a reply, she tucked a gloved hand within Elaine's arm and drew her out of the press of carriages to a point a little behind the general mêlée. Elaine did not see how she could stop herself being kidnapped, although nothing could have been further from her wishes—especially in the light of recent events!—than a tête-à-tête with this would-be Countess of Wytham.

The woman's manner was caressing, and she had begun with a compliment, which made Elaine instantly chary. Belinda was herself prettily clad in a great-coat dress of Indian cotton, dyed pink and ornamented with scarlet ribbon bows which matched the feathers in her neat round bonnet.

It was unsurprising to discover that it was not for a friendly chat that Elaine had been dragged aside. No sooner were they comparatively out of earshot of the crowd than Miss Tarrington opened fire.

'I am glad to have this opportunity to talk to you alone, Elaine.'

Elaine eyed her warily, for a certain quality in her voice gave warning of what was to come. 'Indeed?'

The thin features became pinched, the smile forced. 'You have intruded upon a situation of some delicacy.'

A faint tremor started up in Elaine's bosom, but she maintained an air of calm. 'How so, Miss Tarrington?'

'I allude to Charles,' said Belinda, at her most clipped and metallic. 'Oh, do not misunderstand me. I acquit you of any base design. I believe Harriet to be mistaken in you.'

Astonished, Elaine gazed at her blankly. 'You do?'

The abrasive laugh came. 'Do not look so amazed. I have observed you closely.'

'On two occasions,' said Elaine flatly.

'It was enough. The second time I met you, I became convinced that you had been speaking the truth all along. I am very sorry for you, dear Elaine, but I am afraid you cannot have Charles!'

Elaine kept her gaze steady upon the woman's face, but the riot in her bosom was deafening in her own ears. She hoped that her voice did not quake.

'I do not understand you.'

Belinda's smile did not reach her eyes. 'I think you do, Elaine. You see, Harriet has kept me well informed. Boating on the river? Wanderings in the night?'

'But that was accidental!'

'I believe you. And I know you have Meg to thank for much of it, and that her design is supported by Matthew. That would scarcely matter. Meg has tried before and failed. But with you, it is different.'

Elaine fought to stop anticipation rising in her bosom. And signally failed. The intensity of passion underneath the woman's words was compelling. Elaine's pulse continued its uproar. Had not her own instincts told her that there was substance in Belinda's jealousy?

'How—is it different?' she managed to ask.

A pitying glance raked her. 'Tush, are you so naïve? You are living in his house! You are in a unique position to break down his barriers. And you are beginning to do so, for I have seen it for myself.'

Then she was not the only one to think it! A surge of feeling rushed through Elaine. She did not speak, for she could not. All she could hope for was that she was not giving herself away.

'That is why I wished to put you upon your guard,' pursued the woman. 'I should hate to see you hurt any more than you have been. You see, Charles is promised to me.'

Elaine's mind went blank. 'I beg your pardon?'

'We have an understanding. I have ever regarded it as binding.'

It was on the tip of Elaine's tongue to ask whether Charles did so, but she held her peace. Yet it little accorded with what she had herself observed. Her spirits rose.

'You are making this up,' she said coolly.

'Am I? I am five and twenty, Elaine. I have had offers. Do you imagine that I would have remained single if I had no surety that Charles would marry me?'

Elaine's blood chilled. 'What surety?'

Belinda smiled, smug at last. 'He had my maidenhead, Elaine. That is my surety.'

Chapter Seven

Charles tossed and turned in his bed, unable to sleep. That he had lost his self-assurance was bad enough. Worse that he had acted like a sulky youth consumed with a fit of jealousy! It had been that which had held him silent, fighting the urge to stop the carriage once again to enforce a second confrontation. One with an outcome more attuned to his desires!

Had Elaine made the slightest move at reconciliation, he would have melted instantly. But she had remained stead-fastly aloof. He had tried to be glad of the breach—and had failed dismally.

Guilt rode him, because she had been distressed by that revelatory memory. But chiding himself did not mend matters. He should have made an effort to do so. It cut at his gentlemanly instincts as much as his burgeoning and mis-placed feeling for Elaine. But he had been unable to make the first move. This, he was forced to realise, had its origin in that Elaine had shown herself to be wholly indifferent to him.

From the moment she had intimated that she did not wish to be drawn into condoning Meg's patent matchmaking, he had felt shut out. And when she had announced her intention of travelling back in the landaulet, he had been so resentful he could not trust himself to speak.

Matt, who had joined him in the phaeton, had not helped matters. They had, by mutual agreement, stopped at an alehouse to refresh themselves. Charles had soon regretted it.

'Now you can tell me what has made you as surly as a bear,' Matt had remarked, the moment they had seated themselves in a quiet corner outside the inn.

'What is that supposed to mean, confound you?'

'That's just what it means,' had said Matt frankly. 'Can't say a word to you without having my nose bitten off!'

Charles had stiffened. 'I beg your pardon.'

'Never mind begging my pardon. What has put you all on end?'

'It was Elaine, if you must know,' Charles had confessed, goaded.

'Thought as much. Quarrelled, have you?'

'I would hardly call it a quarrel.'

'Oh? Then why aren't you speaking to one another?'

Charles had sighed. 'Is it that obvious?'

Matt had lifted his tankard, and winked. 'What's obvious, m'boy, is that you are more than half in love with the girl!'

Charles had disclaimed in no uncertain manner, cursing his brother-in-law with a will. Matt had only laughed, leaving him more than ever indignant. In love! He admitted to a strong attraction. Who could remain unaffected? Elaine was beautiful by any standards. But love? No, indeed.

But the idea obstinately persisted, roving in his mind long after he had denounced Matt's supposition with all the eloquence at his command.

To prove his brother-in-law wrong, if nothing else, he had forced himself to address several commonplace remarks to Elaine through the evening. She had replied with reserve, and Charles had been chagrined at Harriet's evident pleasure in the breach. Meg had said nothing, but she had looked well satisfied, and Charles must suppose her to be in Matt's confidence. Confound the man! And confound Elaine, too!

At length, sheer exhaustion put him upon the point of falling asleep, when he was roused again by the faint, but unmistakable sound of the harp.

Wide awake in a second, Charles sat bolt upright in bed. She was playing the harp at this hour? Was she mad?

'She will wake up the whole house!' he muttered aloud.

That it might not be Elaine playing did not even cross his mind. He was out of the bed and striking a flint to light his candle before he had even realised that the sound had ceased.

He paused with the candle just flickering into life. She must have come to her senses and recalled that it was the middle of the night.

Come to her senses? Did that mean that she had again fallen victim to her demons? Confound it, what was it to him? She would not thank him if he went to her. He made a move to slide back under covers. But he could not do it. Elaine was in trouble, and that alone commanded him.

Elaine sat over the harp, her forehead resting against the wooden frame. She fought with the tears that would persist in rising. Of what use to weep?

But she felt so alone! Meg's smirking satisfaction had enraged her, so that she had withdrawn the slight urge to confide in her the muddled thoughts that plagued her.

'You don't have to tell me,' had said that matron, an all-too-knowing look in her eye. 'Matt said that you quarrelled with Charles, and I can see for myself exactly why.'

'You are mistaken,' Elaine had lied in a shaking voice, 'if you suppose my upset has anything to do with him.'

'Does it not?' The glee she had exhibited had slain at once all desire in Elaine to share with her Belinda's horrifying testimony.

She did not want to believe it. Yet had not Charles himself spoken of the traps that had been set for him? She recalled mention of a female who had attempted to coerce him by waylaying him in a bedchamber. Elaine would not put such a scandalous proceeding past Miss Belinda Tarrington!

What had so wrought upon her was that his lordship the Earl of Wytham had not seen fit to explain how he extracted himself from that encounter. If he had indeed done so. Or had he instead taken advantage of the occasion? He need not have been compromised by it. He might take his pleasure, and refuse to abide by the rules. Society would say that the female had brought it upon herself. If the Earl had not offered marriage there and then, dare the woman risk her reputation by crying that he had seduced her?

But Belinda Tarrington, if it were she, might cherish that moment, only waiting her chance to wield her weapon of blackmail. Only Elaine could not bring herself to believe that Charles could truly be so little the gentleman as to reject a female whom he had already compromised. If her faith was justified, then Belinda had lied!

The uncertainty of this last had nagged at her half the night. And when she had slept at last, it was only to fall victim to the dream of that unknown pursuer, chasing her through the forest.

She had woken in a sweat of fear, the whole hideous vision of the carriage accident rising up in her mind. The tormented questions surrounding her past had surged back.

Her instinct had been to run to Charles for succour. But no sooner had she risen from her bed and donned the silk wrapper over her nightgown than the quarrel had come back into her mind…and with it, the dread tale thrust upon her by Belinda.

Swept with a feeling of isolation, Elaine had sought refuge in her parlour, and solace in the strings of the harp. But the tears bubbled up, and she could not play.

A footstep outside the room roused her. She rose quickly from the stool, and shrank back into the shadows by the harp, straining her eyes towards the door on the other side of the glow thrown by her candle, which she had left upon the mantel.

The door opened, and a single candle lit the face of the man who entered. Elaine's heart jerked, and she scuttled to the far wall, a protest bursting out of her.

'What do you want here? Why have you come?'

'I heard the harp,' he answered.

'I am sorry I woke you, but pray go away again. Leave me alone!'

Charles crossed to the mantel and laid his own candle down at the other end. He could only just see her, but her hasty movement and the nervy quality in her voice were enough to show him that he had not been mistaken.

'I will not leave you when you are in this state.' He took a step towards her. 'What is troubling you, Elaine?'

She shifted to the day-bed, and sat there, huddling into the green silk wrapper. Why must he come now, just when she needed him? For she could no longer trust him, and it was impossible to tell him why. She fell back upon the obvious, taking advantage of the strained relations between them.

'What should it be? What is it ever? I thought I had opened a key when I found that accident, but I have only more questions unanswered.'

'Tell me,' he said steadily.

'So that you can provoke me into argument?' she snapped uncontrollably. 'You will not succeed, Charles.'

Charles paused a moment. She was brittle—and cagy. He must tread with care.

'It is the last thing I want.'

He dared to approach a little closer. Even in the shadows of the day-bed he saw her shrink slightly, and hurt rose up. Sternly, Charles repressed it. He tried to cultivate that bland note that had always stood him in such good stead.

'It was a foolish contretemps that we fell into today. Can we not forget it, Elaine? I spoke irrationally, and I am heartily sorry for it.'

Elaine held her breath. An olive branch? And delivered in that old tone of indifference. Had she been mistaken, then? Had it all been in her mind? Her instinct was to repudiate him—and with violence. She must not resume that former ease of intercourse. It was dangerous, and unsettling. And now that the predatory Miss Tarrington had spoken—with such incredible candour!—she was the more determined to remain distanced.

Yet his presence soothed her spirits. That he had come to find her, had been woken by her incautious playing of the harp, and known she was distressed, could not fail to warm her heart. And if Belinda had left her uncertain, she ought to recognise how Charles had felt at her own advent. To be faced with an unknown suspicion to which there was no way to find an answer was, she had discovered, hard indeed.

She did not respond directly to his plea, instead seizing upon what she might with impunity impart to him. 'I had that dream again. That a man chased me through the forest. It woke me, and I could not sleep again for the questions.'

'What questions?'

The gentle note disarmed her. Without will she spoke the tremblings of her mind. 'I fell from a carriage, Charles. I was unconscious. Why did no one help me? There was a man in that coach! And the coachman, the groom. Did they leave me there to wander through unknown woods? I cannot think it.'

Elaine had not noticed his approach, but as she ended, she found him seating himself beside her. Her heart performed an unnatural dance, and she shifted unconsciously a little away from him.

'I agree,' Charles said, aware that a frigid tone of formality had entered his voice. He tried to control it, but her retreat could not do other than pain him. He concentrated his thoughts upon the matter in hand. There was more than one possible explanation of her visions.

'The coachman must have been obliged to look to his horses,' he suggested. 'It may have been some time before he brought them under control. He could have travelled some distance. Perhaps you arose in a hazy state, and wandered.'

Elaine looked at the darkness of his features beside her. His nearness was altogether unsettling. She could feel a tremor in her voice, and hoped he might take it to be caused by fear of her visions rather than himself.

'And then he chased me?'

'If you were dazed—if you had already lost your memory—it is natural that you would be frightened. If they looked for you, calling, perhaps you ran further away.'

But this, abruptly, would not do. She felt a resurgence of that frantic feeling that had attacked her when she woke that horrid morning with no vestige of a notion how she had come to be lying under bushes in his forest.

'Then why did they not continue looking? Why did they leave me? All night, Charles!'

'If it was late, and darkness came upon them, perhaps they had no choice.'

'No choice,' she repeated bleakly.

Had he had no choice, when Belinda offered herself to him? Shocked at the waywardness of her own thoughts, Elaine jumped up, crossing to the mantelpiece—anxious only to get at a distance from him. Why could she not keep her attention on what mattered? As if wrenched from her tongue by her unruly mind, she asked an impossible question.

'Would you have left me, Charles?'

Charles drew a ragged breath, his eyes riveted to the strained features that had come abruptly to life as she stepped into the glowing candlelight. Must she ask him that? Why should she think of it? She had risen to escape from him. He knew it! Yet she challenged him with a question that could have but one answer. Without will, he made it.

'Only until I had fetched torches, and men to help me. No,

I would not have left you. I would have found you, however long it took.'

There was a deathly hush. Elaine's mind refused to operate. It felt clogged. All that forced itself upon her notice was the desperate jumping of her pulses.

At length a numbing thought pressed its way in. *She must find out her history.* A wash of despair engulfed her. What was the use? Without that background, there could be no future to the promise contained in his words. Or was she merely reading it there? And then there was Belinda!

Nevertheless, the yawning gap of her past sprang at her in a way that it had never done before. The impossibility of her situation became suddenly disastrous.

'But that man did leave me. He did not fetch torches, nor men to help him. He did not return at all—not even on the following day. Why not? A man in search of me ought to have hunted the area, calling upon every household. But no one has come looking for me here.'

Charles watched her pace, dull with disappointment. For one instant she had looked as though it mattered that he cared. Had she even realised it with her attention so concentrated? The tenor of her words began to penetrate.

'Did I jump from the coach? Or—did he push me? If that was it, he would not stop. He would have driven on.' Unthinkingly, she moved closer to Charles, anxiety in her voice. 'But I do not think that is it. The horses were in difficulties, that much I saw. I might have fallen, but I might equally have taken opportunity to jump. To get away.' Slowly, she repeated it. 'Yes—to get away. Else I would not have run from him in my dreams.'

Charles rose, alive suddenly to the implication. Had she stumbled upon the truth?

'What is it you are saying, Elaine?'

Her eyes, glittering in the feeble candlelight, filled him with a haunting apprehension. 'I am a runaway, Charles. He gave it up then, but it cannot last. Sooner or later that man will come for me.'

Elaine having driven out with Meg on—so ran his sister's excuse—a shopping expedition, Charles had been inveigled into playing a game of bowls with his brother-in-law. Matt had dragged him out to the smooth lawns beyond the downstairs saloon, having sent a couple of footmen to unearth the ancient wooden balls from a lumber room in the attics. Both men had discarded their coats, Charles sporting a fancy waistcoat of linen with a floral design against Matt's plain brown corduroy.

Charles' interest in bowls was but tepid, for it was too desultory a sport for his taste. But any diversion was welcome in his present state of mind.

Matt had conceived a liking for the pastime due to the enthusiasm of his twin sons, whose skill was legendary. It was, Charles knew, the delight of his nephews to beat their father at this game—which they invariably did—and to pour upon his hapless head all the derision at their command.

'I meant to practise every day,' Matt said, watching with a jaundiced eye the recalcitrant behaviour of the bowl he had just sent rolling down the green. 'Look at that! I made sure it would close in on the centre, but the angle is wrong.'

'Take comfort from the fact that Nick and Dick are not here to point out your failings,' said Charles, taking his ball in hand and lining up his shot.

'Monsters!' muttered Matt. Then he cheered as Charles'

bowl went wide. 'I am consoled. However bad I am, I am at least better than you, m'boy.'

'Why do you imagine I refuse to play with my nephews?' demanded Charles. 'If you take my tip, you would do the same.'

'And have them call me coward? No, by God!'

'Why in the world do you allow them to make a mockery of you? In your place, I should know how to deal with them!'

A cheerful grin was cast at him. 'Ha! It will be a different tale when you have boys of your own.' Matt winked. 'Which day, I venture to prophesy, is not so far distant.'

Charles shifted away. 'Will you have done? There can be no question of— Who knows if she is even free, let alone— Oh, confound you, Matt!'

He glared at his brother-in-law, who was convulsed with merriment. But a sudden hail from the French windows open to the saloon brought Matt's amusement to an abrupt halt.

'The deuce! What does Rob want here? Lay you any odds he's got wind of Elaine.'

Charles glanced to see, with a rise of exasperation, his cousin and heir coming through the French windows, and heading towards them. He spoke as one with Matt.

'Harriet!'

Charles cursed. Confound it, this was all he needed! It was undoubtedly Harriet who had let the cat out of the bag. She was as thick as inkleweavers with Bella, and Lady Sway would inevitably have passed on the news to her husband. Was it not enough to be plagued by his siblings? With a growing feeling of frustration he watched the approach of his cousin.

Robert Clevedon, created Baron Sway for services to his

country, was a gentleman close on forty summers who cut an imposing figure in a sober blue frock over buckskins and boots. He was tall, and a slight tendency to corpulence was evident in the protrusion of his waistline under a blue silk waistcoat. He had an air of grandeur and was a natural orator, qualities which fitted him for his ministerial position, much as they hampered him in normal conversation. Charles valued his gifts, thought he might well lead his country one day, and otherwise rated him a dead bore. Today, however, he was more inclined to stigmatise the politician as a busybody who would do better to attend to government affairs, and leave him to manage his own!

'No need to ask what brings you here,' grumbled Matt the instant Robert was within earshot.

'Matt, how d'ye do?' said the newcomer formally, ignoring this remark. He gave his hand to his cousin. 'My dear Charles, you are looking remarkably well, under the circumstances.'

'Did you expect to find him prostrate with shock and anxiety?' Thus Matt.

Charles gave a grim smile, inwardly seething. So Rob had come to interfere. Had he not known it?

'I hardly know what I expected,' said Robert loftily, 'except to hope that my cousin has not, at his age, been taken in by as mischievous a dupe as I have been privileged to encounter.'

To hear Elaine referred to in such terms served to deepen Charles' fury. He was forced to remind himself that his own suspicions had been as condemnatory. Yet he could not trust himself to answer. Fortunately, Matt spared him the necessity.

'You can't have encountered her. Nobody has, as far as we can discover.'

'I thought as much.' Robert frowned. 'By what means have you attempted discovery, may I ask?'

Charles was disinclined to say anything at all, but he bit down on a retort calculated to send his cousin up into the boughs, and answered as shortly as he could.

'First by local enquiry, and then by advertisement.'

'Yes, I saw it,' stated his cousin in a derisive tone. 'If you got anything other than cranks and opportunists by it, I shall own myself astonished. You would have done better to go to Bow Street.'

'I did. So far they have come up with nothing.'

He did not add that he was in two minds whether he wanted them to come up with anything. His cousin launched into a comprehensive speech covering the efficiency and otherwise of that body of men on occasions when he had used their services.

Charles paid little heed to it, his mind running back to last night. Though he wanted the mystery of Elaine's identity to be solved, everything in him revolted at the unpalatable possibility she had outlined. She had been herself inordinately distressed by the notion. Yet she had shrunk from him, permitting him neither to touch nor to comfort her—even with words.

He had tried to persuade her that she could not be sure of anything; that she had no reason to believe—if he had indeed chased her—that the man had been ill disposed.

'You cannot know for certain that you have run away.'

'I do know!' she had cried frantically. 'He chased me, I tell you, and he will come here! He will wrest me from your protection, and you will be able to do nothing about it.'

Charles had been unable to disabuse her of this conviction. And when he had said he would allow no one to remove her until he was certain of their credentials and rights, she had startled and disturbed him by bursting into tears.

'How can you stop them?' she had cried. 'You have no rights over me. You could never have such rights. If a man comes here claiming me, if he proves my background, what could you possibly do, Charles?'

He had been unable to answer her. For there was indeed only one way, and until he knew what she was, and that she was free, he could not even contemplate it. He did not even know if he wanted to. All he did know for certain was that he could not bear to see her in such distress. What folly he might have committed if Meg had not entered the room, he dared not say.

Their voices had woken her—by good fortune!—and she had come to investigate.

'As well,' she had said sternly, though with a smugness in her features altogether irritating to Charles. 'All it needs is for Harriet to wake. She would be scandalised, and we should never hear the end of it.'

Meg had marched Elaine off to bed. It had not seemed to Charles that she exhibited any dismay at leaving him. Indeed, she had gone, he thought, with alacrity.

She had woken late, and Charles had been troubled at breakfast to see the blue smudges under her eyes. Declaring that she looked peaky, Meg had insisted on a shopping spree to 'take her out of herself'.

Her absence had chafed Charles, despite the fact that she showed no disposition to prefer his company. Matt's gibes had done nothing to soothe. And now he must be plagued by Rob into the bargain!

He interrupted his cousin's long-winded discourse on Bow Street. 'It is of no use to weigh up the merits of my having called in the Runners, Rob. It is done.'

'If your sister had written sooner to Bella, you might have had the benefit of my advice before doing so.'

'I knew it!' Matt exclaimed.

'I might have guessed Harriet would drag you into it,' Charles said testily.

His cousin's arm was placed about his shoulders. Charles experienced the greatest difficulty in refraining from throwing it off. Though he knew Rob meant well, he found the gesture as patronising as the speech that accompanied it.

'My dear fellow, my only regret is that you did not see fit to drag me in. You should have laid the whole before me at once. I believe I am not nobody.'

Charles moved out of his embrace. 'It is scarcely a government matter.'

'Hardly,' said his cousin with a dismissive laugh. 'However, I could certainly have used my resources on your behalf. My fellows would have had the woman off your hands within days.'

'How do you know he wants her off his hands?'

'Be quiet, Matt!'

Robert puffed out his cheeks. 'By God, it is just as I feared! Charles, I do most earnestly beg of you to consider well before you commit this rash act.'

Charles suppressed his rising anger and held his cousin's eyes. 'What act? Do you suppose me to be upon the point of offering for a female of whom I know nothing?'

'I'll lay my life that is what Harriet told him!' Matt broke in. 'Lord, Rob, you should know better than to pay any attention to my sister-in-law! She is—'

'It is of no use your ranting at me, Matt,' cut in Robert scathingly, 'for I am well aware that you and Meg between you are doing your utmost to bring about a match here.'

Matt burst out laughing. 'Do you see Charles being influenced by any one of us? He will do as he chooses. I may have cut a couple of jokes with him on the subject, but—'

'Matt, I do wish you will hold your tongue!' snapped Charles, exasperated. 'I am perfectly capable of dealing with Rob's queries for myself.'

Matt subsided, still chortling. But when Charles turned to his cousin again, he found he was being regarded with serious concern. Was Rob reading him too well? His manner might irritate, but he was as shrewd a man as one could meet, else he would not have risen to his present status. Charles found himself suddenly grasped by the hand.

'Charles,' said Robert earnestly, 'you know I am only concerned for your welfare.'

'Or your own,' muttered Matt irrepressibly.

'If you mean that I covet the Wytham inheritance, Matt,' said Robert in aloof tones, 'then I have only to say that Charles knows me better.'

'I do know you better, Rob,' Charles interposed, 'and I know what motives bring you here. Rest assured that I do not contemplate matrimony—at this present. I have as much regard for what I owe to my name as do you.' His grip tightened on his cousin's hand. 'But my honour is involved here. I cannot abandon Elaine. Indeed, I would never let her leave unless I could be certain that her happiness and future were secured.'

Both men were staring at him. Matt in delight; Robert in mingled shock and dismay.

Robert gave a heavy sigh, withdrawing his fingers. 'I had supposed you were settled upon Belinda Tarrington.'

Charles exploded. 'By what sign you supposed it I cannot imagine! I have never had the least *tendre* for the woman, and I never shall. She is and always was Harriet's choice. Never mine. The notion seems to be in everybody's head but my own!'

'Not in mine,' countered Matt. 'Nor Meg's, I may say.'

A direful frown blackened Robert's brow. 'According to Harriet, Miss Tarrington considers herself more than half promised to you.'

'Miss Tarrington is mistaken,' said Charles flatly. 'I have never by word or deed offered her the slightest encouragement.'

'Which does not prevent her from battening upon you,' commented Matt, indicating the French windows with a thrust of his head. 'For there she is!'

Turning, Charles beheld his sister Harriet and Belinda stepping out on to the lawn. He cursed under his breath, and tried unavailingly to suppress a bubbling fury, as he moved automatically to retrieve his coat.

'Is not Elaine here?' queried Belinda the moment greetings had been exchanged.

'She is out with Meg,' Charles said shortly, dusting stray snippets of grass from the forest green frock. That Belinda was as disappointed as she sounded he frankly doubted. He watched her turn to his cousin.

'You must meet her, Lord Sway, indeed you must. She is the most delightful enigma. I told Charles at the outset that it was romantic, but of course he would have none of it.'

A flirtatious glance was flung in his direction, and Charles had to clamp down on a sarcastic retort as he shrugged on his coat. Fortunately, Robert saved him from speech.

'Romantic? By God, I should think not indeed! Sort of flummery you females were bound to think, however.'

Belinda gave that laugh of hers that never failed to irritate.

'What else do you expect? We have not affairs of state to occupy us, Lord Sway.'

'No, you occupy yourselves with quite other *affaires*,' put in Matt, reluctantly shuffling on his fawn frock-coat, in apparent recognition that the bowls must be abandoned.

'Matthew, how dare you!' struck in Harriet, outraged.

But Belinda was laughing. 'No, no, Harriet, you must not take umbrage. Matthew is right, I fear. If we had not the latest morsel of scandal to amuse us, I declare we should be heartily bored.'

'Speak for yourself, Belinda,' Charles said, unable to bear her inanity. 'Not all females are as gossip-hungry as you. You should have married long ago. It would have given your thoughts another direction.'

A short silence ensued, and Belinda's cheeks grew pink. Charles realised what he had said, and gave himself a mental kick. What possessed him to mention marriage to the woman?

Just as he might have expected, Belinda became arch. 'It is not for want of opportunity, Charles. Only I happen to be particular.'

'Markedly so,' said Matt drily.

'Matthew, will you be quiet?'

'M'dear Harriet, what have I said?'

Robert coughed in a pointed fashion, and Charles regretted allowing Belinda to goad him. Especially so when his sister turned upon him instead.

'I am even more upset with what Charles has said!'

'I will not have you berate Charles!' cut in Belinda, tucking a proprietary hand into his arm. 'Is he not plagued enough at this present?'

'Uh-oh!' uttered Matt under his breath.

Charles had stiffened. He wanted to jerk his arm away, but he controlled the impulse, endeavouring to recapture his apparently lost ability to speak to her with studied calm.

'By what?'

She turned with a flutter of her muslin petticoats, stationing herself so that his view was not obscured by the brim of the straw bonnet she wore, and he was thus obliged to meet the pity in those pale eyes.

'Dear Charles, I know how difficult this sojourn of Elaine's has been for you.'

'Do you?' asked Charles dangerously.

Belinda seemed oblivious. 'It has thrown you into a good deal of ill temper, and no wonder! To be obliged not only to house this female, but to be forced into seeking out her background. To endure in the meanwhile the avid interest of the curious. I have not said so, but you have had all my sympathy.'

'I thank you,' Charles said ironically.

A melting smile was cast upon him, and her eyelashes fluttered. 'You know I have your interests wholly at heart.'

'His—or your own?'

If Belinda heard Matt, she affected not to have done so. 'Charles, I do not agree with Harriet. I believe in Elaine.'

He was thrown off guard by this apparent volte-face. 'You believe in her?'

'Implicitly,' declared Belinda in the sincerest voice he

had ever heard her use. 'I am at one with you in thinking that her lost memory is genuine.'

'Careful, Charles!' came from Matt just behind his shoulder. 'She is up to something.'

'No such thing!' snapped Harriet. 'It is perfectly true, if you want to know. Belinda has even said as much to Elaine.'

'I don't understand any of this,' complained Robert.

'No more do I,' said Charles, his eyes never leaving the girl's features. 'What are you at, Belinda?'

She gave a bewildered laugh and showed him a face of innocence. 'I do not know what you mean. Why should I feign compassion for Elaine?'

'Who said you were feigning anything?'

A flush stained her cheeks. 'You spoke to me accusingly.'

'But I did not say that, nor imply it.' Charles arched his eyebrow. 'Yet it does not surprise me.'

'Charles!'

'Yes, Harriet? What arguments have you against Belinda's own slip of the tongue?'

Harriet looked daggers, but she refrained from making any answer. But Belinda was only temporarily discomposed.

'That is unkind,' she complained, making play with her lashes and sniffing. 'Some would say I had been remarkably magnanimous. I might have taken a very different attitude towards Elaine. But when I saw that you were inclined to—'

'Favour her?' interrupted Charles flatly. 'Is that what you were going to say?'

Belinda stared at him, bereft of words. There was a hushed expectancy in the air. He could feel Robert's eyes upon him, and saw Harriet's mouth was at half-cock. Behind him, Matt had drawn a quick breath.

It was too late to pull back. His anger was misplaced. Yet he could not endure to hear Belinda patronise Elaine.

Before he could speak again, his cousin intervened.

'I think, Charles, that you would do better to hold your tongue before you commit yourself irrevocably.'

'Yes, for God's sake, Charles!' came from Harriet in an appalled tone. 'You do not know what you are saying!'

'Let him say it!' urged Matt.

Belinda jerked out a protest. 'No, pray don't!'

Charles stepped back, trying to control the surging fury. 'You are all very free with your demands. I am well able to manage my own tongue, and I will thank you to keep your views to yourselves!'

In a hasty way, Belinda seized upon his arm. 'You have mistaken me, Charles! It was not what I was going to say. It had not crossed my mind that you were developing any sort of feeling for Elaine.'

'Then yours must be the only mind thus free!' declared Charles. 'Let it console you to know that your reading of my mental state is as inaccurate now as it has ever been. Your long-running campaign made no dent in my defences, Belinda. But they crumbled at Elaine's first onslaught!'

He was only half aware of what he had said, driven by his desire to be rid of her clinging hand, and the importunities he had long endured—and could no longer tolerate!

A shocked silence surrounded him, and glancing round, Charles beheld Meg and Elaine herself, standing just within earshot.

His heart sank, and across the distance he met Elaine's eyes. Her look was compound of reproach and bewilderment. He wanted to thrust through Belinda and his relatives, and catch her to him. But pandemonium was breaking out.

Emitting a tortured sob, Belinda whirled away, and ran off down the lawn. His relatives broke into voluble comment and protest.

'How could you, Charles? After all these years, to treat her so badly!' Thus Harriet.

'She asked for it,' averred Matt.

'No such thing! She was—'

'Charles, you cannot have meant it!' said Robert heavily. 'No man in his right mind—'

'This is all your fault, Elaine! He would never have behaved thus before you came.'

'Harriet, that is grossly unfair!' chided Meg, entering the lists.

'And I should have thought anyone in his senses would have realised that to make such an announcement—'

'Meg, you should have heard the way the silly woman badgered him. Anyone would suppose—'

'Nonsense, Matt! She said nothing that—'

Elaine stood outside the hubbub, unaware that she crushed the delicate lawn of her gown in each clenched fist. Her heart hammered in her breast, and a curious blend of dismay and elation grew within her. Then it was true. He did care for her! Hard on this thought came the remembrance of Belinda's warning. She wrenched her eyes away from Charles' face, flaring into sudden anger. What right had he to subject the woman to so public a rejection? Whatever might have gone before to goad him, it was cruel!

She thrust her voice into a lull in the battle. 'Is not anyone going to go after her?'

Several pairs of eyes turned upon her, but Elaine was affected only by that one she felt, rather than saw, for she could not look at Charles.

'You can ask that, Elaine?' said Meg blankly.

'Why should I not? Has she deserved such treatment?'

'Is that to my address?'

Charles' tone was biting, and Elaine flinched. She forced herself to meet the smoulder of the hazel gaze. Though she longed to throw at him the accusation that was burning in her brain, she could not. Instead she spoke with forced calm.

'If Belinda regards herself as in some sort promised to you, has she not reason?'

'Not to my knowledge!' said Charles emphatically.

'Then your memory must be as faulty as my own!'

Charles checked the hot words that rose to his tongue. He was both hurt and incensed at an attack from this quarter, but a thread of common sense served to remind him that if Elaine had been fed some nonsensical story, it must come either from the mouth of Harriet, or Belinda herself.

But before he could respond, Meg intervened. 'Elaine, this is nonsense. Charles has never—'

'Thank you, Meg, I have had enough of others speaking for me,' Charles snapped. He drew a breath, and turned back to Elaine. 'I have no understanding with Belinda, if that is what you think. It was ever Harriet's notion, not mine.'

'I can vouch for that,' Robert said. He bowed in Elaine's direction. 'We have not met. I am Robert Clevedon, Charles' cousin.'

Elaine was in no condition to acknowledge introductions. She barely nodded, her attention fixed upon Charles. She had begun to relax during the expedition to the Twickenham shops. But now all the dreadful symptoms of last night had revived; all the distress that had brought on her bad dreams, culminating in that fateful intimacy in her little parlour.

Bad enough was the panic that had overtaken her at the conclusion she had reached. Worse, Charles' futile promise of protection. And now?

Oh, now it was impossible—if that declaration was to be credited. Whatever he meant, there was no future to be looked for. She had no right to care—to be jealous! But nothing could prevent the turmoil that gripped her at the thought that Belinda might have been speaking the truth.

'Was she lying then, Charles?' she uttered involuntarily. 'Do you ask me to believe that a female could say such a thing of herself, if it was untrue?'

Blank with incomprehension, Charles stared at her. 'If what was untrue?'

The words hovered on her tongue, but Elaine could not bring herself to say them. She turned quickly away. 'It does not matter. I will go after her myself.'

'You will do no such thing!' snapped Charles, stepping forward and seizing her by the arm.

'Charles!'

'Keep out of this, Meg!'

'Yes, keep her close,' chimed in Harriet, gathering up her sprigged muslin skirts, and moving off in the direction her protégée had taken. 'Belinda does not need her sympathy. I shall go.'

'Good riddance!'

'Matt, hold your tongue! I wish the lot of you would follow Harriet's excellent example and go away.'

'No, by God, Charles! Not while you are in this mood.'

'I am perfectly well able to control my temper, Rob.' Charles pulled Elaine closer, unaware of the strength of his own grip.

'Let me go, Charles,' she pleaded, low-toned.

'By no means. You are going to explain that remark.'

Elaine met the scorching anger in his eyes. 'I cannot. Pray don't ask me!'

Charles ignored the tug she made against his strong hold. 'What was it Belinda said?'

'I will not tell you! It is of no use to manhandle me like this. You are only making things worse.'

His hold loosened, but he did not let her go. His voice softened a little. 'Elaine, understand this, once and for all. I have never given Belinda any reason to suppose that I cherish any uncommon regard for her. I am, I trust, enough of a gentleman not to raise expectations in any female breast which I have no intention of fulfilling.'

'Then how is it that you came to compromise her?' Elaine threw at him.

Charles released her, barely hearing the shocked gasps emanating about him. He stiffened, and his voice was ice.

'I *beg* your pardon?'

Cut by his tone, Elaine hit back, as cynical as he had ever been with her. 'Was she the female you boasted of who waylaid you in a bedchamber? Was that how it came to pass?'

In stunned silence, Charles regarded her for a moment, his outrage giving way a little to confusion. 'Elaine, what are you talking about?'

Too angry to think any longer, Elaine spat it out. 'I am talking about your having taken Belinda's maidenhead!'

The instant the words were out of her mouth, she gave a gasp of shocked realisation. The hazel eyes flashed fire, and Elaine backed involuntarily. She looked wildly round for succour. But Meg was speechless with shock. The newcomer—a cousin, was it?—stood rigid with disapproval and disgust. And it looked to be all Matt could do to stifle an unseemly snort of laughter.

Unwillingly dragged, her gaze returned to Charles. His features were white, and he was tight-lipped with anger. There was a deadly quiet to his voice, more alarming than a shout.

'Are you mad? What possessed you to say such a thing?'

Fright made her defensive. 'I did not say it. It was what Belinda told me.'

'And you believed her?'

The deep reproach hit an uncontrollable nerve. Tears leapt to Elaine's eyes. Her voice was husky.

'Why not? Is it any worse than what you believed of me?'

Then she turned from his gaze, and ran for the French windows.

Chapter Eight

'**Y**ou don't understand, Charles,' pleaded his sister almost tearfully, one arm about the heaving shoulders of Belinda Tarrington as she sobbed noisily into a lace handkerchief.

Charles eyed her smoulderingly, his arms folded. He was glad of his cousin's presence at his side, for Rob's stern outrage both backed him up and kept him from the insanity of striking the wench.

'It is you who fails to understand, Harriet,' he said, clipping off the words. 'Belinda has traduced my character, and I am entitled to an explanation.'

Belinda reared up, flaring into speech. 'That creature lied! I never said any such thing. Charles, you cannot think I would vilify you!'

Robert cut in, relieving Charles, who was ready to murder the woman. 'My good girl, that will not fadge! You have been caught out in one lie already. And if you think to foist this preposterous story upon Wytham, you have mistaken your man.'

'I thank you, Rob.'

'I am far from approving your conduct, Charles,' said his cousin austerely. 'In my view, you have today behaved with an intemperance that is to be deprecated. But that I could be mistaken in your integrity I refuse to believe.'

At a wail from Belinda, he added testily, 'Cease your lamentations, woman! Harriet, you would be better employed in advising your friend to frame an apology, than to attempt to argue with Charles.'

'You are full of good advice, Robert,' responded Harriet acidly. 'I trust I know how to deal with my own brother.'

Charles was still smouldering, and this only served to fan the flame. 'Do you, indeed? Let me tell you that if I was not bound by the obligations of a brother and a gentleman, I should know how to deal with you both.'

Harriet was not noticeably chastened. 'Merely because I espoused Belinda's cause—'

'And what was the use of that to me, pray?' came suddenly from Belinda. 'You have no influence with him, I have always known that. It was useful to call you friend, but I had never a hope that Charles would listen to you!'

'Belinda!' gasped Harriet, stunned at this unprecedented attack.

But Belinda was not attending. She threw off Harriet's arm, and moved towards Charles, the pale eyes taut with menace.

'You will hear no ill of your precious Elaine! I knew she would turn you against me. But what if I were to shout it from the rooftops, Charles? What if I should tell the same tale to all the world?'

'Good God!' exclaimed Robert, horrified.

Charles met the challenge of Belinda's pale eyes with

steel in his own. 'You may try. I think you will be taken at fault, Belinda. You don't know it, and none would say it to my face—except Matt, from whom I learned of it—but your determined pursuit of me has made you a laughing-stock. I doubt if anyone would believe you.'

'I can vouch for that!' Robert said. 'Wytham's character is too well established.'

Belinda's thin features became pinched. 'Is it? Well, hers is not. I am not finished, Charles. She shall not benefit from my loss!'

Charles would have slapped her then, but Rob evidently divined his intention, for he seized his right arm and held it powerfully. Belinda was already marching away towards the house. Charles shook his cousin off.

'You need not fear me, Rob.'

'By God, what a venomous female! And to think I had it in mind that you might wed her.'

Glancing at Harriet, Charles felt almost sorry for her. She was staring after Belinda, looking thoroughly bemused.

'That was unkind of her, Harriet.'

His sister looked at him, saying hastily, 'She cannot have meant it! The heat of the moment, I am persuaded. I shall catch up with her, and talk to her.'

Charles did nothing to prevent her from hurrying after the woman. If she chose to blind herself to the truth, that was her own affair. For himself, there was a more urgent matter to be dealt with.

Elaine's first thought was escape. She raced to her bed-chamber and slammed the door, leaning against it as the blinding tears gathered at her eyes. She dashed them away.

She must act! And quickly, before anyone tried to prevent her. Shifting from the door, she swiftly turned the key.

Then she ripped off her bonnet and flung it upon the bed, crossing to throw open the doors of the clothes press. Immediately she was brought up short by the realisation of her dependency.

How could she leave? How was she even to transport the clothes that had been procured for her? She had not so much as a bandbox to her name! Even if she had, by what means was she to remove from this house?

She dropped back from the press, staring at it in mingled frustration and dismay.

The place and everything in it belonged to Charles. His horses, his carriages were the only means of transportation. Would his servants furnish her with those means, without checking first with their master? No, that path would not run.

Then she must walk!

She reached into the press and seized a handful of clothing—and froze, clutching it uselessly.

Walk to where? She had no destination. An inn? The thought gave her a momentary thrust of hope. Yes, she could go to an inn. Only—how would she pay her shot? She had no money. Not a penny in the world.

The garments fell from her hands. Elaine turned from the press and sank down upon the coverlet of the bed, staring sightlessly out of the window.

Was she truly so little mistress of her destiny? Must she remain here, plagued by doubts and feelings that she could not indulge? The picture of Charles' face came to her, and the stinging tears pricked once again at her eyes.

How had she dared to say it? Such a dreadful slip! She

felt more humiliated by revealing the words Belinda had used to her, than Charles could have done on receipt of them in public. But how could he have taunted her so? What, was she to trust him implicitly—while he had a monopoly of distrust?

Oh, no. Charles might with impunity speak disparagingly of her *alleged* lost memory! He might view her with cynical disdain. Look upon her with eyes that made of her a liar and a cheat. That was acceptable—to be expected even. But she? Not knowing him, beholden to him for her very existence, she must be endowed with supernatural powers to *know*, without possibility of doubt, that Belinda Tarrington had lied!

Oh, she would not endure it! Must she remain here, to be insulted and slighted? He had been magnanimous indeed! What had he said to Belinda? That his defences had fallen at her onslaught? He might as well have been speaking of that supposed plot of which he had earlier accused her. Could it be that he still thought her an adventuress?

No, she would not believe it. He could not have behaved to her with such generosity and care. He could not have shown her so tender a manner that she had all but fallen into the way of believing that he…

Her thoughts died. The word lingered in her mind. But she could not give it breath. It was a word untenanted—long gone. A feeling from another time…irrevocably lost.

Elaine stood at a graveside, her heart full, her eyes misted over. A flash of the inscription flitted across her mind, and a name: 'Dymock'.

Then a violent knocking made her jump almost out of her skin. She leapt from the bed, and turned, staring at the door.

'Elaine! Elaine, are you in there?'

Meg! What should she do? Instinct bade her keep silent. She neither moved nor spoke. There came a rattling of the handle, and then Meg called again.

'Elaine, do you hear me? Pray come out! That hateful girl is leaving. Elaine!'

Belinda was leaving. What, then, had occurred? As if she heard the question, Meg spoke once more.

'Charles was furious with her. Don't imagine he is angry with you, Elaine. Come out, pray!'

But Elaine remained perfectly quiet, her determination to be gone from this house building up again. She could not face Charles—especially now.

A muttering came from behind the door, and then she heard footsteps retreating. Elaine waited until they were to be heard clattering down the wooden stairway, and then darted to the door. Unlocking it, she cautiously opened it, looking swiftly up and down the passage. The coast was clear, and she slipped out, moving silently in the opposite direction, towards her parlour.

Her parlour. As if anything was hers in this alien house! With a vague hope that it would be supposed that she was still locked in her bedchamber, she hastened along the corridor.

In the parlour, she paced, restless as she thought again of the vision she had recaptured just as Meg knocked on the door. What was that name? Dymock. It had struck her with the utmost familiarity. What of that French name she had earlier discovered? Was she then Dymock and not St Vigians? But she had been French, and the name meant nothing if it was not hers. It was hers, for she had lived at the Château de St Vigians!

Her heart dropped. It was as she had suspected from the first. She had changed her name, which meant only one thing. Was it her husband from whom she had run away? But then what was she doing by a graveside? And there was the name, clear as day on the engraved stone at its head. A feeling of bewilderment enveloped her, curiously mixed with sadness.

The complications seemed to multiply. She wished she might have seen more in that brief glimpse of her unfathomable past. Who was that Dymock? And why should it sadden her?

A hollow opened up inside her. How futile were her wayward emotions! As wayward, as beyond her control, as was this accursed memory.

She must leave here! Somewhere she had a husband. That man? The thought of giving herself into his keeping was not one that she could contemplate with anything but misgiving. But even less could she bear the thought of remaining here—where she must be always in the vicinity of Charles Clevedon.

With no thought beyond removing from the Earl's house, she crossed with feverish haste to the door. It opened, and Charles stood in the aperture.

Elaine fell back, her heart leaping into life, and racing for all it was worth. She tried to control her unruly breath, but the sight of his drawn features made it all but impossible.

'Elaine…'

It was barely a murmur, but some quality within it wrought havoc inside her. She wafted a vague hand, as though she would stop him from speaking.

'Pray don't—'

He shut the door and moved into the room. 'There is so much I must say.'

Elaine backed. Her voice shook. 'No! It is best you say nothing, Charles. We can afford no further words.'

'What does that mean?' he asked, fierce all of a sudden. 'I must and will clear things up with you!'

'It is useless, Charles,' she cried frantically, shifting to the day-bed, as far from him as she could get.

He made no attempt to follow her, but stood in the middle of the room, regarding her with eyes that burned. 'Do you think I have come to reproach you? It is not your fault that Belinda should have—'

'Don't!' cut in Elaine, involuntarily covering her ears. 'It was none of my concern, whether it had been true or not.'

'Except that I have made it your concern,' he said flatly.

Elaine turned away, the image of that gravestone looming abruptly in her mind. With it, a confusion of sadness and pain, which forced on her a single certainty. It must not be her concern! She could not care for Charles—*for her affections were already engaged.*

Behind her, Charles hesitated, unsure how to continue. She did not appear to be angry, merely distressed. But there was withdrawal here. Doubt seized him. Had it not been, as he had instantly imagined, an instinct of jealousy when she had cut at him? Had his own desires led him to deceive himself? If so, his task must be the harder.

'I never meant it to come to this, Elaine. If I had not been plagued beyond bearing by my abominable family—'

'Say no more!' Elaine pleaded, turning. 'Do not begin on explanations that must inevitably lead you to speak of—'

'My feelings?' he broke in, unable to help a surge of

passion. 'It is too late, Elaine. I have said it too publicly, and I will not now retract.'

Desperation flooded Elaine. She must not fall into a situation she knew to be fraught with danger. Coming away from the window, she passed around him, heading for the door.

'It makes no matter, Charles. I am leaving. I cannot stay here.'

'Leaving?' Charles moved to bar the way. 'Confound you, Elaine! You can't leave. Where will you go? What will you do? Are you afraid of me that you are so eager to escape?'

'Yes!' Her lip trembled, and she strove to contain the rising tears. 'Yes, I am afraid of you.'

Charles gazed at the misting of her blue eyes, at the quiver of her lip, and his heart contracted. Without thought, he moved to her, catching her before she could evade him. One arm encircled her. With his free hand, he cupped her face.

'Don't weep! Don't you know that I would never hurt you?'

The softness in his voice all but destroyed her. A ferment of guilt rose up to torment her. Her hands came up to thrust at his chest, but she did not push him away. There was so much tenderness in his gaze that her heart turned over.

'Let me go,' she begged huskily. 'This can never be, Charles! I must leave here. I have seen my name. Not St Vigians as I had thought—though it was that once. It is Dymock. There can be no longer any room for doubt. I am a married woman.'

An uneasy atmosphere pervaded the house. In her private parlour, Elaine plucked restlessly at the strings of the harp. She improvised, producing here and there a snatch of half-remembered melody that fell upon the air but briefly. Whether she persisted in this occupation in so dedicated a fashion to keep herself from thinking, or to drown out Meg's question and commentary, Elaine was not sure. She knew only that while she was concentrating on the harp, the nagging ache at her heart was dulled.

'It is of no use your holding to it that Charles has not upset you,' Meg stated flatly from her position on the day-bed. 'You would not otherwise be so distant with each other.'

'You are imagining things.'

'I am not imagining it!' Meg averred crossly. 'Do you think I don't know my own brother? He has barely looked at you these two days, never mind spoken to you.'

The reminder served to jerk the pain into life. Elaine's fingers faltered on the strings, producing a couple of patently false notes.

'You see!' accused Meg. 'You are upset!'

'Meg, pray leave it!' begged Elaine, gripping the hard, gilded surround of the instrument.

Meg rose and came quickly across the room to pull the harp away and set it upright. 'I wish you will stop playing that thing, and attend to what I am saying.'

'Can't you see that I cannot bear it?' cried Elaine, leaping up from the stool and jerking away across the parlour.

'What can't you bear? It is not my persistence that troubles you, but the feelings you are trying to suppress. What occurred between you, Elaine? Tell me, pray!'

Elaine turned to face her, trying to contain the impatience that had thrust her into protest. 'It is useless to press me. I know you only mean to be kind, but there is nothing you can do, Meg.'

Nothing anyone could do, she might have said. Least of

all herself and Charles. He had been brought up short by her conviction. He had released her, with obvious reluctance. Elaine had moved quickly away. For long moments—which had stretched endlessly into the vacuum left by an impossible dream—neither of them had spoken.

Charles had shifted aimlessly to the mantelpiece, leaning his elbow upon it and kneading at his brow. At length, he had turned his head. The faint smile upon his lips had caught at Elaine's heartstrings.

'It is ironic, is it not? Half inclined to believe that you were in a plot to entrap me, I indulged in a reckless intimacy. With the result that I have entrapped myself.'

She had replied only with an agitated waft of one hand, begging his silence. Charles had straightened, looking away.

'No, very well. You are right. The less said, the less need for reproaches.'

'I do not reproach you.'

'I do not accuse you of it.'

'My reproaches are for myself.'

'You have no need of them, Elaine.' He drew, she thought, an unsteady breath. 'And, so that you shall have no reason for them, I will hold aloof. Which will be preferable to what I must feel if I permit you to leave here.'

At that, Elaine experienced a resurgence of distress. 'I cannot remain here!'

'You have no choice, I fancy. Besides, as you once said, sooner or later someone will come for you. What will I tell this—' the word seemed to choke out of him '—*husband* of yours, if you are gone?'

Elaine flinched. 'You need not speak as if you do not believe in his existence.'

'I don't want to believe in it!' Charles retorted.

She looked at him with pain. 'But you must, Charles.'

He said nothing for a moment, taking a hasty turn about the room. At length, he fetched up at his usual position by the mantelpiece, and turned to her a face taut with tension.

'I am tied by circumstance. But I will not permit you to leave my house, Elaine. Whatever the truth, I will see you safe. We will wait until the Runners have unearthed a clue. Unless I am given reason to believe otherwise, you remain in my charge.' He arched an eyebrow in the old, cynical fashion. 'Meanwhile, rest assured that my emotions will not tempt me to violate the sanctity of your refuge!'

With that he had walked out of the room. Elaine had been left with a dawning realisation. Charles little suspected how those emotions were reciprocated, if he supposed that her wish to leave sprang from a fear that he might importune her. In vain had she since tried to persuade herself that it was as well for her that he had not fathomed her heart.

That Thursday night the presence of his cousin—who had stayed to talk of nothing but politics!—had kept Charles wholly aloof. Elaine had seen him thereafter only at meals, or in the company of members of his family. She had been glad of his promise, but had not bargained for the aching loss occasioned by its being adhered to. Plagued by a useless yearning, which followed her into the long nights of emptiness, she had opted for the doubtful balm of her musical talent.

It did not help to be obliged to endure Meg's incessant quest. She might have confided in her, were it not for the fact that she knew Meg cherished dreams of a bridal. Elaine could not bear to listen to the inevitable expressions of disappointment, nor the notion that there might yet be hope. She was with difficulty preventing herself from indulgence in that insanity. She was not free, of that much she was certain.

It was not difficult to find a subject that would divert Meg from her purpose.

'Have you heard anything of Belinda? Or rather, do you know if Harriet has done so?'

Meg threw up her hands. 'Why in the world should you care? And after the way in which she spoke to Harriet, I can tell you that even my sister is disinclined to enquire.'

Elaine frowned, moving to take one of the chairs grouped about the day-bed. 'I thought Matt said that Harriet had made it up with her.'

'Tried to,' amended Meg, reseating herself on the day-bed. 'But Belinda was so extremely rude to her that Harriet is disinclined to forgive. She is even talking of returning to her home, and I wish she would!'

'I thank you, sister!' said Lady Harriet's voice from the doorway. 'But I think you will be glad that I am still here when Matthew has given you his news.'

As she entered, Elaine saw Matt come in behind her. But she did not hear his first words because he was followed into the room by Charles.

A pulse in Elaine's throat set up such a tumult that she was unable to utter a sound. She could feel her fingers shaking, and surreptitiously slid her hands together so that she might grip them tightly to prevent Charles from seeing how she reacted to his presence.

He glanced once at her, and then shifted to his favourite stance at the mantelpiece, his gaze turning to his brother-in-law, who had flopped down beside his wife upon the day-bed.

Elaine looked fixedly at Matt, trying to take in what he was saying. She became aware of Meg's shocked countenance, and hearing Harriet's voice again, flicked a quick look at her.

'It is only what was to be expected,' she was saying, from the chair she had taken next to the day-bed.

'But it is mad!' exclaimed Meg. 'How could anyone suppose such a thing with both Harriet and myself living in the house?'

'Should know better than to ask that, m'love,' said Matt. 'When has probability stopped the gossips?'

'Very true,' agreed Harriet. 'For my part, I am astonished that people have not said so before.'

Elaine's pulses quickened now with apprehension. She stared at Meg and Matt. 'What has been said?'

'Lord, did you not hear Matt say it, Elaine?'

For the first time since the party's entrance, Charles spoke up. 'I fancy not, Meg, since she is asking. The news, Elaine, was gleaned at Matt's favoured hostelry. You had better tell it again, Matt.'

Elaine found herself the recipient of a pitying look from Meg's husband. 'Hate to be the bearer of bad tidings, m'dear, but no sense in beating about the bush. The word down at the Anglers is that bets are being laid on whether you will oust Belinda from the lists.'

'Which presupposes that Belinda has not spoken of the happenings here on Thursday,' put in Meg. 'Otherwise, everyone would know that—'

'That will do, Meg! Go on, Matt.'

Unable to help herself, Elaine cast a quick glance at Charles, and caught his eye briefly. She looked swiftly away. Had Meg been about to mention what he had said in public that day? Did he wish to spare her embarrassment? A pointless exercise, for how could she be other than embarrassed?

'Rumour has it, Elaine,' Matt continued on an apologetic note, 'that you have become Charles' mistress.'

A queer blankness invaded Elaine's mind. She stared at him as though the words he had used made no sense. There was stillness in the room, as they waited upon her reaction.

'Well, Elaine? Have you nothing to say?'

Her eyes turned upon Charles. Why had he to speak so harshly? 'What should I say?'

'Does it not shock you?'

'Shock? Yes, I suppose so.'

'You suppose so! Confound you, Elaine, don't you understand what this means?'

At a loss, Elaine merely gazed at him. But Meg broke in sharply.

'Don't speak to her like that, Charles! Lord, what is the matter with you? Besides, I have even less notion what you mean than does Elaine. Unless you are suggesting that Belinda started these rumours?'

Harriet drew herself up. 'What nonsense! Why should she do so?'

'Do you still champion her, then?' put in Matt, raising his brows. 'If so, you are destined for disappointment. Belinda is known to be leaving for Brighton today, which has shortened the odds on Elaine's chances with Charles.'

'And lent colour to the other rumour, I don't doubt,' said Harriet in a waspish tone.

'Oh, then it is certain that she did start it!' averred Meg. 'Depend upon it, she is bent upon revenge. Did she not expressly inform you, Charles, that she had not finished?'

But Charles was eyeing Elaine's set features. She had not leapt to the same conclusion as he had done, that was plain. But her face was drawn and pale. Too much like she had looked in those early days for his present comfort. He came away from the mantelpiece and moved towards her. 'Do you not see it, Elaine? There is nothing for it but to announce our intention to marry. And immediately!'

If Elaine had been capable of saying anything, she would not have got the chance. Uproar broke out.

His relatives leapt up as one, launching into argument, and Charles was obliged to turn to face them. For several minutes, he was unable to get a word in edgeways.

'Are you mad, Charles? When it has been suggested that Elaine is already married? You cannot possibly do so.'

'Loath as I am to agree with her,' said Matt, 'Harriet is right. You don't want to be had up for bigamy!'

'He could only be a bigamist if he married her *knowing* that she was already married,' objected Meg. 'To announce his intention of it can only—'

'And what happens when we are faced with proof that she is married?' demanded Harriet. 'Charles will look even more of a fool than—'

'What I think is that you should ignore the rumours, Charles,' Matt advised. 'After all, it is only conjecture.'

'To which he ought to put a stop. It is the most sensible thing to do.'

'Meg, you can't have thought—'

'It was what she has been thinking from the outset! I might have known it would come to this.'

'What I wish you to understand, Meg,' pursued Matt, riding over Harriet, 'is that Charles cannot make such a commitment. Lord, he knows virtually nothing of her back-ground! The few scraps that have emerged don't amount to—'

'I don't give a fig for her background!' Charles said, breaking in at last.

'Yes, that is all very well, but—'

'Matt, will you have done?'

'Yes, be quiet, Matt!' snapped Meg, slapping his arm. 'It is of all things the most romantic, and I will not have you—'

'Confound you, Meg, will you let me speak?'

His sister paused with her mouth at half-cock. Matt grinned, but refrained from comment. Only Harriet, stiff with disapproval, ventured to interrupt again.

'If it is your intention to explain yourself, brother, you might wish to do it in the presence of your bride elect. Perhaps your scheme is not to her taste.'

Frowning, Charles turned. Elaine was gone from the room.

Elaine sped down the winding avenue that flanked the drive, screened by the trees. She was rapidly running out of breath, but she kept moving, spurred by her determination to be far enough away before her absence should be discovered.

That Charles would look for her she could not doubt. She was unsure why she had dashed in so precipitate a fashion from the refuge he had called it. But it was no haven from the promptings of her unwary heart.

Her sides were heaving, and her steps slowed. Pausing briefly, Elaine dragged in great lungfuls of air, leaning on a trunk of one of the great elms that formed an avenue either side of the drive. She looked back towards the house, which was hidden now. Ahead of her lay the gates—and freedom. The odd word echoed in her mind as she began to recover her breath.

Freedom? From what? Not from Charles, cried her heart. It was from his wild declaration that she had fled. Oh, why had he said it? He knew well she could not agree to a betrothal. Yet the notion caught at the secret longings that had plagued her. She was enmeshed by the intolerable restrictions of her unknown life.

The oddest compulsion seized her. The forest! Had not Meg suggested it that far-off day—how long ago it seemed!—when Doctor Gorsty first came to her? She had been drenched in fear at the notion. But now, dogged by a relentless fate, and the knowledge that there was that in her past which she had been too afraid to remember, it was the only possible course.

How to get to the forest? She was dressed only in a white muslin gown, her feet slippered in light shoes unfit for walking. How could she go there in this guise? And alone. As well return to the hideous exposure she had endured that dreadful day!

Looking again to the gates, she noted to one side the lodge that housed the keeper. Might the man be induced to help her? A faint wisp of apprehension curled into her breast. Would he instead question her, attempt to return her to the house? No, he would lay no hands upon her. At worst, she had only to leave him, and walk through the open gates.

She discovered that she had been moving on these thoughts. Turning off the drive, she headed towards the lodge, looking for its front door.

A youth in a smock opened it, staring at her with round eyes and his mouth at half-cock.

'How do you do? Are you the lodgekeeper's boy?'

'Ay,' agreed the lad, his mouth still suspended.

'Is he here?'

The boy shook his head. 'Gorn up the 'ouse.'

Elaine felt somewhat at a loss. What should she do? By now it was likely that the family would be in search of her. The sane thing would be to go back—ask Charles to take her to the forest. No, not Charles. She must do this alone!

The boy was regarding her blankly, much as he might a freak in a side-show at a fair. Elaine smiled at him, and he blinked rather rapidly.

'Do you know the way to Lord Wytham's forest? It is near here, I think.'

'Ay.'

'Could you tell me how to get there?'

But this appeared to be beyond the lad's powers. His eyes finally left her face, travelling down her person to her shoes and back up again.

'Was you meaning to walk, miss?'

She had no other choice. 'I must.' A thought occurred. 'Unless you have a vehicle that I may borrow?'

'There be cart out back,' said the lad to her surprise. 'Pa done borrowed it fer to go to market early, an' that's done with.'

'But if he has gone up to the house…'

'I could take yer,' offered the youth with a sudden grin.

'Are you not keeping the gate for your father?'

'Ay, but gate's open.'

Then without more ado, the boy came out of the house and

shut the door behind him. Elaine felt a trifle guilty. She was certain the youth should not leave his post without permission. But her need was too urgent to permit of rejecting this heaven-sent opportunity. She followed him, and was soon ensconced on the uncomfortable wooden plank that served for a seat, in a vehicle pulled by an ancient cob with his own ideas about speed.

Elaine ascertained that the name of her guide was Sim, but beyond that he had nothing to say, only casting her an awestruck glance from time to time. Elaine could not but be glad of it, for her thoughts were distracted, and the slow pace chafed her.

It could not have been much more than a couple of miles to the forest, but when at last she found herself at the edge of a considerable thicket, Elaine almost gave way to a craven wish to run away from the place. But it would not do. She had come this far. She would not give up now.

Where to enter she did not know, for she had no idea where she had been found. It mattered little. She had run through this place incontinent, until she was far from the spot where the accident had occurred. That dream was all too real for her to disbelieve its evidence.

She alighted from the cart, staring apprehensively into the thick woodlands. She was loath to enter the place alone. And she was bound to lose her bearings.

'Do you know these woods?' she asked the boy, on a sudden thought.

'Ay,' came the usual response. 'Come here when I were nobbut a lad, I did, often and often.'

Poaching, or merely to play? The stray thought passed quickly. Sim knew the woods, and that was enough.

Within minutes of entering the forest, she had reason to be glad of the boy's company. She found herself crushed by a resurgence of feelings that were all too hideously familiar.

She was wading ankle-deep in rough gorse, her muslin petticoats clutched tightly and held out of harm's way. Her stockings were scratched, and her light shoes clogging with dirt. Above her loomed trees so vast that she felt dwarfed, their huge swathing branches rustling unpleasantly.

Her heart beat unnaturally fast, and she felt sick with fear, despite the stalwart form of Sim tramping steadily close behind. Indeed, his swishing progress troubled her not a little. Growing, as it appeared to her overwrought mind, into the sound of several feet. She could hear them thudding behind her. Distant in her ears at first, increasing in volume as they seemed to gain upon her.

Nearer they came. They? No, not they. *It was he!* He had found her again! She had not shaken him off. He was so close that she could hear his coarse breathing, his crashing progress through the undergrowth behind. Oh, God, but he pursued her still! And echoing through the darkening shadows about her, someone cried out her name.

'Elaine! *El-aaaine!* Elaine, where are you?'

She began to run, heedless of the sudden shout behind.

'Miss! Missie, wait!'

But Elaine was lost in the nightmare, her hands loosening from the muslin, and thrusting at the brambles and branches that came in her way. About her legs, the long freed petticoats caught and twisted, hampering her movements.

She could hear the pursuit gaining on her. Footsteps hard behind, pounding in her head. The cries, so mixed in voice and timbre that she no longer distinguished the words. She only knew that if she did not run her hardest, he would catch her, and drag her back.

Then abruptly the footsteps ceased. Only her own motions registered in her ears. Above the agonized hammering in her chest, her thoughts flew.

Was she then safe? Had he given up? She could slow her pace. Hold hard. Rest for a little, only to catch her breath. Desperate, she grasped at a passing branch and halting, hung there, panting painfully. For an uncountable period, she had no room for thought. The whole concentration in her head was on recovery. Presently, the urge to gulp in draughts of air was sated, and she felt her way down the saviour branch to the hard ridges of the trunk. Here she leaned, pressing her fingers to her hot cheeks.

Her eyes opened upon the dappling shadows of the forest. Ahead of her was a collection of thin trees, the moss on their grey trunks picked out by stray beams of light. All was quiet. She was unharmed. Looking down, she found her gown to be intact. A little ruffled at the bosom, and perhaps a stray twig caught about the hem, but that was all.

Slowly Elaine's eyes wandered about, and came to rest upon two figures standing at a distance, and watching her. The whole hideous nightmare receded.

Charles! He was grasping the arm of the boy Sim, holding him fast. But Elaine was in no state to wonder why. With a cry, she stumbled towards him. Vaguely she saw that he let the boy go, and then he was moving. Elaine fell straight into his arms, and burst into sobs.

Chapter Nine

∽∽∽◆∽∽∽

For several minutes Elaine was too overcome with the fact of Charles' presence to think beyond the relief occasioned by the strong embrace that cradled her. But the fit of weeping was brief, and the croon of his voice began to penetrate.

'Hush, my darling. You are safe now. There is nothing to fear. Softly, my lovely girl.'

There was balm in the endearments, and for a while Elaine succumbed to the insidious pull of her heart's desire. Nestling where she had longed to be, she forgot the dread murmurings of her erratic memory.

At length, however, it occurred to her to wonder how Charles came to be there at all. And as she raised her head to ask him, the sequence of occurrences that had led to her seeking out this place came tumbling into her mind. With a distressed cry, she thrust away from him.

'No! We must not, Charles. Let me be!'

Charles made no attempt to recapture her. He was in such relief at discovering her at all that he would do nothing to alienate her again. That she had come to him voluntarily was balm to the wounding conviction that she did not care for him. But it proved nothing. She had been, he guessed, in the throes of her painful memories, which was why he had himself halted and prevented the boy from continuing to chase her.

He glanced behind to find his lodgekeeper's son regarding him with a mixture of fear and chagrin. Did he think there would be retribution for his part in this reckless escape? Charles could not be angry with him, for he had no doubt that Elaine's beauty had overwhelmed the lad. He had said as much to Creggan when the fellow had ventured to suggest that the missing cart and his son with it, at the precise moment that the young lady had vanished, too, told its own tale.

For Charles, apprehension had mingled with relief. He and the family, together with the female servants, had searched the house from top to bottom while the rest scoured the grounds. His anxiety had known no bounds. Yet the discovery that Elaine had sought to escape him in a cart—a cart, confound it!—had thrown him into confusion.

'But where?' he had demanded blankly. 'Where could he have taken her?'

It had been Matt who had brought him to a semblance of rationality. 'Can't have got far. She's either headed for the river, or away from it. You'll catch up quick enough, even if you try both. Get Parr to fig out your phaeton, and go after her, man!'

He had been upon the point of turning for the river when it had abruptly occurred to him to try the forest. He had come upon the abandoned cart within a few minutes. At least the lad had been astute enough to accompany Elaine into the woods. But his presence at this reunion could well be dispensed with.

'Go back to where you left your cart, boy,' he instructed, moving towards the lad. 'There you will find Parr, my groom. Tell him, if you please, that the lady is safe with me and he should await my coming. We shall be with him presently. Then you may drive the cart home.'

Sim tugged at his forelock, cast one last yearning glance at Elaine, and took himself off. Charles watched him out of sight, and then turned back to find that Elaine was looking about her with puzzlement in her face.

'Are you trying to find the place where you woke up?' he asked, going to her. 'Is that why you came here?'

Elaine shifted a little away from him, in a pretence of looking between two trees towards a patch of clearer ground. 'I thought I might spring open my memory. I did not truly think it through. It was a foolish impulse. I have gained nothing by it, but a resurgence of that nightmare.'

'I thought as much,' Charles said. 'I probably frightened you into it by calling out.'

She turned to him. 'Was that you?'

He nodded, his eyes fixed upon her face. His voice dropped. 'Elaine, did you run away because I said we must announce that we are to marry?'

The blue orbs clouded. Her voice was a thread, twisting his heart. 'We cannot marry, Charles.'

'Not now, I know.' He gave a wry smile. 'I fancy my partiality had obscured my common sense. I lost my head. It was foolish of me to say it at this time.'

She looked away. 'It would be foolish at any time.'

Charles clamped down hard upon the protest that boiled

up in his chest. He must stay calm. He must not frighten her, or drive her further away. Yet he must know!

'Do you say that because you would not wish to marry me? Is your heart against me? Only tell me it is so, and I will never speak of this again.'

Elaine knew not how to answer him. Her pulse quickened. Had he truly not divined how she felt about him? If not, it behoved her to lie! She must tell him that she could never care for him. Let him think her indifferent. Surely it must make it easier—for both of them.

'Elaine, your silence tortures me!'

It was too much. 'What should I say, Charles?' she cried involuntarily. 'In either case you are asking me to do what I know to be wrong!'

'How so?' he demanded, closing in on her. 'How can it be wrong to tell me the truth?'

Elaine withdrew a little. 'Don't come near me! You destroy my ability to think.'

He dropped back, a frown appearing between his brows. 'I have no wish to do that. I only want you to be safe—and happy. It is all I could ever want. I love you, Elaine.'

Tears sprang to her eyes. 'Don't! *Ne le dis pas!* I cannot bear it, Charles.' She swung away, shifting back and forth among the trees as words tumbled from her lips. 'I had rather you had remained suspicious of me. How can I endure to be the cause of your suffering as well as my own? It is bad enough to have the guilt upon my own account, for it is wrong. I know it is wrong!'

Charles watched her with pain for the distress of mind that she exhibited, but a dawning hope took from him all power of finding words to soothe. He felt a tremor in his own voice.

'What precisely is it that is wrong?'

She threw up agitated hands. 'You know as well as I! If I were to give voice to those feelings—as you have done!— we had as well fall into that relationship of which rumour already accuses us, Charles.'

'You mean that you had as well become my mistress,' he said bluntly. 'I would not so insult you!'

'What else could there be between us? I owe my duty to some other man—a stranger now. For I am married. I know it as surely as I know that my heart is false to him.'

'If that means what it seems to mean—'

'I cannot love you!' she cried wildly. 'It is wrong to love you!'

Charles crossed the intervening space between them, and seized her shoulders, driven by so fierce an intensity that he knew not how to contain it.

'But you do!'

The tears spilled over. 'Yes, *Dieu me sauve*!'

'It is too late for prayers,' uttered Charles gutturally, and his mouth came down hard on hers.

Shock held Elaine still for several seconds. The pressure at her lips startled her with the violence of its impact.

Then Charles released her mouth, and, gasping, she flung her head back, staring at him with eyes wide and fearful.

'Don't look at me like that!' he begged. 'Oh, Elaine!'

His hands came up and cupped her face, drawing her to him. He bent his head to hers, and with his lips, caressed her skin, travelling featherlight about her enchanting features. The tautness of her muscles began to relax, and Charles sought her lips again, exploring her mouth with his own.

Powerless to gainsay him, Elaine gave herself up to his

pleasurable assault. Warmth crept stealthily down her veins, heating her blood. The soft touch of his lips increased its pressure, and without will, she admitted the intimacy of that velvet sweetness within. Heat swept through her, and her arms, unbidden, snaked around him.

She heard his sharp intake of breath, and then she was dragged against the full length of him. A torch flared into life inside her. Elaine melted into his tightening embrace, her mouth questing hungrily at his lips. Thought had sped. There was only sensation.

All at once, Elaine felt herself falling, slipping away from him into a half-conscious limbo. Her jellied bones refused to engage and she slid from the slackening support. Above her, an anxious face looked down, its features uncertain. Like two separate countenances, neither clear. They melted one into another, their identities changing so that she knew not to whom they belonged.

He was calling again. *'Elaine.'* Calling through the trees. For there were the trees, high above her. She ought to escape, but she had neither will nor power to haul herself from this overwhelming lassitude. Besides, how could she run when her legs refused to hold her up? Well, if he found her, it would serve. If she could not stand, she could not marry. The priest would refuse to perform the ceremony, if he must do so with the bride prostrate upon the ground.

'Elaine!'

'I cannot marry you,' she told him. 'Not like this.'

'There is no question of marriage, Elaine. Not yet awhile.'

'Then why have you pursued me?'

'Did you think I would leave you to wander in the forest alone?'

She frowned up at him. 'How did you find me? I ran and ran. I did not think you could find me here. Do you know that I hit my head? It is bleeding. I think I need a doctor.'

There was silence for a moment or two. Then the voice started up again. It spoke with authority.

'Elaine, wake up! You are talking wildly.'

A light slap struck at her cheek. It was sharp, and stung a little. She protested, blinking up at—

'Charles!'

He sighed with relief. 'Thank God!'

It came to Elaine that she was lying at full stretch on the ground, and that Charles knelt beside her. She struggled up on to her elbow.

'Easy!' He slid a supporting arm under her shoulder, letting her rest against him. 'You may yet be a trifle unsteady.'

'What are you doing?' she asked weakly, aware of his fingers brushing lightly at her hair.

'You have gathered a quantity of debris,' he muttered, picking off dead leaves and small twigs from her short locks.

'But what happened to me?'

'I was kissing you when you half-swooned,' he told her, and grinned as the bewilderment spread across her face. 'You may well look confused. I had no notion that my embraces were thus overpowering.'

Elaine laughed, and groped for his hand. It closed reassuringly over hers and she clutched it, filled with the realisation of what had been in her head. 'I was recalling that man. I thought you were he. That he had found me.'

'I believe you were a little mixed up, Elaine. For you answered me as myself, when you spoke of marriage.'

'Did I speak of it? But you were not constraining me to marriage.'

'Would that I could!' Charles lifted her fingers to his lips, and then shifted a little, helping her to sit up. 'How are you feeling? I fear I will undoubtedly constrain you to a worse fate, if we do not leave this place soon!'

His words threw her into consciousness. She was as fully alive to the danger. But a more pressing concern made her grip the fingers that held hers.

'Charles, this must be forgotten. The moment we leave here, we must put it all behind us. You must not speak of it. Oh, I don't mean to the others, for I know you would not do so. To me, Charles. Don't mention it again. Nor attempt at any time to renew those caresses which—*à mon risque!*—had such a shocking effect upon me.'

Charles drew her fingers to his lips and kissed them. 'You think me stronger than I am, I fancy. My darling, though I would do anything to spare you further pain—'

'Don't call me that! Pray, Charles—'

He put his fingers lightly to her lips to silence her, unable to bear the poignant pleading of the clouded eyes. 'Elaine, I think I am incapable of what you ask. To know that you return my regard makes it ten times worse. I can only curse the day that your past chooses to catch up with you.'

She withdrew her hands from his. 'You should rather curse the day we met.'

His smile was rueful. 'That were impossible.'

That look disarmed her utterly. A dry sob escaped her, together with a hopeless utterance. 'I know, Charles.'

He was looking at her with such tenderness that her heart melted within her. Impulse took over. Reaching towards him, Elaine drew his face to hers and softly kissed him.

Charles wanted to weep. How he refrained from seizing

her to him once again, he knew not. It was all he could do to remain still, for he knew if he touched her again, there would be no end. His passion, unleashed, would take her to perdition along with him. He cared less for his own conscience than for the burden he would lay upon hers.

As she drew away, he got hastily to his feet, and held out a hand to help her up. 'Come, we must go back.'

The return journey was accomplished in relative silence, for the presence of Parr up behind put a curb upon conversation. As well, Charles felt. In the light of his new knowledge, at once a source of elation and distress, he was unable to think of anything to say which did not hark back to their impossible situation. Elaine appeared the more subdued the closer they came to his home. It was inexpressibly painful to see it, and to be unable to do or say anything to cheer her.

Elaine was glad of the enforced moments of quiet. The happenings in the forest had thrown her into turmoil. Bad enough to have experienced those longings when she had no example to guide her. Now, with the imprint of his lips upon her own, how could she do other than yearn for that fulfilment which could never be permitted? How was she to continue living in his house, pretending an indifference that he knew to be untrue? Worse, how was she to face Meg's penetrating eye?

In the event, these troubled questions were destined to remain unresolved. As the phaeton bowled down the drive, nearing the entrance to the white stone mansion, it was to be seen that a reception party awaited them upon the pillared veranda outside the front door.

'Your arrival has been looked for with impatience, it

would seem,' remarked Charles, frowning as his brother-in-law came leaping down the steps.

'We've been on the watch for you!' called out Matt, as the phaeton came to a halt.

Elaine saw both Meg and Harriet were leaning anxiously over the low stone wall. She allowed Matt to take her hand, and began to climb down from the phaeton.

'You need not have been concerned,' remarked Charles, preparing to alight as Parr ran to the bays' heads. 'I found her easily enough, just as you predicted.'

'It is not that,' said Matt, guiding Elaine to the steps. 'Don't go in for a moment, I charge you!'

Elaine gazed at him, dazedly recognising the oddity of his behaviour. 'Why, what is amiss?'

'Tell you presently,' he said in a lowered tone. 'Only wait until Charles is with us.'

Parr began to lead the equipage away, and Charles let it pass him, and then crossed to the steps. He had not heard what Matt said to Elaine, but his manner had been enough to alert an intuitive chord. He dared not put a name to it, but his voice had sharpened considerably.

'What's to do, Matt?'

'No use trying to soften it.' His brother-in-law's eyes were for once sombre. 'Some fellow has come for Elaine.'

The jolt was shattering. Like a blow in the stomach. Charles' glance went automatically to Elaine. The blue eyes were fixed on Matt, and her face was draining of colour.

'Who is he?' Charles shot out.

Matt grimaced. 'A deuced plaguey parson! Name of Dymock.'

Elaine felt herself trembling, and put out an automatic

hand. She felt Charles take it in his strong clasp, and her fingers clung. Just outside the periphery of the numbing blanket that had settled on her mind, she could feel the charge of emotion that emanated from him. From somewhere, she found strength, and turned to face him.

'It is over.'

The tragic little smile she gave was more hurtful to him than the hideous knowledge that she was to be torn away from him. As she withdrew her hand from his, Charles felt as if he was losing the world.

Elaine turned to Matt. 'Where is he?'

'I left him in the saloon, but—'

Above them sounded hasty footsteps, and a glad cry. Elaine looked up. From the top of the steps, a black-clad gentleman was starting down.

'*Madeleine!* My poor, dear Madeleine! Thank heaven I have at last found you!'

Elaine could neither speak nor move. Shock held every faculty in suspense. That face! It was a face she knew, that one from several visions. A face seen dead.

From his customary stance at the mantelshelf in the downstairs saloon, Charles eyed the stranger, trying to keep a vibrant hostility in check.

The Reverend Mr Dymock was a stocky gentleman, about half a head shorter than Elaine. He was seated on the long sofa, his back to the window so that light filtered like a halo about the brown hair, worn unfashionably confined in a queue. His face was a trifle shadowed, but Charles had seen that it was a young, if serious, face. A face that Elaine had recognised.

After a moment of silence, when the fellow had presented himself before her, she had emitted a whimpering cry and delivered herself of a terrified utterance.

'It is he!'

Then, before Charles could think to do or say anything, she had picked up her skirts, and fled up the steps, vanishing into the house. He had seen Meg take off after her, and had turned irately upon the intruder.

'Confound you, look what you have done!'

Dymock had looked upset. 'I do beg your pardon, sir. It was witless of me. In my anxiety to see Madeleine, I had forgot that she might not remember me.'

Before Charles had been able to respond to this, Matt had butted in, unwontedly belligerent. 'Well, evidently she does! And in no friendly spirit, if you ask me.'

The tone had brought Charles up short. Recollecting himself, he had fought down his fury—born of anxiety and an overriding feeling of imminent loss—and had done his best to recover his poise. Introducing himself, he had invited the man to come with him to the saloon, adding that nothing could be decided about Elaine's future without discussion.

The Reverend Mr Dymock had agreed with alacrity. 'Indeed, my lord, I should not dream of expecting it.'

Charles had excluded both Matt and Harriet, insisting that the gentleman and he would do better in private. Beyond a mental vow that he was not going to give Elaine up to this creature without a fight, he'd had no idea what he was going to say to the man. He had preferred to say it, however, without his family's interference.

In the event, it was Dymock who opened the discussion, bringing up the subject of Elaine's lost memory.

'I wonder it did not occur to me that something of the sort had happened. How did it come about, Lord Wytham?'

'She received a knock on the head. My physician, who attended her, suggested that she fell upon a heavy stone and suffered a concussion. She had lain in my forest all night.'

The reverend gentlemen expressed his horror at it, adding, 'I am profoundly thankful that she fell into such good hands.'

Charles would have found it easier if the wretched man had not been so confoundedly civil! He adjudged the parson to be four and twenty or thereabouts, with, it presently became clear, a deal more good sense than his age warranted.

'You have taken us somewhat by surprise,' Charles began.

The man shook his head, his expression regretful. 'I should have written first. But once I had word of Madeleine's whereabouts, you will appreciate my impatience.'

'I fancy you must oblige me with a comprehensive explanation of your claim, sir,' Charles told him, tight-lipped.

'I intend to do so. You have been so solicitous of my wife's well-being that it certainly behoves me to satisfy you.'

It took a few seconds for the fateful word to penetrate Charles' awareness. When it did, he surprised in himself the most murderous desire to slaughter the Reverend Mr Dymock where he sat. Quashing it, he took a hasty turn about the room before he dared trust himself to speak.

Aware that the other's eyes had followed him, he cursed himself. The last thing he needed was to betray his intense disquiet. Should this indeed be Elaine's husband, it was imperative that he guessed nothing of her dealings with her host. An oddity that had been hovering at the back of his mind suddenly surfaced.

'You call her Madeleine,' he said, stopping short before

the man. 'Yet the only name she was able to recall was Elaine—and she does not know if that is her own.'

A heavy sigh answered him, and the visitor drooped. 'We do not use the shortened form. It was what her family called her, and could not but be a painful reminder.'

Charles felt a chill inside him. 'Of what?'

Dymock looked up, a world of sadness in his face. 'You might not think it from her speech, but Madeleine is French. Her entire family was lost in the unfortunate doings across the Channel. She is the only one left.'

It was a serious blow. Though Elaine had never indicated that the memory had returned to her conscious mind, Charles had heard her speak of this that day on the river. If this man was not who he claimed, how could he know all this?

He shifted, and found himself back at the mantelpiece. 'Elaine is not herself aware of those facts,' he said, turning his gaze once more upon the man who now threatened his life's happiness. 'Indeed, she is aware of very little, so I beg you will take care how you speak in front of her.'

Dymock nodded sagely. 'You need not fear me. Ever since my attention was drawn to your advertisement, I have been filled with dread upon that account.'

Charles realised that his preoccupation with the man's fateful arrival had thrown him completely off balance. Why in the world had he not questioned this at the outset? He made haste to remedy the omission.

'If you made the connection through my advertisement, why did you not come sooner? It is some time since it was inserted in the newspaper.'

The parson threw up one hand. 'I only wish I had seen it earlier! My anxieties would have been laid to rest days ago.

Unfortunately, I was myself too much debilitated by my injuries to be reading such frivolous items. How could I have guessed that there would be mention of Madeleine?'

Charles began to feel physically ill. Yet he was not to be so easily satisfied! This man had lost Elaine. If he had been hurt, had that been in the accident that she recalled? Was it he who had chased her through the forest? All the details of Elaine's dread nightmare came hurtling back into his mind. He stepped forward.

'This is all extremely glib, Mr Dymock, but if you are indeed connected with Elaine, you have a trifle of explaining to do, I fancy.'

The parson spread one hand wide. 'I am entirely at your service, my lord Wytham. Pray ask me anything you wish.'

He was well prepared, then? They would soon see.

'First you may tell me how your Madeleine came to be lost,' said Charles grimly.

'Alas! The most unfortunate accident to our carriage. I do not know how it was, but my coachman supposes it may have been a flash of lightning. The horses bolted. The coach rattled about in the most dreadful way.' He put a hand to his chest as though the memory was painful to him. 'The door became loosened. Poor Madeleine was thrown! There was nothing I could do, for I was a prisoner. Until, that is, a severe rut in the road caught the wheel and we went over.'

'Very well, but you must have gone back for her,' said Charles, irritated that his story should so closely have mirrored Elaine's slight memory—and his own suppositions.

Here the Reverend Dymock appeared to lose some of his assurance. He threw his hand over his face, and shuddered.

'Would that I could have done so! But I was myself

injured.' He indicated his left arm, and Charles realised for the first time that it had rested in his lap, unmoving. 'Even now I am unable to manage the most childishly easy tasks. The fingers are active, but the arm is largely useless.'

Charles watched, fascinated, as he first wiggled the fingers, and then lifted the wrist with his other hand to show how paralysis had affected it.

'You have my sympathy,' he said shortly.

'Pray do not say so! I would have given both arms rather than have lost Madeleine.'

'Yet you made no attempt to discover her whereabouts.'

'Believe me, sir,' insisted the other in a protesting voice, 'I made every possible attempt. At least, my servants did so. Even injured as I was, when she was found to be missing, I joined in the search for some little time, until I was overcome by my personal agonies. But she had vanished, seemingly without trace. My fellows hunted as long as they could, but darkness defeated us.' He lifted the good hand in a gesture of dismissal. 'You will say that I should have resumed the search, and you are right. You cannot reproach me more than I have done myself.'

'Then why didn't you resume it?' Charles demanded, unable to keep a note of anger from his voice.

'I lost consciousness. My fellows took the decision out of my hands. They deemed it of more importance to bring me home, for apparently I became delirious. It was days before I was myself again. By that time, it was too late.'

Charles was so disgusted he wanted to hit the man. 'For God's sake, why could you not have sent your servants back to the area? Someone might have made enquiries on your behalf.'

'Believe me, I wanted to,' said Dymock with an earnestness that ought to have convinced. 'But my lawyer advised me that it would be useless. My home is distant—we are near Bath, you must know. By then, Lorling thought she must have been rescued, and that I must hear of her soon enough. I was less satisfied of this. Indeed, on occasion I could not rid myself of the hideous fear that she was no more.'

He covered his eyes with one hand. Charles watched him with a lessening of sympathy. Up to now, he had been growing more and more convinced of the truth of Dymock's identity. But this last had awakened his distrust.

If Elaine was his wife—if he loved her!—how could he act in so irresponsible a fashion? Why, in his position, Charles knew he would have moved heaven and earth to find her.

This flaw could not easily be glossed over. Either Dymock had not as much common sense as he had supposed—or he was not who he claimed to be.

He waited until the parson showed an apparency of recovery. Mr Dymock had recourse to his handkerchief, and then, begging Charles' pardon for his weakness, stated that he thought that the sight of his dear Madeleine had shaken him more than he had supposed.

'Allow me to offer you something that may help you to compose yourself,' Charles said, crossing to the bell-pull.

In his own frantic trouble, he had forgotten his duties as host. He was more master of himself now, for the faint hope engendered by his suspicion had put heart into him.

His butler entered so quickly that Charles guessed he must have been waiting almost outside the door. No doubt Matt and Harriet were similarly hovering! He wondered how Elaine might be faring, and whether she had allowed Meg to stay with her.

'Pray bring some Madeira to this room, Moffat, and some cakes—' turning to Dymock '—if you should be hungry.'

The parson declined the cakes, but said, with a sigh, that a glass of wine would be welcome. Moffat bowed himself out, and Charles went to take a seat in a chair opposite his unwanted guest. From here, the light did not fall directly behind Dymock, and he could see his face more clearly.

It did nothing for his self-control. The fellow was all too personable! He had that fresh look of prettiness that females found appealing. But his eyes were a trifle hard for his calling. Or was that wishful thinking?

The habitual bland tone slid a little more readily off Charles' tongue. 'I am bound to state, sir, that your story tallies with the few scraps Elaine has so far recovered. But I fancy I shall require more concrete proofs.'

The Reverend Mr Dymock remained quite unruffled. 'Yes, I had anticipated as much. I have brought what I hope may satisfy you.'

Charles was tempted to say that no items could serve to satisfy him were they to help this man to remove Elaine. He tried another tack.

'How long have you been—' the word caught in his throat, and he was obliged to pause and take a steadying breath before resuming '—married?'

'A little over three years,' answered the parson without hesitation. 'You must know that Madeleine had only just left school in Bath. She came to stay with a friend who resided then in the same vicinity as my living. I was fortunate enough to be in a position to console Madeleine in her appalling loss.' He coughed. 'One thing led to another.'

Charles discovered that this touching little history did

nothing to foster his doubts. On the contrary, it was all too believable. He was glad that the door opened just then to admit Moffat, bearing a tray with glasses and a decanter. He waited while the butler served them both, and took his own glass in fingers that were not quite steady.

Leaving the tray upon a table set in the niche beside the fireplace, Moffat crossed to the door. Charles looked up again to confront his guest, and saw that he was rising to his feet, his gaze fixed in a different direction. Turning his head quickly, Charles saw with a sickening thud at his chest that Elaine had entered the room.

She stared across at the man without speaking. Vaguely she was aware of Charles moving towards her, but the face took all her attention.

'Come and sit down, Elaine.'

She heard him, and walked where he led her. At his command, she seated herself in the chair he had just vacated, but she neither acknowledged his aid nor glanced at him.

It had taken a deal of resolution to come downstairs. She had been too distraught either to understand or to answer Meg's eager questions. She had swished up and down the little parlour, her vision filled with images that totally contradicted the appearance of the man who had accosted her. She had run incontinently from him, as from a ghost!

But little by little, the fright had left her. She had spoken to Meg, but with no real wish of communicating.

'It must be my memories which are at fault. He was standing there, was he not? I did not dream it?' Meg had assured her that the man was all too real. 'Then I know him, for I have seen his face.'

'But you don't know who he is, Elaine!' Meg had pro-tested. 'You can't go off with him, just because you have seen his face. And he called you Madeleine.'

She had remembered it then. 'But I think that could be my name. It is French, and it is close to Elaine.'

'Which proves absolutely nothing!'

It had not mattered. Here at last was someone who might explain the hidden mystery of her past. She had turned to go, and caught sight of herself in the mirror. Her gown had been dirty and crumpled. Recalling events in the forest, she had looked down, and discovered the caked dirt on her shoes. She could not come before that man in this guise! Who knew but what he might notice—and become suspicious. If he demanded an explanation, she would have to tell him about Charles.

Charles! Her heart had taken a dive. She had kicked off her shoes, and with quaking hands, had tried to remove her gown. Her fingers had been all thumbs.

'Help me, Meg!'

While Meg had assisted her to take off the gown, and had sought for another, Elaine's mind had been all on the memory of those stolen caresses in the forest. If only she had not gone there! She might then have spared herself—and Charles, too!—from the hideous sensations of guilt that now attacked her. Just as she had foreseen, someone had come for her. But what was he to her? A parson who bore her name, who called her his 'dear Madeleine'. Who could he be but the man to whom she was irrevocably vowed?

The thought had caused a wash of misery to gush into her breast. Her legs had threatened to give way beneath her, and she had grasped at Meg for support.

'Oh, Elaine, you cannot go down to him!' had wailed that matron, as she had held her comfortingly tight.

But this had served only to strengthen Elaine's resolve. 'Whoever he is, Meg, I must know.'

She had paid no heed to that lady's protests, but had only dressed in silence, in another white muslin with her new overgown of blue. But when once ready, she had stood for several moments, frozen in the doorway, willing herself to go down and meet her fate. As for Charles, she must put him from her heart and mind.

Such fright possessed her by the time she entered the room that she was numbed to the thought of losing Charles. Now she sat before the man with the face, and addressed him directly from the deep-seated fear that had her in its grip.

'You are the face, but the face was dead.'

Stirred to the core by her tense white features, Charles intervened. 'Can you explain that, Mr Dymock? Why should Elaine remember a dead man who looks as you do?'

The Reverend Mr Dymock fetched another deep sigh. 'My brother. My poor Madeleine, did you think it was I?' He looked towards Charles. 'She was sincerely attached to him. Alas, his untimely demise followed so closely upon those earlier griefs she had endured. I am not surprised that the incident is engraved upon her mind.'

From the mantel, where he had laid down his glass, Charles cast a troubled eye upon Elaine. Confound the man! He had promised to mind his tongue. And here he was mentioning her lost family. Elaine was deathly still, her gaze fixed upon Dymock's face. Had she picked up on it, or was it the new idea that was affecting her?

'What happened to your brother?' he asked, in the hope of deflecting her thoughts.

The parson's hand came up, and he pressed the back of it against his mouth as he looked again at Elaine before he answered.

'The most terrible accident. Such a silly thing to happen, too. He fell down the stairs. His neck was broken. It happened just over a year ago. Madeleine felt it deeply. Indeed, she has scarce touched the harp since his death. My poor brother was used to listen to her with so much pleasure.'

Elaine uttered a cry, and threw her hands over her face. It was all too like! She had remembered it all. The face that watched her at the harp; the man falling down the stairs; and the dead face. No wonder she had been confused—unable to know if that face had belonged to her husband.

'You are so like him!' She dropped her hands to her lap, gazing at the man.

'We were much alike, yes. But I think, when you can bring yourself to look more closely at me, that you will define the differences. You were always used to do so easily, Madeleine.'

Elaine got up, hardly knowing what she did, and took several steps towards him. He had sat when she did, but he rose quickly and stood before her, with an odd gesture that threw his head back. Elaine halted abruptly.

She knew not where the words came from, for she was not thinking. A creeping unease settled into her guts, and her pulses thrummed unevenly.

'He was taller. And he laughed. His cheeks were leaner, and his eyes were grey. You are the more handsome, but you have not his warmth. I do not know you!'

She turned on the words, seeking instinctively for Charles.

He was beside her in seconds, his arm about her shoulders drawing her to him, while over her head his eyes raked the parson's figure.

'She does not recognise you, sir. I cannot release her to you!'

The Reverend Mr Dymock was evidently altogether unsurprised by this outburst. He gestured resignedly with his good hand. 'Pray allow me to send for my servant. I believe my coach was taken to your stables. I have some items which I shall show you both, if you will permit me?'

Elaine shifted back a little, looking up into Charles' strained features. 'What does he mean?' Charles' arm tightened about her, and she was caught by a sudden presentiment. 'Does he say he is my husband?'

Charles' chest caved in as he met the dawning horror in her eyes. He wanted to kick the man down the front steps!

'He says he has proofs. We will have to let him produce them.'

Elaine stiffened in his hold. Dismay came into the cloudy eyes. 'Oh, *bon Dieu*,' she whispered.

Then she twisted out of his grasp, and shifted quickly to drop into a chair. In a daze, she saw Charles cross to the bell-pull. Then she wrenched her gaze from him, though she could not look at the man who had come for her. If he could make good his hateful claim, it was vital that she did not let him see what Charles meant to her.

The small box lay open on a table that had been put by her chair. Elaine sat with a sheet of paper held loosely in her fingers, staring at the plain gold band that fitted exactly upon the third finger of her left hand.

It felt odd, and at the same time, chokingly correct. For the feeling with which it was associated made her want to weep.

Her eyes lifted to the portrait which had been laid on the floor to lean against the table, by a serving-man whose face meant nothing to her. Unlike the face in the portrait, which was incontrovertibly the one that she saw in the mirror.

'It is a little unwieldy, but it is a good likeness,' said the Reverend Mr Dymock from where he still sat in the sofa opposite, regarding her with an expression of kindly concern.

Elaine forced herself to look at him, though the sick disgust within her nearly choked her. 'Why was I not wearing this ring?'

She did not glance to Charles for his reaction. She was resolved not to look at him again, for fear that she must give herself away.

A gentle smile entered the parson's face. 'Your troubles must have caused you to lose weight again, Madeleine. The ring had become too tight. I was taking care of it for you, with the intention of having it made a trifle larger.'

It hardly mattered that the explanation was plausible. It was enough that he had one at all. Elaine had not wanted him to have one. With a feeling of dumb despair, she read again the details on the paper in her hand. It told her, without possibility of argument, that one Madeleine de St Vigians had been wed upon a certain day some three years since to one Lancelot Dymock, of the parish of Southwick.

'The signature is mine,' she muttered.

'Are you sure?' came from Charles.

He almost snatched the document from her hand, and read it all over again. But there was no possible way he could refute its evidence. He wanted to cry out that she could not be sure that the signature was hers. She had never called herself Madeleine. But the cumulative pieces of information allied to these solid objects could not be gainsaid. Only one thing militated against it, and it was not an argument that he could use. Elaine did not love her husband.

He folded the fateful paper, and passed it back to Elaine, his eyes turning upon the man who was undoubtedly entitled to take Elaine away from him. The words were forced from him, through a jaw that felt stiffly alien.

'You seem to be adequately furnished with means of identification, sir. I am obliged to accept that you are who you say you are.'

Elaine heard him without resentment. He was going to let her go, but what choice had he? A stone lodged in her chest. With infinite care, she laid the folded certificate in the box. Then she took hold of the ring, and slid it from her finger.

As she did so, she had an instant vision of doing the exact same motion once before. She could see her own fingers in an image that seemed to overlay them as she stared at her hands. Her eyes pricked. She had taken off the ring—and thrust it into the hand of another.

'Elaine?'

She started, looking quickly round to find Charles' concerned hazel gaze upon her. She shook her head slightly. Then she laid the ring in the box, on top of the paper that declared her wedded state. It was her ring, of that she was certain. Wear it again she must, but not yet.

Her legs were unsteady as she rose from the chair. Movement across from her told her that the alien creature to whom she must give herself up rose also. She took a breath and raised her eyes to meet his. Her voice sounded hoarse in her own ears.

'And still I do not know you. You must forgive me if I cannot at first bestow upon you those marks of affection that belong to you by right. I will learn them again—in time.'

'After what you have suffered, my dear, you deserve infinite patience,' he replied, in so saintly a voice that Charles was hard put to it to refrain from striking him.

He heard Elaine murmur something about fetching her belongings, and then she turned and quickly left the room.

Chapter Ten

Unable to help himself, Charles turned on the man whom he could not think of as other than an intruder.

'Confound you, Mr Dymock! You may have proved your claim, but nothing will make me believe that Elaine has ever loved you!'

A sad little smile entered the priest's face. 'You are right, my lord.'

Charles blinked, feeling the wind had been taken out of his sails. 'I beg your pardon?'

He received an oblique response. 'You have become fond of Madeleine, I think?'

A tightness at his chest warned Charles to be careful how he dealt with this. He had betrayed himself!

'She is a very lovely girl,' he said, trying for a bland note. 'Yes, I have become attached to her. We all have. I could not wish to see her unhappy.'

Whether he succeeded in veiling the true strength of his feelings, he did not know. But the Reverend Mr Dymock nodded understandingly.

'She has that effect on people. Let me set your mind at rest. I will force nothing on Madeleine. Honesty compels me to admit that ours was not a love match. Had circumstances been different, it might have been my brother who—' He broke off, coughed delicately, and resumed. 'But he is at peace now, and that is neither here nor there. The fact is, Lord Wytham, that I wished only to offer protection to an unfortunate female whose future could not be other than uncertain. Madeleine is beautiful, as you have noted, and I am excessively fond of her. Yet I knew that her affections were not engaged.'

Charles listened with amazement. He could not tell just what this speech was supposed to make him think. He suspected that Dymock had been more smitten than he made it appear. As for Elaine, was he suggesting that her affections had been instead engaged by his dead brother? A pang smote Charles.

He became aware that Dymock was regarding him, and hastily broke into speech, hardly knowing what he said. 'I must honour you for your confidence, I suppose.'

The parson smiled gently. 'I thank you. But pray do not imagine me to have been...' a slight hesitation and a straight look felt to Charles like an accusation '...betrayed. I was well content. Madeleine and I achieved no small degree of ease together, and I have missed her dreadfully. I have no doubt that with care and devotion, these unhappy events will fade and her memory will gradually return.'

It was a moment before Charles was able to speak for the uncomfortable sensations that attacked him. This hateful interview could have but one conclusion. It had been implicit from the start, and only his own dread of the outcome had prevented him from acceptance.

'You cannot wish to rush away, sir,' he said at last, with an unformed idea of delaying the inevitable. 'Allow me to offer you the hospitality of my home until Monday at least.'

Even as he said it, he realised that he could not endure this man to remain in his house—especially if he had the intention of sharing Elaine's bed! The thought blanked out everything, and he heard only vaguely the parson's response.

'Out of the question, but I thank you for it. I do not wish to hurry Madeleine, but I may not travel tomorrow—the Lord's day, you know—and I have business in London which is long overdue. We were, you must know, on our way to the capital when the accident occurred. I am anxious to have the matter done with so that Madeleine and I may resume our former life as soon as possible. I must take her away at once.'

He found Elaine seated at the harp, plucking notes at random. Her face was pale and set, her aspect so distressing that Charles was able only to stare silently for a moment or two.

He had been obliged to run the gamut of his family's involvement as he had pursued her to the little parlour. Matt had followed him, demanding to know what right 'this parson fellow' had to remove Elaine. Even Harriet had been caught up in the general panic of the situation, evidently unable to decide whether or not this development boded good or ill.

Meg had been guarding the parlour door. 'She wanted to be alone, poor Elaine. Is it true, Charles? Must she indeed go?'

'Stand aside, Meg!' he had ordered tersely, his mind too concentrated upon the need to see Elaine to trouble himself with answering questions.

'Come away, Meg!' had echoed his brother-in-law to his relief. 'We'll hear it all soon enough, I don't doubt.'

His way clear, Charles had thrust open the door, only to be brought up short by the sight of Elaine at the harp.

He shut the door upon his relatives, and moved into the room. 'I wish this might have happened a couple of weeks ago.'

Elaine's fingers dropped away from the harp strings, and she summoned a tiny smile. 'When you still thought of me only as an adventuress.'

Charles did not return the smile. 'I have been taken at fault, I fancy. And with a vengeance.'

She rose from the stool, and shifted towards the day-bed in the window embrasure. It was an aimless movement, but for the sharp necessity to refrain from looking at him.

'It is unfortunate that we had to meet in such a way.'

'Don't say that. Whatever else, I could not regret finding you, Elaine.'

She turned at that. 'It seems that I am not Elaine.'

Charles' voice sounded hollow in his own ears. 'He says it is a pet form of Madeleine, no longer used.'

'Well, I must suppose him to be right. My identity is certainly proven. *Je suis sa femme.*'

The words jerked Charles' pain into life. He stepped forward, seizing her by the shoulders. 'No! You will never be his wife! If you were so once, then you are no longer the woman who knew of it.' He caught her hard against him. 'Elaine, Elaine, I cannot let you go!'

Elaine's bosom was too full for speech, and she clung to him. Creeping into her mind came the insidious thought that she had come to rest at this safe haven after a stormy passage—and now she must put out again into rough seas. The worse for the fact that she was leaving her heart behind.

Pulling away a little, she looked into Charles' ravaged features. 'I do not wish to go, Charles. What choice have I? Or you, for the matter of that?'

'I would we might make the choice!' he said fiercely.

She shook her head, reaching up her fingers to his lips to stop the words. 'You know it to be impossible.'

Charles kissed the fingertips. 'I know only that I cannot bear to lose you. And I know that you love me.'

Elaine's eyes pricked. '*Et je t'aimerai toujours.* It may be wicked of me to say so, but if I loved that creature, I do not remember it.'

He loosened his hold, taking her fingers in his and holding them tight. 'You have no reason to reproach yourself, Elaine. Indeed you never loved him. Dymock admits as much. He says that it was not a love match. Confound it, why should you live with a stranger whom you do not love?'

She shifted her shoulders. 'Why ask me, Charles? Because he is my husband. Because I have no alternative.'

Charles cradled her to him. 'I wish I might beg you to leave him, and stay with me.'

She nestled within his embrace, but her voice shook. 'With what object? That I become your m-mistress?'

'Do you think I would so disgrace you?' he asked tenderly.

'For my part, I wish that you had! Or better, that your hasty words on that account had not caused me to run away today. I should not then have betrayed myself to you.'

Charles' fingers were playing in her hair. 'If you regret it, I do not.' He withdrew a little so that he might look at her, a faint smile in his eyes. 'I never thought I would have cause to regret the passing years. If only I were a callow youth still, and not a man of sense, I should be begging you to divorce him.'

A tiny laugh escaped her. 'Oh, Charles. And be as much disgraced?'

'That is just it,' he sighed. 'It would be useless—and worse than giving you up. For even if I then married you, no one would receive you.'

Elaine drew back, her hands moving to his shoulders. 'This is only prolonging the agony, Charles. Let me go!'

He did so, shifting quickly away to the mantelshelf, which he gripped in a way that made his knuckles whiten.

'If I could only think that this wretched parson cared for you, it would not be so bad.'

'Don't, Charles. Whatever his feelings, it does not lessen my guilt at having betrayed him with you.'

Charles frowned. 'I don't think he regards it thus. He even hinted that it was his brother with whom you betrayed him—or for whom you cared as you did not care for Dymock.'

A sudden intent look in her eyes gave him pause, awakening a sliver of feeling that he recognised to be jealousy.

'What is it, Elaine? Was he right? Did you indeed love his brother?'

Elaine's pulse began to beat in an unsteady rhythm. She stared at Charles' face, at some dim corner of her mind aware of what drove him to the questions. But the idea that was burgeoning in her mind was so bewildering that she dared not give it utterance. It was not that she had betrayed this unknown man with his brother—but that she had betrayed his brother with Charles!

'*Mais, ce n'est pas possible,*' she whispered.

'What is not possible?'

Elaine shook her head. 'I was thinking aloud.' She drew a deep breath. 'Charles, let us say farewell now. In his presence, we will have to dissemble—and it will break my heart to pretend to be indifferent.'

'I cannot say goodbye to you,' Charles uttered raggedly, unable to tear his eyes from hers.

There was silence for a moment. Then he saw Elaine make a slight movement towards the door, and he could not help himself. Next instant, she was in his arms, and he was kissing her with an intensity that spoke his anguish more clearly than any words.

When he released her, the clouded eyes were drowning. A husky whisper reached him. 'Remember me!'

Then she was running from the room. Charles remained just where he was, staring bleakly at the harp. As if he could forget!

'Anyone would suppose,' said Meg crossly on the family's return from church, 'that there had never been the slightest cause for gossip. It is all Harriet's fault!'

Charles did not answer. It was sufficiently trying to be obliged to appear unaffected, without engaging in a postmortem with his sister. He had attended the service at St Mary's, his mind on the letter from his cousin sent by special messenger that morning, and walked straight into the sort of curiosity he dreaded—for which Harriet was undoubtedly to blame. She had left for home yesterday after Elaine's departure, but not before paying a farewell visit to the Tarrington household, which was itself in the throes of removal. He did not doubt but that her tongue was responsible for these spurious expressions of regret.

'Why should we be obliged to listen to people bemoaning the loss of Elaine?' complained Meg. 'Just as if the wretches had not been coupling your name with hers in the most insulting fashion only two days since!'

Touched on the raw of his too-recent wound, Charles retreated to the French windows, staring out at the grey drizzle—so much in keeping with his mood!—that had descended within hours of Elaine being taken away from him.

'The worst of it,' Meg was continuing, 'is that my dreams for you, Charles, have come to nothing. I made sure of a match between you! It is too bad.'

Charles did not turn. Nor could he reply. He was rescued by his brother-in-law.

'Will you have done, Meg?' said Matt, uncharacteristically sharp. 'If you had more regard for your brother than for your own silly romantic notions, it would be a better thing!'

'Matt!' cried Meg, shocked. 'How can you say so? I have a great regard for Charles.'

'No one would think it to hear you!' declared her husband. 'If you will but look at him for once, instead of prosing on and on in a way that must grate upon his ears.'

Charles turned at that. 'Don't, Matt.'

But Meg was regarding him with some regret. 'No, Matt is right. The mistake he makes is in thinking me unaware of what ails you. You miss her very much, I know.'

Miss her? How inadequate a term to describe the aching void her going had left in his life!

'If you know it, m'love, you shouldn't plague him.'

'How can I have plagued him?' objected Meg. 'I have scarce seen him these four and twenty hours.'

Which was true, Charles reflected. He had shut himself up in his study the moment that fatal carriage had driven away, emerging only at dinner, of which he had partaken little. The night had left him numb, a state from which he had been roused only by the letter from his cousin.

Remembering it, he withdrew it from his pocket. 'Rob has written to me.'

Meg stared at him, blinking, but his brother-in-law moved towards him, eager. 'Has he found something?'

'Nothing to change the circumstances.'

'What are you talking of?' demanded Meg.

'Charles set Rob on to see if he might discover something of the family St Vigians,' Matt explained.

'You mean through the Foreign Office?'

Charles nodded. 'It seems that St Vigians was a marquis. He must have been the grandfather she spoke of that day on the river. He, together with all his family, were among those executed within the first two years of the Terror.'

'How dreadful!' exclaimed Meg. 'Poor Elaine!'

But Matt was thoughtfully scratching his chin. 'The granddaughter of a French marquis, eh? I'll warrant Harriet would have sung a different tune if she'd known our little upstart was an aristocrat!'

'Lord, yes!' agreed Meg, casting round eyes at her brother. 'Eligible indeed!'

Charles did not respond. What did Elaine's eligibility matter when she was lost to him?

'What I can't make out,' pursued Matt, frowning, 'is how she came to be married to that weasel of a parson.'

'Well, if she had no family, my love, an *émigrée*—'

'I'm not saying she'd make a good match. But that fellow!'

'I daresay Mr Dymock is not so bad a man,' suggested Meg, 'if only Elaine and Charles had not fallen in love.'

'Must you?' said Charles, wincing.

'There is no point in mincing words.'

'No need to rub his face in it!' protested Matt. 'For my part, the fellow was presentable enough, but he had a sanctimonious way with him. Can't abide that sort of fellow! I wouldn't trust him.'

Charles frowned. 'No more would I. Only I suspect that is merely wishful thinking on my part.'

'Had doubts about him, did you?'

'Don't be silly, Matt,' broke in Meg. 'Why should there be any doubt? He had enough proof to stand up in any court.'

'I don't say he didn't have proof,' said Matt testily. 'I'm saying the fellow was too dashed smooth-spoken for my money. Surprised a woman like Elaine could stomach him.'

Something leapt in Charles' chest. 'She couldn't!' He remembered suddenly the way Elaine had turned from the man, saying that she did not know him. 'She shrank from him, confound it! And I let her go with him!'

'How could you have stopped it?' demanded Meg. 'He had every right to remove her, Charles. What could you have done?'

Charles began to pace, restless all at once. 'Rob might have helped. Or I could have gone to Bow Street. They could at least have checked out his credentials.'

'Fat lot of use they've been,' snorted Matt. 'Have they found hide or hair of Elaine's background?'

'No, they have not,' Charles answered, but he was frowning, filled with misgiving. 'Have I been duped? Was I stupid to let her go without making more effort to search out the truth of what he told me?'

Meg made haste to reassure him. But the more he thought about it, the more Charles became convinced that he had given in too tamely. It was Matt who clinched the matter, coming over to lay a hand on his shoulder.

'Nothing to be done about it now, m'boy. Sorry I ever said anything. Face it, Charles. Whatever kind of man he is, his claim is at least more valid than yours.'

It was scarcely comforting, but Charles was obliged to acknowledge that his brother-in-law had a point. Besides, it was a hopeless exercise to beat himself over the head for something which could not now be mended. Elaine had been gone only a day, but he had as well reconcile himself to the notion that she was gone forever.

On the thought, the door opened to admit his butler. Glad of almost any interruption to his unsatisfactory thoughts, Charles crossed to his usual place by the mantel.

'What is it, Moffat?'

The butler sniffed. 'A person has called, my lord. He insists upon speech with you. I would have showed him in to Mr Shawbury, but that he is accompanied by a Lady Ventnor.'

'On a Sunday?' exclaimed Meg. 'And who in the world is Lady Ventnor? I have never heard of her.'

'Nor more have I,' said Charles, alert all at once. 'But it must be something urgent to make her travel on the Lord's day. Who is this person that brings her?'

The butler looked pained. 'His name is Merrick, sir. He claims to be a Bow Street Runner.'

His relatives delivered themselves of expressions of surprise, but Charles could only stare. A distinctly hollow sensation opened up inside him, and he experienced a premonition of disaster. He pulled himself together.

'Admit them both, Moffat.'

The butler withdrew, returning in a moment to announce the visitors.

A young lady entered the room, clad in a bronze linen pelisse opened over apricot muslin petticoats. She was closely followed by a thickset individual with brawny arms under a brown frieze coat, and a nose that looked to have been broken at some time in its owner's career. Slouch hat in hand, he remained in the background, a trifle ill at ease, while Lady Ventnor tripped daintily forward.

She was of average height, with a neat figure, and decidedly pretty. Her dusky hair was largely concealed by a straw bonnet decorated with a frivolous cluster of artificial flowers, but was to be seen curling in ringlets down her back from underneath it. Her eyes, which were of dark brown, looked enquiringly from one to the other of the two gentlemen, having passed over Meg without apparent interest.

'Lord Wytham?' she asked, in a light voice in which anxiety could readily be detected.

Charles took a pace forward, bowing slightly. 'I am Wytham.'

'I hope you will forgive this intrusion, my lord, but this affair cannot wait!'

'Certainly. How may I serve you, Lady Ventnor?'

'It was you who placed the advertisement, was it not?'

Charles eyed her. 'Is that why you have come?'

'That, and—' she gestured behind her at the man allegedly from Bow Street '—what I learned from Mr Merrick here.' She hesitated, glancing at Matt and Meg, as if she wondered whether to say her piece in their presence.

Charles performed the introductions, and Meg invited the lady to sit down, offering refreshments. She declined them, saying that she would first like to settle the business upon which she had set out, and travelled such a distance.

'How far have you come?' asked Matt.

'From near Bath.'

Charles exchanged a glance with his brother-in-law, but Meg looked at the stolid Merrick, standing by the saloon door. 'Don't tell me you have travelled all the way from Bath with only a Bow Street Runner for company?'

Lady Ventnor smiled, a trifle of mischief leaping into her face. 'No, indeed. My husband would have had something to say to that! I brought the housekeeper to play propriety.'

'Your husband could not accompany you?'

'I did not come from my own home, you know. I was staying with my parents at Southwick.'

The name caught instantly at Charles' memory. 'Southwick? Then you had heard of—' Realising that he was jumping the gun, he caught himself up. 'You have not yet explained what led you to come here, ma'am.'

Lady Ventnor bit her lip, eyeing him doubtfully. Signing to both Meg and Matt to keep silent, Charles waited.

'You see,' said the visitor at length, 'I could scarce believe it possible that you could be harbouring my poor Elaine. Or that she had been so unfortunate as to lose her memory.'

'You know her as Elaine?' Charles said quickly.

'Why, yes—if it is indeed she. She is my very dearest friend. But I cannot conceive what she could have been doing in this vicinity. And—and why her loss had been, as I must now suppose, concealed.'

This was altogether intriguing, but Charles was wary. Let them first establish that they were talking of the same person.

'One moment, Lady Ventnor. Before we get down to cases, let me confer with the man from Bow Street. Merrick, is it?'

The Runner came forward. 'Right it is, me lord.'

'How is it that you have brought this lady here?'

'It weren't my notion, me lord,' averred the man in an aggrieved tone.

'That is true. It was entirely my own idea, but how could I help it?' put in the young lady.

'Pray allow the man to speak without interruption, ma'am.'

Lady Ventnor apologised, and the Runner resumed. 'I was only wishful to get a confirmation, me lord, that the young lady as we has been a-searching of was the same young lady as we heard of in one of they Bath seminaries.'

'Is that where you started looking?' asked Matt.

'Yes, sir. According to your lordship's information as were sent to my guvnors, they reckoned as she must've done her schooling down Bath way. My instructions, me lord, were to question in all of they seminaries as aforementioned for a French miss of the name you give us. And I found her quite easy. When I arst for a new address, the individuals there referred me to this good lady's parents.'

'And I happened to have arrived to stay just that day,' put in Lady Ventnor, taking up the tale. 'In fact, we'd had talk of your advertisement, because they had themselves shown it to—' She broke off. 'But I am interrupting.'

'This lady's parents confirmed as the lady was one and the same as she we were a-searching of, and give me to know as how she had upped and married, and they proceeded to arst me what were my business with this enquiry.'

Lady Ventnor cut in again. 'You may imagine our astonishment to hear that Madeleine was not, as we had been led to suppose, in Somerset, but was instead here with you with her memory gone.'

'The good lady and myself,' went on Mr Merrick, 'took and checked for her straight at the house as I was give to know as being that of her 'usband, meaning to find the truth of it. Only she weren't there, nor anyone to say where she was.'

'Just a moment,' broke in Matt. 'When was this?'

'Two days agone, just about, sir.'

'I knew it. Just before—'

'Hold hard, Matt!' interrupted Charles. He turned questioning eyes upon his visitors. 'Are you saying that no one in the area knew about Elaine's disappearance?'

It was Lady Ventnor who answered. 'No, for my parents were told positively that she had been taken to Somerset and left with her husband's godmama for a short visit.'

'Why in the world had he to lie?' asked Meg blankly.

'He?' queried the visitor in a puzzled tone.

'She means Dymock.' Charles turned briefly to Meg. 'Presumably he lied because he did not wish anyone to think him callous for not searching for her more thoroughly.' He looked again at the youthful Lady Ventnor. 'Did not your parents hear that Dymock was suffering from an injury?'

'You mean the fall he took?' she asked casually. 'Oh, yes. We talked of it, for Mama thought how unlucky the poor man had been, considering the past. It seems he had fallen upon his paralysed arm, and dislocated the shoulder.'

Anxiety began to gnaw at Charles. The man had lied again! Was it to curry sympathy that he had pretended that the accident had caused his paralysis?

'But it was certainly from him that they understood Elaine was in Somerset,' went on Lady Ventnor, 'for naturally they met him at church.'

'Elaine has not been anywhere near Somerset,' said Charles grimly. 'She has been here these three weeks.' Remembering, he amended with difficulty, 'Or rather, she had been. She left yesterday, in company with her husband.'

Lady Ventnor gazed at him in the liveliest astonishment. 'But that is not possible.'

Charles felt a chill gathering in his breast. 'What do you mean? Why is it not possible?'

'Elaine's husband is dead.'

'What?'

It was Meg who screeched. But it might as well have been Charles. An irregular beat had started up in his chest. His brain felt hazy with the shock of it, but he forced himself to concentrate.

'Explain, if you please. The Reverend Mr Dymock came here to collect Elaine—his wife, as he claimed. He had proofs, both of his marriage to her, and of her identity.'

Lady Ventnor was looking more and more blank. 'I don't understand. Lance Dymock died more than a year ago! Why should Niall pretend to be Elaine's husband?'

'Niall?' Charles frowned. 'The name on her marriage lines was Lancelot.'

'Yes, he was Niall's elder brother.'

'Are you certain of this?' demanded Meg.

'Of course I am certain!' declared the lady indignantly. 'Why, I was maid of honour at their wedding. Indeed, it was to me she turned upon her widowhood. I rushed to her, poor thing, as you may guess. I stayed many weeks, until she was able to bear up under the loss. So tragic! They had only been married two years. It was the most unfortunate thing. And so stupid! That is why Mama commented upon Niall's ill luck. Though he was luckier than his brother.' She shuddered, gripping her gloved fingers together. 'I go cold when I think of it. You see, Lance took a bad fall. He tripped, and tumbled down the stairs. His neck was broken. Poor Madeleine! How could she be expected to endure it? After all she had suffered!'

Charles listened with a tortuous mix of emotions. While he grieved for Elaine's agony, there was elation, too. She was *free*. He felt a burgeoning fury against the wily Reverend Mr Dymock. His instinct of dislike had not been at fault. He should have checked further! Yet underneath it all, a pang smote him for Elaine's first love, which must have been sweeter than that she bore towards himself. It was an unworthy thought, and he tried to dismiss it.

'Then, when he gave me to understand that Elaine might have preferred his brother to himself,' he mused slowly, 'he must have meant to throw dust in my eyes because he had seen that she did not favour him.'

'Favour him? She was afraid of him!' said Matt bluntly.

'Oh, surely not?' protested Lady Ventnor. 'Elaine afraid of Niall? Why, that must be nonsense. Niall succeeded to the property—it is not much, of course—and Elaine has been living under his protection during her period of mourning.'

'Well, it would seem that his protection leaves a good deal to be desired,' said Meg crossly. 'What in the world can he hope to gain by it?'

Lady Ventnor had been looking puzzled, but at this, she gave a little gasp, as though a sudden thought had occurred to her. Charles eyed her.

'You know something, ma'am.'

She looked up, her expression changing to anxiety. 'But how might he—? Unless he intended only to— How dreadful! I would not have thought it of him. And he a parson!'

'What is it you have in your mind?'

Lady Ventnor glanced at the Bow Street Runner, who had once again taken up his stolid stance at the door, apparently divorced from the proceedings once he had performed his part. Charles caught the look, and at once wondered if the lady suspected Dymock of some criminal intent.

'Mr Merrick.'

The Runner came alert, stepping smartly forward. 'Me lord?'

'I must thank you for having brought Lady Ventnor to me here. By and by, you and I will talk again. I think we need not trouble you any further for the moment. Pray ask my butler, on my orders, to furnish you with some refreshment.'

The man executed an awkward bow, thanked his lordship, and left the room. Charles went to take a seat beside his visitor.

'Now, Lady Ventnor, tell me plainly what you suspect.'

She looked at him in a troubled way, fingering her pelisse in an agitated fashion. 'Lord Wytham, how much have you discovered of Madeleine's background?'

'She remembers very little.' He hesitated, undecided whether to tell her what he knew, or to wait to see whether her story backed it up.

'Isn't it better if you tell us?' suggested Meg, taking the decision out of his hands. 'Then we can judge if your knowledge of her corroborates what we have found out.'

'There is also the problem,' Charles put in, 'that Elaine often recalled things without even realising it. For example, she breaks into French, and does not know it.'

Lady Ventnor nodded. 'Yes, she was always used to do that, even at school.' Her manner became even more fidgety, as she clasped and unclasped her fingers. 'Oh, dear, this is all so confusing! Now I see that Niall must have been pretending when my mama showed him the advertisement. He laughed off the possibility of it being Madeleine, you must know.'

'If he did, he was certainly prevaricating,' said Charles, 'for he told me it was the advertisement that led him here. But you do not explain what further villainy it is of which you suspect him, Lady Ventnor.'

'Villainy! Yes, it must be that.' The young lady sighed. 'I had best start at the beginning. You might not think it, but my dearest Elaine is of aristocratic birth. She was brought to England and left at the academy by her grandfather.'

'The Marquis de St Vigians?'

'How did you know?'

'I received information from my cousin in the Government only this morning. I know that the rest of her family were killed.'

The dark eyes blinked rapidly. 'So tragic, poor Elaine! But this was a little before the horrors broke out in France. Madeleine was only eleven years old. She had no English then, but since there was only the French mistress—who was not even French!—with whom she might converse in her own tongue, she quickly learned to speak English with fluency. By the time we were both in our teenage years, Elaine had no trace of an accent, but she would still fall into French in the middle of a sentence. It was most disconcerting. And she never knew that she was doing it!'

'So we found,' agreed Meg, 'only we thought it had to do with her lost memory.'

'Go on, Lady Ventnor,' said Charles.

'What was I saying?'

'You were leading up to explaining your suspicions of Dymock,' Charles reminded her.

'Oh, yes. Well, Madeleine had lived in fear of the fate of her family for years. At last someone brought the dread tidings—a lawyer who acted for her grandfather. He told her she had been established here for her protection, for the Marquis had foreseen the troubles in his own country.'

'How dreadful for Elaine!' exclaimed Meg, distressed. 'To become utterly alone at one blow.'

'Yes, and I suspect that is why she fell for the first man to come in her way,' opined Lady Ventnor.

'Why, what do you mean?' asked Charles, with a resurgence of that uncharitable feeling of jealousy. 'Dymock gave me to understand that he was a comfort to her in her loss of her family, and—to use his own words—one thing led to another.'

Lady Ventnor stared. 'But that is nonsense! She knew Niall, for he presides at the local church. But Lance she met in my parents' house. You see, I had insisted they invite her to live with us. Not that they minded, for they were sorry for her, and she had nowhere to go, poor Elaine.'

'Lord, what an unenviable situation!' said Meg. 'Then she had no means of coming out, either.'

'Well, as to that, my mother would have brought her out with me. Only she fell head over heels for Lance, and he was perfectly eligible. She would have done anything for him, you know. She even changed her religion.'

'I never thought of that!' Meg threw a glance at her brother. 'Of course, she must have been Catholic.'

'It was no small sacrifice, I believe. But Elaine was so very much in love with Lance. I should think she would never love anyone again.'

Charles inwardly cursed, holding both his breath and his tongue. He willed her not to say any more. But he reckoned without his sister.

'Why shouldn't she?' demanded Meg, bristling. 'She is young enough, after all.'

'You did not know Lance,' said the visitor, with all too firm a conviction for Charles. 'Oh, he was such a gay young blade. Full of life and laughter. And he absolutely adored Madeleine! They were the most devoted couple. No, I cannot see her loving anyone else.'

Charles fought down his own doubts. Had he been but a substitute for this Lance? When Elaine at last recalled that deeper love, untainted by lies and treachery, would she then reject Charles who claimed her love anew?

'Poor Lance!' sighed Lady Ventnor. 'No one could have foreseen that he would die so tragically young.'

Except perhaps the Reverend Mr Dymock, thought Charles. Or was he letting his imagination run away with him? However that might have been, it seemed he had taken advantage of his brother's untimely demise. But for what purpose? The chafing at his heart found expression in a burst of irritation.

'While we sit talking, that villain has Elaine in his power! He told me he planned to go to London.' He bent a frown upon Lady Ventnor. 'Do you know why?'

The visitor was looking troubled. 'I think he must be intending to go to her lawyer. You see, I must suppose Niall meant all along to pretend to be married to Elaine. Or—' She broke off, and a look of deep distress overspread the pretty features. 'He could not have been trying to wed Madeleine, surely?'

Charles dismissed this. 'Hardly. It is against the law.'

'Yes, and a parson of all men must know it,' agreed Meg.

'But did Elaine know it?' demanded Matt shrewdly.

A memory snapped into Charles' head, and his breath stopped in his chest. In the forest! When he had kissed her, and she had fainted. Had she not said it then? She could not marry him! He had responded that there was no question of marriage, and Elaine had asked him why then he had chased her. She must have thought she was talking to Dymock. And he, fool that he was, had taken it to himself.

'No, she did not know it,' he said, hardly aware that he spoke aloud. 'He must have meant to force her into a fraudulent marriage.'

'Iniquitous!' exclaimed Meg. 'But for what purpose?'

'There is only one answer to that,' stated Lady Ventnor, her dark eyes burning with wrath. 'He must be wishing to get his hands on her inheritance.'

Laying down the borrowed comb, Elaine regarded herself in the mirror atop the dresser conveniently placed for the use

of patrons to the inn. Mr Dymock had commented several
times upon her pallor, and she did indeed look pale. There
was a bluish tinge about her eyes which Elaine attributed to
the sleepless nights, though she had not said so to Mr
Dymock.

The name sent that now familiar riffle of unease through
her. She ought to have overcome it. Instead, she felt it more
every moment in his company. He was her husband, but she
could not think of him as other than that distant 'Mr
Dymock'. Two days, was it? Three? She could not count
them. They merged into one long emptiness wherein the
single most pressing awareness was of the constant aching
loss.

A stabbing within made her catch her breath. She must
not think of Charles! Beyond her control were those dreams,
that granted her unlawful desires a fulfilment which could
never be, and which woke her to tears. But by day, she must
learn to banish him. He belonged to that fantasy world
wherein she had dwelled too long, unknowing that the reality
she sought to remember was this prison to which she had
returned. With Dymock her gaoler. How she hated him!

Guilt consumed her, and she thrust herself up from the
dressing-stool, going to the bed where the items of her
meagre wardrobe were folded, ready to be placed in the portmanteau.

She must not speak of hate—even to herself. He had been
kind, and overwhelmingly considerate. He had brought this
container and various articles of clothing, including a couple
of plain gowns selected by a maid, from her belongings.
Elaine had been more relieved than dismayed to recognise
nothing, for Meg had thrust upon her everything she had been

using at Clevedon House. Elaine could not have borne to put off the gowns of Charles' provision, the only tangible mementos of that forbidden life.

Though her duty was clear, she had been dreading that first night, when they had arrived at this inn. Mr Dymock had evidently divined her fears, setting them instantly to rest.

'You need not suppose, my dear Madeleine, that I will impose upon you in your unfortunate situation. It must be difficult enough to be thinking of me as a stranger. We will take separate chambers.'

Elaine had been too thankful to wonder at his forbearance. But alone that night, as she had damped her pillows in her misery, she had recalled what Charles had said—that this had not been a love match.

A horrid night had been followed by a bleak day. For Mr Dymock, being unable to pursue his business on Sunday, had instead taken her to church and they had spent a dull day thereafter together, watching the rain. It had stretched Elaine's nerves to screaming point. She had pleaded a headache that she might go early to bed, only to lie awake half the night with her mind on the inhabitants of Clevedon House, and her heart weeping for its owner.

Today Mr Dymock intended to conduct his business, and he had requested Elaine to accompany him. Until this moment, lost in a morass of grief, she had not troubled to wonder why he should wish for her attendance. Now it struck her oddly. What business could need her participation?

Picking up a thin Norwich shawl that had belonged to the deceased Lady Wytham, she draped it over her elbows and braced herself to face him.

He was waiting for her in the private parlour, where breakfast had already been laid out on a central table. Mr Dymock rose with alacrity, and bowing, pulled out a chair for her with his able hand.

'I trust you slept well, my dear?'

'Thank you, yes.'

Elaine approached him with a resurgence of discomfort, aware of moving in a fastidious fashion to ensure that he had no occasion to touch her—even accidentally. The thought of him brushing against her made her skin crawl. How was she to tolerate that intimacy to which he was entitled, and which he must sooner or later require of her?

He resumed his seat at the other side of the table, and she breathed a little more easily. She watched with a sense of morbid fascination as he poured coffee for her, first lifting his unwieldy left arm to rest upon the table so that his fingers might steady the saucer. He passed her the cup, and then removed a silver cover from one of the dishes, and invited Elaine to partake of its contents.

'You have adapted remarkably quickly,' she observed on a wistful note, as she served herself with a modest helping of ham and eggs. 'I wish my memory had been as obedient.'

The parson smiled as he took up the serving fork. 'Perhaps I was the lucky one. The mind is a tricky patient. Physical injury is more easily dealt with.'

Elaine spread butter on a slice of bread, wishing he was not so understanding. The more gently he spoke, the less at ease she felt. There was some comfort in the business of eating, since she was not obliged to look at him.

'I dare say you have been wondering why I wish you to come with me today,' he began, as soon as he had provided himself with a sustaining repast and begun upon it.

—

'Yes, I had,' Elaine answered involuntarily, looking up.

Mr Dymock nodded. 'I have sent to the lawyer that we intend to pay him a call. We will set out the moment I have confirmation that the fellow is there and ready to receive us.'

'Lawyer?' echoed Elaine, puzzled. 'What lawyer?'

'Folingsby is his name. Does it mean anything to you?'

Unease awakened. 'What has it to do with me?'

Mr Dymock smiled ruefully. 'Everything, my dear. You see, it was to Folingsby we were headed when the accident occurred.'

The accident! As clearly as if it was happening, Elaine saw it again. She had pulled away—from this man!—and thrown herself upon the handle of the door, dragging it down. He had hoisted her back as the door burst open, the sudden uneven weight upon that side causing the coach to sway alarmingly.

She saw herself struggling, the violent lurching coming to her aid as they were together flung this way and that. Then she was breaking away—and launching herself at the open doorway in a hazardous leap for freedom.

Chapter Eleven

Elaine came out of the memory and saw Dymock waiting. Had she given her thoughts away? She sought for what he had said that had triggered the image. A lawyer—he had spoken of a lawyer to whom they were travelling. What had occurred—some quarrel, perhaps—to make her escape him in so drastic and violent a fashion? Her heart beat fast, and an instinct of caution caused her to play for time.

'Mr Dymock, I—I recall very little of anything. You will have to tell me why we undertook that journey, for I do not know.'

He nodded understandingly. 'It is hard to know what you may or may not remember. Do you, for example, know anything of your family?'

Elaine felt a rush of sickness to her stomach. 'I have no family. *Ils sont tous morts.*' It came to her what she had said, and she gasped. 'Is that true? That my family are all of them dead?'

Dymock laid down his utensil, and spread his good hand.

'What can I say, Madeleine? Lord Wytham said you know nothing of it, although you had spoken of it once.'

Charles had known? And he had said nothing! Only to protect her from knowledge which must necessarily distress her. And had not Doctor Gorsty warned that she must be allowed to recall things by herself?

'I do know it,' she said slowly. 'I have recalled pictures of my home in France. But it has only just come to me that my family are all gone. Who told me? Was it you? No, it cannot have been you.'

'Assuredly not,' he affirmed. 'We met some years after these events.'

Elaine thrust away the question. What did it matter who had told her? He had begun with something quite other.

'What has any of this to do with this lawyer?'

'It is a pity that you do not recall him. Folingsby, I mean. It is to be hoped that he will at least know you. In any event, I have all the proofs of your identity that we may require. And since you have resumed wearing your ring—'

An elusive thought played at the contours of Elaine's mind, and she unconsciously felt with her thumb the gold ring upon her finger. She did not need proofs of identity. If she was who she was, then there was someone who knew it. She frowned in an effort of concentration, a forkful of ham poised halfway to her mouth.

'What are you thinking?'

The question made her jump. The fork jerked, sending its contents flying. Elaine came to herself with a flurry of apprehension. One certainty overcame everything else. She must not tell Mr Dymock anything of what was in her mind!

He was fussing over having startled her, urging her to drink a little coffee. 'It will steady your nerves, my dear.'

With no idea in her head but to keep from answering his question, she obeyed, sipping at the coffee while she hunted her mind for some legitimate response.

'I was—trying to remember the lawyer,' she said, a trifle breathlessly. 'You say that I have met him, but I have no picture in my head.'

'Don't concern yourself. As I said, I have brought proofs enough.'

Elaine resumed her meal. She was only toying with the food, but she hoped it might conceal her inner turmoil. The memory continued to elude her, but she felt a growing certainty that there was a momentous discovery to be made.

He spoke again. 'And still you do not ask me why we are visiting this lawyer.'

'I thought I had done so, only you evaded me,' Elaine protested, unable to suppress a rush of anger.

Dymock's brows rose. 'There is no need for such heat, my dear Madeleine. I was about to tell you.'

Elaine thought she must choke on the food in her mouth. She wanted to be angry with him! Had she not been so, that day of the accident? So angry that she had taken her life in her hands only to get away! But why? What had he done?

She looked at him with a resurgence of hatred. 'Well?'

A faintly sneering expression crossed his face. 'Almost you tempt me to believe that my first suspicion was correct.'

'What does that mean?'

'But I don't think so,' he said, without further explanation. 'Had you been pretending to forget, the outcome would have been markedly different.'

Bewilderment began to dissipate the convictions that had been driving her. Elaine wilted a trifle, reaching for her cup and taking a sustaining draught of the strong brew.

'I do not understand you.'

'How should you?' He resumed the sick-bed manner he had adopted towards her. 'Dear Madeleine, I did not mean to speak in riddles. Perhaps it does not occur to you that this is almost as difficult for me as it is for you.'

It had not occurred to her. She fought against the upsurge of guilt. Should she have thought of it? Only he had the advantage of her in every way, for he remembered! Was he waiting for her to beg his pardon? She could not.

'I would be glad if you could just tell me why you require my presence at this lawyer's place of business.'

'Because our going there is entirely on your account, Madeleine,' said Mr Dymock, with a smile altogether saintly. 'There is something left, it appears, from the wreck of the fortunes of the family of St Vigians.'

Elaine gazed at him. Something left? Did he mean money? Then this man—Folingsby, was it?—must be an executor. The riddle tapped at the edges of her mind again. This was a key, if she could only grasp it for the turn.

'You deserve to have it, my dear,' Dymock was saying. 'You came to me with nothing—not that I minded it. You must not think that I am motivated by self-interest. I took you without any fortune at all, most willingly.'

'Thank you,' Elaine managed, in a hollow voice. For there was a grinding in her head, as if the key, long rusted and useless, was beginning to turn.

'What I hope for is a little that you may settle upon your children, if you do not wish to avail yourself of it.'

'But anything that comes to me,' she said, obeying the instinct that put the words into her mouth, 'must necessarily go to you—as my husband.'

Dymock smiled. 'There is that.'

Elaine stared at his face. Something odd was happening. She seemed to see it detach itself, rippling as if it sought to shift away, revealing another face beneath. A face that came clearer every second. One of warmth, genuine and open. A face that broke apart in a gay outburst of laughter that echoed in her head. And words, easy and full of life, given in a ringing tone that caught her up and danced her heart away.

'To hell with France, sweetheart! You are an Englishwoman now, my darling wife.'

And he was lifting her into his arms, kicking open the front door as she broke into delighted protest.

'Lance, what are you about? Have you run mad?'

'Tradition, sweetheart. I am carrying you over the threshold.'

He had staggered into the hall and lost his balance so that they had fallen together, collapsing to the floor in an ungainly heap. They had lain shrieking with laughter, completely unhurt, and Lance had ended by kissing her, so passionately that he had almost taken her there and then, full on the flagstoned floor, in exactly the place where he had lain again on that dreadful day—*dead*.

Elaine's lips quivered, and the tears fell unheeded from her eyes. Across the table, the face she hated slipped back into place. She heard the hoarse whisper of her own voice.

'You are not my husband!'

His eyes grew hard. 'I was wondering how long it would take.'

She sucked in a breath, clamping down on the scream that threatened to erupt from her throat. 'For me to remember?'

'It was inevitable,' he said. 'Only I had hoped we might have got through the business of today beforehand.'

'So that you might cheat me the more? What is it you want? Money? Take it! Only let me go!'

'Ah, but I cannot take it. That would be dishonest.'

Elaine let out a laugh of amazement. 'And you balk at it? You made me believe I was married to you!'

'So you will be, my dear Madeleine.' He waved his good hand in a placatory gesture. 'Oh, in name only, my dear. We will tell no one and continue our lives just as before.'

She rose abruptly. 'I will never marry you!'

A sudden thought took her, and she pushed away from the table, moving quickly behind her chair, her horrified eyes upon him as he got up also.

'Do not come near me! I did not dream it, did I? You did chase me. I had jumped from the coach and run away, and you chased me! Was there even an accident?'

'One that you caused, Madeleine.'

He moved a little around the table towards her as he spoke, and Elaine slipped in the opposite direction. Then she saw that he was heading for the door, and made a dash to beat him to it. Her arm was seized as he caught up with her and swung her away.

'No, you don't!'

He had surprising strength for a man virtually one-armed. Elaine tried in vain to wrench free. Beyond the door, she could hear the sounds of footsteps and voices, muted but within range. She was not alone! This was a public inn. If she yelled for aid someone would hear.

'Let me go, or I will scream!'

His fingers dug deeper into her arm. 'Only be still, and I will do so. I have no wish to hurt you. But you must keep away from that door!'

Elaine ceased her struggles, swallowing on the panic that had driven her. 'Very well. Loose me, pray.'

Dymock released her, and she shifted quickly away to the other side of the room, massaging her arm. He remained near the door, watching her. Elaine's instinct was to shout to whoever was in the vicinity beyond that door. But this man was thought to be her husband. He had recourse to any number of excuses. Who would interfere? She tried for a measure of calm. She must be cagey, if she hoped to outwit him.

A worse thought hit her. She was dependent upon the man! She was in no better position to run from Dymock than she had been when she had attempted to run from Charles.

Pain smote her heart. Charles! If only he had not been duped. Only how could he help it? This wretch had been all too plausible. Useless to long for him, to dream of his aid.

She became suddenly aware of a medley of voices immediately outside the door. And then, as though she had conjured him up, it opened, and Charles stood in the aperture.

At first Elaine thought it must be another figment of her imagination. She stared as blankly as Dymock was staring, chagrin all over his face. And then Charles spoke.

'You blackhearted villain! Elaine, this man has been lying to you!'

A wash of feeling made her almost stagger, and she caught at a chairback for support. 'It is you! Oh, Charles, thank heaven you are come!'

Charles strode into the room, closely followed by a gentleman of middle years, whose features had familiarity for Elaine, and a stocky fellow who thrust back a servitor of sorts peering over his shoulder and shut the door. He took up a solid stance before it, folding his arms. She saw the Reverend Mr Dymock shift away from the door, his eyes going from one to the other of the three men.

Then Charles was at her side, catching at her shoulders.

'Has he touched you? I swear if he has, I shall murder him!'

Elaine shook her head dumbly, lifting her fingers to his face, seeking to assure herself of the reality of his presence.

'You came,' she said wonderingly. 'It really is you.'

Charles caught her fingers to his lips. 'Only tell me that you are safe. He has not dared to—?'

'No, no, I assure you he has not attempted anything.'

'He did not try to sleep in your bed?' he demanded bluntly.

She shivered. 'No, indeed. But, Charles, how did you find out?'

'I learned the truth only yesterday. From a schoolfriend of yours. Lady Ventnor?'

The name slipped into place, and another came out of her mouth. 'Dinah! Oh, she was my dearest friend.'

'She is so yet. She had been told of your present whereabouts by Merrick here—he is one of the Runners who has been searching for your identity, you must know—and came to find out the truth. Dymock had told her parents that you were staying with your husband's godmother in Somerset.'

'Her parents? Yes, I remember. It was at their house that I met Lance.' Her fingers clung to his, and her eyes filled. 'He is dead. I am a widow, Charles. I remembered it only moments ago. All the time I have felt ill at ease with this man. Now I know why.'

'And you had reason,' said Charles grimly. 'I have brought your lawyer Folingsby to tell the whole.'

Elaine looked where he gestured. The lawyer was standing on the other side of the table, regarding her with a look of concern. It was a thin face, with a long nose, overlaid with spectacles that gave it an owlish look. An image popped into Elaine's head. Bewigged, instead of the short grizzled hair that this man had. But its features imprinted themselves upon these, and they locked together.

'Folingsby,' she breathed. 'It was you who came to tell me. I was—fourteen? You'd had word from France.'

The lawyer tutted, clasping his hands behind his back. 'Terrible business. Worst task of my career. Never wish to be obliged to do such a thing again.'

Dymock spoke at last. 'Then you do remember her! I thought you would.'

Folingsby turned his head. 'Do you address me, sir? If what I hear is true, you have a deal to answer for.'

Elaine released herself from Charles' grasp, and came around the table. 'I am sure I would have remembered, the moment I saw your face.'

He took the hand she held out in both his own. 'Not likely you'd forget, with the tidings I brought.' A thin smile creased his mouth. 'I'd have known you anywhere, Mademoiselle de St Vigians. More beautiful than ever!'

She smiled, but her mind was on other matters. 'But I do not understand, Mr Folingsby. I am no longer Mademoiselle de St Vigians. I was married to this man's brother.'

'So I have been led to believe,' he agreed, casting a glance over his shoulder to where Dymock stood. 'Only he would have fraudulently taken possession of your inheritance himself, for he wrote to me—as your husband.'

Elaine glanced at Dymock, and back to the lawyer. 'But I know nothing of any inheritance. Or should I? Is this something I have forgotten?'

She found Charles once again at her elbow. 'You will hear it all presently.' He was looking over the remains of the meal upon the table. 'But what is this? Were you at breakfast?'

'We were in the midst of it when I suddenly remembered Lance. But it does not matter.'

'You may at least take some more coffee.'

Pulling out a chair, Charles obliged her to sit, and himself took a seat beside her, thrusting the dishes to one side, and supplying her with her own cup, refilled.

The lawyer, meanwhile, turned to the Reverend Mr Dymock. 'Sir, you will oblige me by coming to the table. This matter must be sifted, before we can decide what action should be taken.'

The parson hesitated, plainly undecided. But the stalwart individual by the door came forward, placing a hand upon his shoulder.

'Just you do as he says, me bucko. And in case as you was wonderin' who I might be to tell you so, the name's Merrick. Of Bow Street, as aforementioned.'

'Damn you, take your hands off me!' snarled Dymock. But he picked up a chair that stood by the wall, and came to the table, sitting at as great a distance as he could conveniently settle upon from the other three.

Folingsby waited until the Runner had stationed himself

behind the parson's chair, and then turned back to Elaine. 'Now, ma'am.'

'One moment,' begged Elaine, turning with the cup in her hand to Charles. 'How did you know where to find us? Come to that, how did you know it was Mr Folingsby that he meant to visit?'

'I didn't. Lady Ventnor knew you had a lawyer in London, and her father had mentioned that your husband spoke once of an inheritance. He was asking, I understand, for advice. But I am indebted to my cousin Rob—'

'Lord Sway, you mean? The Government Minister?'

'Exactly. I went directly to him on my arrival in London, and a Foreign Office clerk was dragged from his Sunday rest to comb through records until we had found that it was Folingsby here who had, some years back, made exhaustive enquiries about your family. We then repaired to—'

'To my house, ma'am,' broke in Folingsby with a wry look. 'But you need not think I objected to be disturbed upon the matter. And his lordship was at my office this morning when I received Mr Dymock's note, written from this hostelry.'

Charles cast an unloving glance at the parson. 'Was this fiend constraining you to marry him, Elaine?'

She shivered. 'He said it again—just now, when I had remembered. He said it was in name only, that we would keep it secret.'

'Very cunning, Mr Dymock!' said Charles grimly. He turned to Elaine. 'My poor girl, he would have tricked you most villainously. In this country, a widow cannot marry her deceased husband's brother.'

Her eyes widened. 'You mean it is a sin?'

'It is illegal, ma'am,' interpolated the lawyer. 'The fellow's whole scheme was fraudulent.'

'Then he would have made me guilty!'

Charles frowned at the parson. 'What I do not understand is how he hoped to persuade you into taking part in a marriage ceremony at all, when he had already fooled you into thinking that he was your husband.'

Elaine stared across at her brother-in-law. 'I think he was waiting for me to remember. I must suppose he had some scheme to persuade me that I was compromised.' Something snapped in her head, and she jumped. 'It was what he said to me before! It was that which caused me to leap from the coach.'

'Stupid female!' muttered Dymock abruptly. 'You made the horses bolt! Lucky for you that you did not suffer a worse injury than losing your memory.'

'Will you hold your tongue?' said Charles dangerously.

'No, let him speak,' Elaine said slowly, for the picture was unfolding in her head. 'Everything he says brings me closer to the truth. I think, Charles, that I did not lose my memory immediately.'

'You could not have done,' he agreed, 'if you knew enough to escape from this scoundrel.'

'I lost consciousness, but perhaps only briefly. It must have been later, after I had been hunted in your forest—'

'That you collapsed. Of course. And when you awoke—'

'I could no longer remember.' Elaine looked at the parson. 'You see, I did suffer an injury, Niall.' She gasped. 'That is your name! You are Lance's brother Niall.'

'And I have protected you since his death, Elaine.'

'No, sir!' broke in the lawyer in an irate tone. 'You have been protecting what you thought of as your own interests. Greed! It has been the ruin of so many. But you are a man of the cloth, Mr Dymock, and your sin is therefore the greater.'

'Am I any the less human for my calling?' demanded Niall with sudden fierceness. 'My brother was lost to me, and I had his widow on my hands. Why should I not benefit?'

Charles almost ground his teeth. 'If I have to listen to much more of this—'

'My lord, have patience!' begged Folingsby.

'For my sake, Charles!'

He took the hand she held out to him, and kissed it. 'I beg your pardon.' Biting down on his frustration, he looked once more at the lawyer. 'We do not let you get your story out, Folingsby. Pray continue.'

The lawyer bowed his head. 'When your grandfather, the Marquis de St Vigians, brought you to England, ma'am, he also brought with him both gold and all his family jewels.'

'Then he meant to come himself!' guessed Elaine, a catch at her throat. 'Why did he not stay? Why did he go back?'

'From what I gathered,' said Folingsby, 'Monsieur le Marquis had it in mind, but saw no immediate necessity for a precipitate departure from France. Few, I believe, of those unfortunates who perished, had any idea of the scale of destruction to which their class would be subject.'

'Who did?' put in Charles drily. 'Bar those who perpetrated the atrocities.'

'In my opinion, my lord, I doubt if even they had the premonition to foresee it. The momentum was beyond what anyone could have imagined.'

Elaine was conscious of a pricking at an old wound. But her puzzlement was acute. 'Then why did *Grandpère* bring me?'

'You were the youngest of the family, ma'am, and it would not, he thought, appear suspicious if he were to establish you at school in England.'

'Then Elaine was merely a blind so that he might transfer his valuables to this country,' Charles suggested.

'Precisely. And most fortunately for you, ma'am, as it turned out. The Marquis was taken, as I heard, close upon his return to France, and imprisoned. His family soon followed. But it was more than three years before I could ascertain that all had perished.'

Charles looked quickly at Elaine's whitening features, and taking her hand, held it tightly. Her mouth was trembling in a way that he knew well, and the blue orbs glistened. A sudden fierce regret came over him that it had not been he, but Lance Dymock, who had met her first. By the time he had banished it, Elaine was again speaking.

'It was then that you came to see me? If you spoke of the inheritance at that time, I do not remember it.'

'It was hardly appropriate, ma'am, in face of the grief occasioned by your appalling loss.'

Elaine found herself staring again at her brother-in-law, who sat with set features, his chagrin easy to be read. 'Then how was it Niall became acquainted with the whole?'

'I suspect that he came to know of it through your husband's papers. You see, ma'am, when I next attempted to make contact with you, I was led from your academy in Bath to Southwick, where you were then residing, having recently married. I wrote to your husband, to advise him that, after exhaustive enquiries, I had concluded that there were no members of your family remaining who might be entitled to a share in the gold and jewels entrusted to me by the Marquis. You would therefore inherit as soon as you came of age.'

'But did Lance tell me of it? If he did, I have no recollection of it.'

'According to his letter, your husband had thought that mention of it could only revive unpleasant memories, and that it should better come as a surprise upon the event.'

'And would you believe it?' cut in Charles drily. 'Just one week before you became lost, you turned one and twenty. Which was when, I surmise, this villain wrote to you, Folingsby.'

'Precisely. I have been expecting you these three weeks and more. I had no knowledge of the accident.'

'No, because Dymock had no knowledge of Elaine's whereabouts. To cover himself, he pretended that she was away upon a visit of duty. He explained his own injury—not to his arm, by the by, Elaine, which was already—'

'Paralysed!' she cut in, with a flashing recollection. She had ever cringed at Niall's disability, an irrational sensation for which she had always felt guilty. 'I thought you had adapted too readily! But why pretend? Was it to awaken my sympathies?'

'Not yours, Elaine,' said Charles. 'Mine, I fancy. And to add colour to his story. If he was so badly injured, he had an excuse for not having continued to search for you.'

A harsh laugh was surprised out of the Reverend Mr Dymock. 'Search? For two days we scoured that damned forest! Yes, and narrowly missed being spotted at least a dozen times by some keepers there. Do you suppose I would have allowed her to slip so easily through my fingers?'

Charles eyed him with loathing, for he had the man's measure now. 'No, Mr Dymock. Nor do I suppose that you would not have enquired for Elaine in the area, had you already been equipped with all your so-called proofs. Only you did not then know that she had lost her memory, did you? For all you knew, she had taken refuge with someone near at hand, and—'

'And thrown myself upon their mercy!'

'Exactly. It was too dangerous. You were constraining her to this criminal marriage, and she might well have told someone. She could even have been already on her way back to Bath to take refuge with Lady Ventnor's parents. It behoved you to make all speed home, that you might cover your tracks until you had word of Elaine's whereabouts.'

Folingsby was looking much shocked, his pained glance upon the culprit. But Elaine was beginning to appear crushed. It must be all too bewildering for her—everything at once!

Charles stood up. 'Merrick, you are acquainted with the law. You too, Folingsby. What charges should properly be brought against this man?'

The Runner scratched his chin. 'For my money, I'd do him for kidnapping. But I dessay as that wouldn't stick nohow.'

'Assuredly not,' affirmed the lawyer primly. 'But upon the charge of fraud, on the other hand—'

'No!'

Charles turned to Elaine, who had risen, her eyes on the parson, whose features had paled. 'What is it, Elaine? You are not thinking of allowing him to get away with this, I hope?'

She did not answer him, but only turned to the lawyer. 'Mr Folingsby, does this depend upon my pressing charges?'

'Elaine!'

'Pray hush, Charles. I must know the answer.'

The lawyer pursed his lips, and settled his spectacles upon his nose. 'I have evidence in my possession, but I have no doubt that you would be required as a witness if a jury was to be convinced. And then it would be your word against his.'

Elaine drew a breath. 'Then I desire that you will let him go. I wish only to be rid of the affair, not to pursue a petty revenge.'

'Elaine, the fellow is a criminal!'

'Charles, only think a little! Versions of the story are bound to leak out. Dinah already knows. It will be punishment enough for Niall to be the subject of gossip and conjecture. There is no necessity to degrade him further. Besides,' she added, turning to look at the man who wore her husband's face—or a version altogether too close to it, 'he is Lance's brother. I could not reconcile it with my conscience to defile my husband's memory.'

Elaine tucked the last of her belongings into her portmanteau, wishing she might rid herself of the garments procured by Niall from her old wardrobe. She must go to Southwick to collect those personal mementos that might serve to re-awaken her memory to something of that other life. But for the future, she would look to Charles for her needs.

The thought caught at her. Charles! He had come to her rescue, and his actions indicated that his intentions were the same. But Elaine had detected a little reserve in his manner, as the aftermath of her involvement with Niall's plot was cleared away. Charles had wished to pursue Niall to the utmost limit of the law, and she had argued at some length with him. She had won, and perhaps it was that which had left him aggrieved. He had insisted upon the Bow Street Runner overseeing the parson's packing, and had himself joined Merrick in escorting Mr Dymock from the premises.

Elaine had then repaired with Charles and Folingsby to the latter's office, where her signature upon a document gave her entitlement to the St Vigians fortune.

Remembering, Elaine gave a gasp. She was not dependent upon Charles! She had not set eyes upon the items of her inheritance, which were safely locked up in a bank, but Folingsby had assured her that the worth of the jewels alone was considerable. She might sell them, or draw upon any bank draft, with a promise of repayment from the store of gold.

It was heartening to have that independence. It could not be that which troubled Charles, could it? Did he suppose that her new estate would prompt her to seek some other life— apart from him? No, that must be nonsensical.

Brushing her doubts aside, she firmly closed the portmanteau, and picked it up, together with a long hooded cloak provided by Meg from the attics. Opening the door, she trod resolutely along the narrow corridor, and down the stairs.

Charles was awaiting her in the doorway to the private parlour bespoken by Niall, which had today remained a convenient headquarters. He came forward, a slight frown between his brows, and took the portmanteau from her, gesturing to the private parlour.

'Come in, Elaine.'

'But are we not going?' she asked, passing into the room.

They had taken a luncheon here with Mr Folingsby, who had accompanied them back from his office on Charles' invitation. But he had soon left them for Charles had been anxious to start for Teddington.

'Presently,' he said, shutting the door. 'I want to talk to you first—in private.'

He looked so serious that a faint tattoo started up in Elaine's breast. Charles made no attempt to touch her, but laid the portmanteau aside and crossed to the other side of the room where he remained for a moment, staring out of the window that gave on to the courtyard of the inn.

Elaine went to lay her cloak over the back of a chair, watching him with a rise of apprehension. Then she had not imagined his unease! She stood silent and anxious.

Charles turned at last. 'I doubt if we shall have another opportunity to settle matters between us.'

'Settle…' A vague whisper.

'You know what Meg is like. And your friend Lady Ventnor is also at Clevedon House. Between them—and Matt will not be slow to put his oar in!—we may look to be thrust into…'

He faded out, balked by the expression on her face. Confound it! How was he to make this right? The last thing he wanted was to hurt her. 'Elaine—'

'Thrust into marriage?' she cut in quickly. 'If you do not wish for it, Charles, you have only to say so.'

'Wish for it? It is all I live for! Only—'

He broke off again, and Elaine saw that there was real trouble in his eyes. Without thought, she moved around the table, and came to him, holding out her hands. He took them in his, but his expression did not change.

'What is the matter, Charles? Is there some barrier? I thought you had been reserved with me earlier, but—'

Charles released one of his hands, and instead cupped her face, searching her eyes. 'Is there no barrier, Elaine? Is there not a ghost whose shadow falls across your heart?'

For several seconds, Elaine stared back at him, while a numbing silence dragged upon her mind. Within her breast crept an empty space, widening as the fell portent of his words sank into her brain. A whisper echoed upon the air.

'Lance.'

Unknowing what she did, Elaine pushed his hands from her, and stepped away. She discovered that her knees were weak, and seized the back of the nearest chair. Her mind began to whirl, a myriad pictures flickering through, one after another, with no time to assimilate their content. Except that they all contained *his* image.

Her eyes closed. 'It was he whom I thought I betrayed. Oh, Lance!'

She felt hands upon her, and allowed herself to be guided into a chair. But in her head she stood by the graveside, and now the inscription was clear.

Lancelot Dymock, beloved husband of Madeleine. Born 1772. Departed this life 1797. '*Je t'aimerai toujours.*'

'And I will!' she uttered vehemently.

'You will always love him.'

Had she then spoken aloud? She became aware of Charles, seated across from her. There was that in his face which thrust her back into apprehension. Was she to lose him a second time?

'Why do you say it like that?' she asked shakily. 'Do you think Lance would not wish me to reach for happiness?

Groping for his memory, I felt that. But now I remember—and it is untrue. Charles, I made the same promise to you. Have you forgot it?'

He shook his head, squashing down the feelings that were rising up to choke him. 'How could I forget? But I cannot be Lance for you, Elaine! I am more than ten years your senior, and I am not he.'

'Why should you be?' she asked, bewildered. 'As for your age, what is that to me?'

Charles got up, pacing away to the window, so that he need not see the distress that he knew he was inflicting. 'I hate to see you hurt, Elaine, but it would be foolhardy for both of us if I allowed things to drift—without question.'

'You had no question before Niall took me away,' came from behind him, so forlorn a note in her voice that he winced.

'I did not then know that you had…loved and lost.'

'But I knew.'

Charles turned swiftly. The hazel eyes were fierce. 'No, Elaine! You had unconnected snatches only to guide you.' He arched an eyebrow in that cynical look. 'Will you try to make me believe now that you settled your feelings upon me because you were heart-free?'

She clasped her fingers together and held them, pressing down upon the polished wood of the table. She could not look at Charles. 'Of what do you accuse me? I had thought your suspicions of me were long ago laid to rest.'

He started forward, seizing the back of one of the chairs at the table. 'I have no suspicion! I do not accuse you. I think only that you do not understand your own feelings.'

She glanced at him then, the blue eyes flashing. 'And you do? You profess to know me better than I know myself?'

'Perhaps!' Charles flung away, beginning to pace. 'How can you know yourself? You have recaptured a few images—'

'Pitifully few,' she agreed.

'And therefore your knowledge of yourself is limited to that in which you have lived only since the accident.'

'Which encompasses my knowledge of you! Charles, my past life is as unreal to me as…as this unknown inheritance. All that is truly real is that short period of time during which I have had to relearn myself—and that discovery is irrevocably bound up with you.'

There was a wealth of sadness in the hazel gaze. 'That is just my point. What is real to you now may not be so later. You will remember, my darling. Little by little, it will come to you. And I can neither shield you, nor replace the loss you will grow to feel more and more.' He drew a painful breath. 'I love you, and I thought I would have you at any price. But that is too high.'

Elaine's blue orbs did not waver from his. But they had misted, and it took all his resolution not to throw caution to the winds. To seize her, drag her up from the table and into his arms. But the very strength of his passion held him still.

'You do not believe that I truly love you.' The husky quality of her voice well nigh destroyed him.

He set his teeth. 'I think I am the re-embodiment of the man you lost.'

The frown became etched between her delicate brows. Elaine had to make an effort to concentrate, for the agony was acute. 'And so you will let me go?'

There was silence for a moment. Then she looked away from him, lifting her fingers to knead at her temples. Why had he rescued her, then? As well might he have left her to her fate! Was this love? Was it for her sake or his own that he intended to release her?

She was barely aware of speaking, for the clouds in her mind mirrored the hideous disorientation of that first day. '*Comme je suis bête!* I tried not to give him my heart, and I lost that battle. His was the first face I saw. Does he think I made then a transference of feeling? *C'est incroyable!* To a man so suspicious of me! I did not even wish to remain in his house—beholden to him for my every need.'

'Elaine—'

'Wait!' She wafted a hand to silence him, aware of significance in her words. 'Beholden…I was so to Lance, for I had nothing then. Or so I thought.' She looked up, seeing Charles' face, yet not seeing it. 'Niall, too. He said "the wreck of the St Vigians fortune".'

A picture broke into her mind. Niall holding out his hand, as she had tugged off her wedding ring and forced it upon him. 'Take it! I shall never wear it for you.'

She rose quickly from the chair. 'Charles, I took off my wedding ring that Niall might not use my wearing of it to prove that we were married, which he intended.'

'But what has that to do with—?'

'Don't you see? I would never have removed it had those feelings I cherished for my husband not been already a fading memory. I must have been a year in mourning before I met you. It is absurd to suggest that my feeling for you is a delusion.'

'Yet you said yourself that it was wrong to feel as you did for me,' he reminded her, involuntarily moving to her. 'And just now you reiterated that you would always love him.'

'The memory of him, yes,' Elaine said, desperation in her bosom. 'But against you—alive and with me day after day? How could it be more real to me than what I feel for you?'

'And if your returning memory makes him live again?' He gripped her by the shoulders. 'You don't understand, my lovely girl! It has taken so long for the right woman to come into my life. How could I bear it if you were to find at last that I was not the right man for you?'

A faint smile wavered on Elaine's lips. She had believed that she was losing him. But the discomfort of his fingers digging into her shoulders was fiercely reassuring.

She reached up trembling fingers and brushed back one of the unruly chestnut locks. 'If the risk is too great, Charles, then you had better settle for Belinda.'

For a few seconds he gazed at her, frowning and bemused. Then the sense of her words sank in. A slow smile dawned.

'Confound Belinda!' he said softly.

Her fingers had shifted to trace the contours of his mouth. He kissed them and Elaine smiled at him. His heart swelled, and his arms slipped down, drawing her closer.

'And confound the risk!'

He sought her lips. They melted into his, and his blood soared. The thought drifted through his mind that he had been unutterably foolish. And then there was only sensation.

Elaine gave herself to his need, half-drowning in the warmth that flooded her, melting her bones. She came to herself breathless, quite sagging in his arms, and opened her eyes to find the hazel eyes tender upon hers.

'Would you really have let me go?' she asked, the cloudy orbs a little anxious.

Rueful, Charles cradled her, dipping his head to drop a kiss on her brow. 'I thought so. But when it came to the point, I fancy I would have recanted.'

Elaine sighed. 'I do love you, Charles. And it is so silly to be throwing our happiness away.'

'That thought would probably have occurred to me sooner or later,' he agreed drily.

'Then pray marry me swiftly, before you have time to think of some other way to make us both miserable!'

Charles laughed. 'Shall we get married at once?'

The blue eyes widened. 'You mean now, before we go home?'

'By special licence. Yes, that is exactly what I mean. I am sure my cousin Rob must have influence with a tame bishop.'

So much light entered her face, the blue eyes shining with happiness, that the doubts that niggled at the back of his mind were crushed.

'Yes, dearest Charles,' she breathed. 'I can do with romantic memories to cherish.'

Charles kissed her again, and for some little while there was no more need of words.

'We are going to cause a deal of talk,' Elaine observed presently.

'Who cares?'

'Harriet?'

'Don't you believe it, my lovely one.' He leaned back a little, arching an eyebrow. 'Now that you are an accredited heiress, and the granddaughter of a French Marquis, my sister Harriet will be the first to offer her congratulations.'

Elaine laughed. 'I had not thought of that. How fortunate that you fell into my trap, after all!'

'How could I have escaped when it was baited with your enchantment?' said Charles lovingly.

But Elaine bethought her of the advancing hour, and urged him to action, that the trap might be securely fastened before the day was out. And Charles, his mind upon the coming night, was moved to speed himself to the pleasurable task of replenishing his lady's store of memories.

* * * * *

For a sneak preview of Marie Ferrarella's
DOCTOR IN THE HOUSE,
coming to NEXT in September,
please turn the page.

He didn't look like an unholy terror.

But maybe that reputation was exaggerated, Bailey Del-Monico thought as she turned in her chair to look toward the doorway.

The man didn't seem scary at all.

Dr. Munro, or Ivan the Terrible, was tall, with an athletic build and wide shoulders. The cheekbones beneath what she estimated to be day-old stubble were prominent. His hair was light brown and just this side of unruly. Munro's hair looked as if he used his fingers for a comb and didn't care who knew it.

The eyes were brown, almost black as they were aimed at her. There was no other word for it. Aimed. As if he was debating whether or not to fire at point-blank range.

Somewhere in the back of her mind, a line from a B movie, "Be afraid—be very afraid..." whispered along the perimeter of her brain. Warning her. Almost against her will, it caused her to brace her shoulders. Bailey had to remind herself to breathe in and out like a normal person.

The chief of staff, Dr. Bennett, had tried his level best to put her at ease and had almost succeeded. But an air of tension had entered with Munro. She wondered if Dr. Bennett was bracing himself as well, bracing for some kind of disaster or explosion.

"Ah, here he is now," Harold Bennett announced need-lessly. The smile on his lips was slightly forced, and the look in his gray, kindly eyes held a warning as he looked at his chief neurosurgeon. "We were just talking about you, Dr. Munro."

"Can't imagine why," Ivan replied dryly.

Harold cleared his throat, as if that would cover the less than friendly tone of voice Ivan had just displayed. "Dr. Munro, this is the young woman I was telling you about yes-terday."

Now his eyes dissected her. Bailey felt as if she was under-going a scalpel-less autopsy right then and there. "Ah yes, the Stanford Special."

He made her sound like something that was listed at the top of a third-rate diner menu. There was enough contempt in his voice to offend an entire delegation from the UN.

Summoning the bravado that her parents always claimed had been infused in her since the moment she first drew breath, Bailey put out her hand. "Hello. I'm Dr. Bailey Del-Monico."

Ivan made no effort to take the hand offered to him. Instead, he slid his long, lanky form bonelessly into the chair beside her. He proceeded to move the chair ever so slightly so that there was even more space between them. Ivan faced the chief of staff, but the words he spoke were addressed to her.

"You're a doctor, DelMonico, when I say you're a doctor," he informed her coldly, sparing her only one frosty glance to punctuate the end of his statement.

Harold stifled a sigh. "Dr. Munro is going to take over your education. Dr. Munro—" he fixed Ivan with a steely gaze that had been known to send lesser doctors running for their antacids, but, as always, seemed to have no effect on the chief neurosurgeon "—I want you to award her every consideration. From now on, Dr. DelMonico is to be your shadow, your sponge and your assistant." He emphasized the last word as his eyes locked with Ivan's. "Do I make myself clear?"

For his part, Ivan seemed completely unfazed. He merely nodded, his eyes and expression unreadable. "Perfectly."

His hand was on the doorknob. Bailey sprang to her feet. Her chair made a scraping noise as she moved it back and then quickly joined the neurosurgeon before he could leave the office.

Closing the door behind him, Ivan leaned over and whispered into her ear, "Just so you know, I'm going to be your worst nightmare."

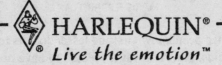

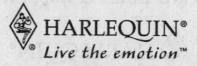

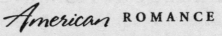
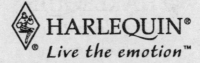

HARLEQUIN®
INTRIGUE®

BREATHTAKING ROMANTIC SUSPENSE

Shared dangers and passions lead to electrifying
romance and heart-stopping suspense!

Every month, you'll meet six new heroes
who are guaranteed to make your spine tingle
and your pulse pound. With them you'll enter
into the exciting world of Harlequin Intrigue—
where your life is on the line
and so is your heart!

THAT'S INTRIGUE—
ROMANTIC SUSPENSE
AT ITS BEST!

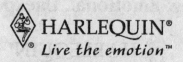

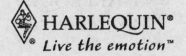

Harlequin® Historical
Historical Romantic Adventure!

Imagine a time of chivalrous knights and unconventional ladies, roguish rakes and impetuous heiresses, rugged cowboys and spirited frontierswomen—— these rich and vivid tales will capture your imagination!

Harlequin Historical . . . they're too good to miss!